英汉对照·中国文学宝库·现代文学系列
English-Chinese·Gems of Chinese Literature·*Modern*

叶圣陶小说散文选
Selected Stories and Prose by Ye Shengtao

叶圣陶 著
Ye Shengtao

中国文学出版社
Chinese Literature Press
外语教学与研究出版社
Foreign Language Teaching and Research Press

图书在版编目(CIP)数据

叶圣陶小说散文选:英、汉对照/叶圣陶著.—北京:中国文学出版社;外语教学与研究出版社,1999.8
(中国文学宝库·现代文学系列)
ISBN 7-5071-0569-5

Ⅰ.叶… Ⅱ.叶… Ⅲ.①小说-中国-现代-对照读物-英、汉 ②散文-中国-现代-对照读物-英、汉 Ⅳ.H319.4:I

中国版本图书馆 CIP 数据核字(1999)第 29617 号

中文责编: 邓锦辉
英文责编: 殷 雯

英汉对照 中国文学宝库·现代文学系列
叶圣陶小说散文选
叶圣陶 著

中国文学出版社
(北京百万庄路24号)
外语教学与研究出版社 出版发行
(北京西三环北路19号)

北京市鑫鑫印刷厂印刷
新华书店总店北京发行所经销
开本 850×1168 1/32 10.375 印张
1999 年 8 月第 1 版 1999 年 8 月第 1 次印刷
字数:155 千 印数:1—5000 册
ISBN 7-5071-0569-5/I·510
定价:12.90 元

总编辑 杨宪益　戴乃迭

总策划 野　莽　蔡剑峰

编委会（以姓氏笔划为序）
　　　　　吕　华
　　　　　李朋义
　　　　　赵文炎
　　　　　凌　原
　　　　　野　莽
　　　　　蔡剑峰

目 录
CONTENTS

大学生读书计划 ················· 编 者（Ⅰ）	
——中国文学宝库出版呼吁	
A Life ··· （ 2 ）	
一 生 ··· （ 3 ）	
Bitter Greens ····································· （ 12 ）	
苦 菜 ··· （ 13 ）	
A Stroll at Dawn ································· （ 30 ）	
晓 行 ··· （ 31 ）	
How Mr. Pan Weathered the Storm ············ （ 48 ）	
潘先生在难中 ······································ （ 49 ）	
The Package ······································ （102）	
一包东西 ·· （103）	
Night ··· （120）	
夜 ·· （121）	
A Trainee ·· （146）	
一个练习生 ······································· （147）	
A Declaration ···································· （178）	
一篇宣言 ·· （179）	
A Minor Flutter ·································· （196）	
一个小浪花 ······································· （197）	
A Year of Good Harvest ························· （214）	
多收了三五斗 ···································· （215）	

目录

Lotus Root and Water Shield ………………………… (238)
藕与莼菜 ……………………………………………… (239)
Before Leaving ………………………………………… (244)
将　离 ………………………………………………… (245)
Traveller's Words ……………………………………… (252)
客　语 ………………………………………………… (253)
Selling Gingkos ………………………………………… (268)
卖白果 ………………………………………………… (269)
Late-Night Food ……………………………………… (276)
深夜的食品 …………………………………………… (277)
Three Kinds of Boat …………………………………… (286)
三种船 ………………………………………………… (287)
Ox ……………………………………………………… (314)
牛 ……………………………………………………… (315)

大学生读书计划
——中国文学宝库出版呼吁

在即将开机印刷这第一批50本名为中国文学宝库的英汉对照读本时,我们的心情竟然忧多于喜。因为我们只能以保守的5000册印数,去面对全国400万在校大学生。

虽然我们并非市场经济的局外者,若仅为印数(销售量)计,大可奋起而去生产诸如TOFEL应试指南,或者英语四六级模拟试题集一类的教辅图书,但我们还是决定宁可冒着债台高筑的风险,也有责任对大学生同胞发出一声亲切的呼唤:请亲近我们的中国文学。

身为向世界译介中国文学和向国内出版外语读物的,具有双重责任的出版社,我们得知目前大学生往往仅注重外语的学习而偏废了母语的提高,以及忽视了中国文学的阅读,放弃了人文知识的训练。有统计表明,某理工院校57%的同学不曾读过《红楼梦》等四大名著,以致校园内外流行着"样子像研究生,说话像大学生,作文像中学生,写字像小学生"的幽默。还有一副这样的对联,说大学生的文章是"无错不成文,病句错句破残句,句句不堪入目;有误方为篇,别字错字自造字,字字触目惊心",横批"斯文扫地"。作为未来社会中坚和整个社会发展关键力量的大学生,这种"文弃"现象的流行,势必导致一场人文精神危机的爆发。对照以科学与人文精神追求为主题的五四新文化运动,八十年的历程告诉我们,以上提醒绝非危言耸听。

我们已经迈入知识经济时代,在追求科学知识的同时,创新精神已成为关键;而创新的源泉其实有赖于多学科多领域知识的交融,依靠的是新型的复合型人才,所以,文学对于新一代的大学生来说绝非装点,而是沟通自然科学与人文科学的桥梁,使我们在汲取知识的同时更能获得智慧,于创造物质的同时还进一步丰富和完善着精神;无怪乎爱因斯坦认为自己受影响最大的竟是陀思妥耶夫斯基。由此证明,一个真正的科学家应该拥有丰富的文学和文化知识以及完整的人格。十年前,七十五位诺贝尔奖得主聚会巴黎,当时他们所发表的宣言开篇就是,"如果人类要在21世纪生存下去,必须回首2500年去吸收孔子的智慧。"确实,十年的时间让我们有目共睹,现代经济科技的飞速发展何尝不是一柄双刃的剑?只有文化的力量才能抵消随之而来的负面后果。可见,知识的获取与技能的训练对于大学生来说固然重要,但文化与修养却尤需关切。正因为大学生代表着社会先知先觉的知识力量,置身当前的文化现实,就应有一分责任感与使命感,力求对知识技能以外许多带有根本性质的精神追求形成明确的意识,从而具备一种对生命意义进行探索与追问的精神,一种以人文精神为背景的生存勇气和人格力量。那么,能够引导我们探索前行的一盏明灯,不就是闪烁着理想光芒的不朽的文学名著吗?

一个人乃至一个民族,从其对文学的亲疏态度,可以衡量出其文化素质的程度。文学应是从人类文化中升华出的理想的结晶,她"使人的心灵变得高尚,使人的勇气、荣誉感、希望、尊严、同情心、怜悯心和牺牲精神复活起来"(威廉·福克纳);无疑,只有文学才能从更高的层次上提升人的文化素质和整体素质,充实人的内心世界,焕发人的精神风貌,带给人们真善美。而亲近文学,特别是热爱祖国灿烂的文学以及文化,正是当代中国大学生加强文化修养,弘扬人文精神的有力脚步。

"越是民族的,就越是世界的",中国文学属于中国,也属于世界。和平是人类的共同愿望,交流与共享则是新世纪的潮流。

中国当代大学生的血液里流动着数千年的文化积淀,没有理由在让世界了解中国大学生聪明才智的同时,却无缘分享我们的骄傲——中国大学生不但能够读懂英语的莎士比亚,而且能让世界感动于中国文学的伟大。

这是我们作为出版者的理想。我们原有一个世纪礼物的构想,是同大学生一起做一个"读书计划"。这一次将中国文学的最新荟萃配设高水平的英语译文,是其中推荐给新世纪大学生的第一批读物。盼望着您——我们无数知音中的5000名先来者,给我们鼓励,也给我们意见和批评。

编者
一九九九年五月三十日

只有文学才能从更高的层次上提升人的文化素质和整体素质,充实人的内心世界,焕发人的精神风貌,带给人们真善美。而亲近文学,特别是热爱祖国灿烂的文学以及文化,正是当代中国大学生加强文化修养,弘扬人文精神的有力脚步。

A Life

Village born she was never waited on or made up, never taught the feudal precepts for women or the bourgeois ideas of equality and freedom. She was indeed a very simple creature.

After leaving her mother's womb, by the time she was able to walk and talk she helped her parents glean paddy stalks and pluck herbs. At fifteen they married her off. For sooner or later she would belong to some other family anyway, and each extra year they kept her meant the cost of an extra year's food, clothing and so on. Better, then, get her off their hands early to save themselves trouble and expense simply to enrich other people.

Her husband's family had so much field work that they needed to hire help. Even if this new daughter-in-law couldn't save them taking on a hired hand, she was worth half an ox to them. In less than a year, to her bewilderment, she gave birth to a son; for it seemed to her only yesterday that she had slept in her mother's arms, and now here she was holding a baby of her own. He had no cradle, no snug clothes, no airy, sunny nursery, and it was only at night that he could enjoy sleeping in her arms; by day he slept in a dark corner of the room. In less than six months he died. She cried and cried as if her heart would break. Her monther-in-law accused her of not knowing how to look after children and inveighed against her for causing the death of a perfectly good grandson. Her father-in-law

一 生

伊生在农家,没有享过"呼婢唤女""傅粉施朱"的福气,也没有受过"三从四德""自由平等"的教训,简直是很简单的一个动物。伊自出母胎,生长到会说话会行动的时候,就帮着父母拾些稻稿,挑些野菜。到了十五岁,伊父母便把伊嫁了。因为伊早晚总是别人家的人,多留一年,便多破费一年的穿吃零用,倒不如早早把伊嫁了,免得白掷了自己的心思财力,替人家长财产。伊夫家呢,本来田务忙碌,要雇人帮助,如今把伊娶了,即不能省一个帮佣,也抵得半条耕牛。伊嫁了不上一年,就生了个孩子,伊也莫名其妙,只觉得自己睡在母亲怀里还是昨天的事,如今自己是抱孩儿的人了。伊的孩子没有摇篮睡,没有柔软的衣服穿,没有清气阳光充足的地方住,连睡在伊的怀里也只有晚上睡觉的时候才得享受,白天只睡在黑魆魆的屋角里。不到半岁,他就死了。伊哭得不可开交,只觉以前从没这么伤心过。伊婆婆说伊不会领小孩,好好一个孙儿被伊糟蹋死了,实在可恨。伊公公说

英汉对照
English-Chinese
中国文学宝库
Gems of Chinese Literature
现代文学系列
Modern Literature

swore that his line would die out — she was too ill-starred to rear children. Her husband merely remarked that he didn't care if ten sons died, if only it would bring him luck in gambling. She didn't try to fathom what they meant, simply crying from morning till night.

One day she made a strange discovery. When she opened her chest to take out the blue cotton-padded clothes that were part of her dowry, she found they had disappeared. Later, her husband when drunk told her he had pawned them. Winter came very quickly. The west wind chilled people to the bone. She screwed up her courage to beg him to get her clothes out of hock. For that he boxed her ears a couple of times. She was used to his knocking her about, which always reduced her to tears.

Today when she wept her mother-in-law snapped, "Crying? Want to drown us all in your tears?"

That made her sob still more loudly. In a rage her mother-in-law snatched up the pestle for washing clothes and thwacked her back several times. For good measure her husband gave her two more slaps.

This was more than she could bear. The thought of tomorrow and the day after ... the future ... filled her with fearful dismay. The next morning before it was light, she slipped out of the house while luckily her husband was still asleep. The west wind was like a knife and stung her face. Never mind, it hurt less than his beatings. She hurried a dozen *li* without stopping for breath till she came to the river bank, then waited for the passenger boat to town.

When finally the boat came, she went aboard. The passengers all

伊命硬,招不牢子息,怎不绝了他一门的嗣。伊丈夫却没别的话说,只说要是在赌场里百战百胜,便死十个儿子也不关他事。伊听了也不去想这些话是什么意思,只是朝晚地哭。

有一天伊发见了新奇的事了:开开板箱,那嫁时的几件青布大袄不知哪里去了。后来伊丈夫喝醉了,自己说是他当掉的。冬天来得很快,几阵西风吹得人彻骨地冷。伊大着胆央求丈夫把青布袄赎回来,却吃了两个巴掌。原来伊吃丈夫的巴掌早经习以为常,惟一的了局便是哭。这一天伊又哭了。伊婆婆喊道,"再哭?一家人家给你哭完了!"伊听了更不住地哭。婆婆动了怒,拉起捣衣的杵在伊背上抽了几下。伊丈夫还加上两个巴掌。

这一番伊吃得苦太重了。想到明天,后天,……将来,不由得害怕起来。第二天朝晨,天还没亮透,伊轻轻地走了出来,私幸伊丈夫还没醒。西风像刀,吹到脸上很痛,但是伊觉得比吃丈夫的巴掌痛得轻些,就也满足了。一口气跑了十几里路,到了一条河边,才停了脚步。这条河里是有航船经过的。

英汉对照
English-Chinese
中国文学宝库
Gems of Chinese Literature
现代文学系列
Modern Literature

seemed to have sixth sense: they saw at a glance that she had run away from home because she had been badly treated.

"You've only yourself to blame if you make your in-laws angry," they told her. "Even if they treat you shabbily, a young wife has to put up with such things. If you're so temperamental and touchy, so much the worse for you! Besides, who can you turn to now that you've run away? You'd better go back with this boat."

She didn't answer, just hanging her head in silence.

In exasperation one of the passengers said, "Who knows what she's up to? She may be eloping."

The others roared with laughter, but she paid no attention.

On reaching town she found an employment agent who got her a job as a servant. A new life began for her. Though she was on the go all day long, it was less tiring than farming, and as no one scolded her, cursed her or beat her, she thought herself extremely well off and wished she could stay there for ever. It was only when she woke at night from dreams of her dead baby that she felt unhappy.

One day while out shopping, to her consternation she met a neighbour from her husband's village. As a result, in less than three days her father-in-law came to find her.

"Run away, would you?" he bellowed. "Now I've tracked you down you won't get away again. If you've any sense, come back with me at once!"

She dared not answer but rushed indoors to cower motionless behind her mistress.

The latter called her father-in-law in and said, "Your daughter-in-law's made a contract to work here. It isn't up yet — so how can

等了好久,航船经过了,伊就上了船。那些乘客好似个个会催眠术的,一见了伊,便知道是在家里受了气,私自逃走的。他们对伊说道,"总是你自己没长进,才使家里人和你生气。即使他们委屈了你,你是年幼小娘,总该忍耐一二。这么使性子,碰不起,苦还有得吃!况且如今逃了出去,靠傍谁呢?不如趁原船回去罢。"伊听了不答应,只低着头不响。众客便有些不耐烦。一个道,"不知伊想的什么心思,论不定还约下了汉子同走!"众人便嘲笑起来。伊也不去管他们。

伊进了城,寻到一家荐头。荐头把伊荐到一家人家当佣妇。伊的新生活从此开始了:虽也是一天到晚地操作,却没下田耕作这么费力,又没人说伊,骂伊,打伊,便觉得眼前的境地非常舒服,永远不愿更换了。伊惟一的不快,就是夜半梦醒时思念伊已死的孩子。

一天,伊到市上买东西,遇见一个人,心里就老大不自在,这个人是村里的邻居。不到三天,就发生影响了:伊公公已寻了来。开口便嚷道,"你会逃,如今寻到了,可再能逃?你若是乖觉的,快跟我回去!"伊听了不敢开口,奔到里面,伏在主妇的背后,只是发呆。主妇便唤伊公公进来对他说,"你媳妇为我家帮佣,此刻约期还没满,怎能去?"伊公公无可辩论,只得狠狠地

英汉对照
English-Chinese
中国文学宝库
Gems of Chinese Literature
现代文学系列
Modern Literature

she leave?"

Stumped by this he surlily ordered his daughter-in-law, "As soon as your time's up, come back! If you run away again we won't have you back. We'll sell you wherever you are or break your legs!"

So this place where she had felt so comfortable, would in no time be an illusion — how could she bear it? She dreaded the thought of the future. For the next few days her eyes were swollen, she couldn't eat, couldn't work. Her master, now that he knew the circumstances, thought it shouldn't be hard according to the new law to get her a divorce.

He asked her, "Do you want to break with your husband's family?"

"Of course I do!" she said.

Thereupon he drafted a petition for her, clearly stating the facts of her case and her request for a divorce, meaning to present this to the magistrate.

His wife, however, demurred, "Of course it's good to get her a divorce. But she may not be working for us all her life. Suppose she leaves us and nobody hires her, what's to become of her? By rights, her own family should take her in, but can they manage it?"

That made him less eager to take up the cudgels for her. "It can't be helped then," he said.

A few days later her father arrived, sent by her father-in-law.

Her mistress asked, "Have you any way to rescue your daughter?"

"Since she's married into their family, it's up to them if they want to beat her or curse her," he answered. "What can I do about it?

叮嘱伊道,"期满了赶紧回家!倘若再逃,我家也不要伊了,你逃到那里,就在那里卖掉你,或是打折你的腿!"

伊觉得这舒服的境地,转眼就会成空虚,非常舍不得。想到将来……更害怕起来。这几天里眼睛就肿了,饭就吃不下了,事也就做不动了。主人知道伊的情况,心想如今的法律,请求离婚,并不繁难,便问伊道,"可情愿和夫家断绝?"伊答道,"那有不愿?"主人便代伊草了个呈子,把种种以往的事实,和如今的心愿,都叙述明白,预备呈请县长替伊作主。主妇却说道,"替伊请求离婚,固然很好,但伊不一定永久做我家帮佣的。一旦伊离开了我家,又没别人家雇伊,那时候伊便怎样?论情呢,母家原该收留伊,但是伊的母家可能办到?"主人听了主妇的话,把一腔侠情冷了下来,只说一声"无可奈何!"

隔几天,伊父亲来了,是伊公公叫他来的。主妇问他,"可有救你女儿的法子?"他答道,"既

英汉对照
English-Chinese
中国文学宝库
Gems of Chinese Literature
现代文学系列
Modern Literature

I'm just passing on her father-in-law's message telling her to go home."

But backed by her mistress she refused to go.

Later her mother-in-law got a neighbour to bring her word that her husband was ill and she must go home to nurse him. She was so afraid to go that her mistress refused for her.

Four days later her father came back. "Your husband's dead," he announced. "If you still won't go back, I can't answer for it. You must come along with me."

"Yes, this time you'll have to go," her mistress said. "Otherwise they'll be coming to make trouble here."

Since everyone told her to go, she felt this time there was no help for it, much as she dreaded it.

At home, the sight of her husband stiff and stark on the bed made her feel rather sad. But she also remembered his cruelty to her. Her in-laws did not tell her to wail or put on mourning; instead they led her to someone's house and sold her for twenty strings of cash.

Her father, father-in-law and mother-in-law all thought this right and proper, in keeping with the maxim: When your ox can no longer till the soil, sell it. To them she was an ox, not entitled to any opinions of her own, so now that they had no further use for her they had better sell her off. The money got from selling her was spent on her husband's funeral, fulfilling her last obligation.

February 14, 1919
Translated by Wenxue

做人家的媳妇,要打要骂,概由人家,我怎能作得主?我如今单是传伊公公的话,叫伊回去罢了。"但是伊仗着主妇的回护,没有跟伊父亲同走。

后来伊家公婆托邻居进城的带个口信,说伊丈夫正害病,要伊回去服侍。伊心里只是怕回去,主妇就替伊回绝了。

过了四天,伊父亲又来了。对伊说,"你的丈夫害病死了,再不回去,我可担当不起。你须得跟我走!"主妇也说,"这一番你只得回去了。否则你家的人就会打到这里来。"伊见眼前的人没一个不叫伊回去,心想这一番必然应该回去了。但总是害怕,总是不愿意。

伊到了家里,见丈夫直僵僵地躺在床上,心里很有些儿悲伤。但也想,他是骂伊打伊的。伊公婆也不叫伊哭,也不叫伊服孝,却领伊到一家人家,受了二十千钱,把伊卖了。伊的父亲,公公,婆婆,都以为这个办法是应当的,他们心里原有个成例:田不种了,便卖耕牛。伊是一条牛,———一样地不该有自己的主见——如今用不着了,便该卖掉。把伊的身价充伊丈夫的殓费,便是伊最后的义务。

1919,2,14

英汉对照
English-Chinese
中国文学宝库
Gems of Chinese Literature
现代文学系列
Modern Literature

Bitter Greens

Behind my house was about a sixth of an acre of vacant land, which, from the frequency with which shattered beams and fragments of brick were turned up there had evidently once been built upon. Short, fleshy wild plants allied to the chrysanthemum and alone fitted by natural selection to occupy the place supported their stems among the rubble and shards, unfurling their unexpected verdure across the leaden earth. A crowd of cheeky youngsters often gathered there to kick metal shot about, its seclusion shielding them from the eyes of parents and teachers, and to fritter away the money their parents gave them for sweets on games of chance, in the excitement of which they would test their aim by throwing the shot in their hands or the brickbats they picked up at the eaves or the sparrows on the roof. These they never hit, though they broke the rear windows, and this more than just once.

Thinking it a great shame to waste this land on a ready-made playground for cheeky youngsters, whom, though scarcely hateful, I could not bring myself to love, I called in a workman to construct a cane fence around it, thereby, as I thought, giving it a newfound calm and security. I went on to speak to a peasant of my close acquaintance.

"I want to hire a man to plant greens there and do odd jobs," I said. "If you come across anyone suitable, send him along for a

苦 菜

我家屋后有一亩多空地,泥土里时常翻出屋脊的碎屑,墙砖的小块来,表明那里从前也建造过房屋。短而肥的菊科的野草是独蒙天择适存在那里的,托根在瓦砾砖块之间,居然将铅色的地铺得碧绿。许多顽皮的小孩子常聚在那里踢铁球,——因为那里僻静,可以避他们父母和先生的眼——将父母给他们买点心的钱赌输赢,他们玩得高兴时,便将手里的铁球或拾起小砖投那后屋的檐头和屋面的小雀练眼功。檐头和小雀都没中,却碎了后窗的玻璃。这也不止一次了。

我想空地废弃,未免可惜;顽皮孩子虽不觉得可恶,究竟没什么可爱,何必准备着游戏场供他们玩耍;便唤个竹匠编成竹篱,将那片空地围起来,这样觉得比以前安静严密了。我更向熟识的农人说起,"我要雇一个人在那里种菜,兼做些杂事,看有相当的人可以荐来试试。"

英汉对照
English-Chinese
中国文学宝库
Gems of Chinese Literature
现代文学系列
Modern Literature

trial."

Once I had someone I put him in charge with myself as helper. Labour would be the true meaning of life. Spiritual fulfillment and happiness would be mine, and the vacant plot would be the wellspring of a new life, which I anticipated with keen ardour.

This was how the peasant Futang was hired and came to me. He differed little from other peasants in his bronzed skin, horny hands, bushy hair, unwavering gaze and short brown beard and moustache, yet a certain gloom overlay his inherent peasant traits and unreflective simplicity.

"You can plant anything?" I asked him.

"Yes, I've been at it since I was a boy. Rice, wheat, greens, beans; anything." His tone was frank, as of one who would retail his experience pleasantly and in detail but could say only so much.

"Excellent, you shall plant greens on the vacant plot behind the house."

"It'll divide up into twenty beds," he said, returned from inspecting his new workplace. "You can get two skeps full from each in twenty days if the seedlings go out right away, and there's time for a second crop with it being warm this year." He smiled as he spoke, as if to demonstrate the immense profit to the owner, and I thought "All glory to the soil in its ceaseless bearing and endless bounty!", an instant convert to pantheism.

Our first task was to pick out the debris. Futang brought a four-pronged, seven-pound rake, which he lifted a foot or so above his head and brought down powerfully so that the prongs bit evenly into the ground, then drew up the handle end in his left hand to lift the

苦菜

我待雇到了人,让他做主任,我自己做他的副手。劳动是人生的真义,从此可得精神的真实的愉快;那片空地便是我新生活的泉源。我只是热烈而深切地期望着。

农人福堂因此被荐到我家来了。他的紫赤的皮肤,粗糙而有坚皮的手,茸茸的发,直视而不灵动的眼睛,口四围短而黄的胡子,都和别的农人没甚分别;但是他还有一种悒郁的神情,将农人固有的特征,浑朴无虑的态度笼罩住。
"你种什么东西都会?"我问他。
"我从小就种田,米麦菜豆都种过,都会。"他的语音很诚恳,兼欲将他自己的经历称述得详细而动听,但是他仅能说这么一句。
"那很好,我屋后那片空地将由你去种。"
他去察看了他新的工作地,回我道,"那里可以画做二十畦。赶紧下秧,二十天之后,每畦可出一担菜。今年天气暖,还来得及种第二批哩。"他说时面作笑容,似乎表示这对主人有莫大的利益。我也想,"土地真足赞颂呀,生生不息,取之无尽。"于此使我更信 pantheism 了。

我们最先的工作是剔去瓦砾砖块。福堂带来一柄四齿耙,五斤多重,他举起来高出头顶一尺光景,用力往下垩,四齿齐没入泥里。他那执柄端的左手向上一提,再举起耙来,泥土便松了

英汉对照
English-Chinese
中国文学宝库
Gems of Chinese Literature
现代文学系列
Modern Literature

15

rake again, loosening a square of ground so that every fragment of rubble stood out. How precious is strength, interacting with nothing while concealed but once applied able to transform anything! After two hours' work he had turned over a sixth of the plot and was sitting on the step taking a break and smoking.

My mood of hope and reverence was fit to brim over with the very first fall of the rake: this time I would indeed taste life's true happiness. The moment he left off, I grasped the handle of the rake with alacrity and set to work copying his stance and action. Yet the rake seemed not to obey me: when I lifted it, it just swayed to and fro and back and forth in mid air; on contact the prongs sank in a mere couple of inches or so; and when I wrenched it up, it left only four loosened trails in the level, solid ground. Undismayed, for this was at least looser than before, I brought it down once more and for some odd reason, its weight increased every time and before the twentieth stroke I was no longer able to lift it. A strand of parching heat spread from my spine to my entire body like a process of cellular combustion. I began to breathe rapidly, almost unable to take in the outer air into my nasal passages. Normal sensation left my hands, which felt as if still grasping the rake — though this was already lying on the ground — so that I could not clench my fists.

"This is no job for a teacher," said Futang, knocking the ash from his pipe on the stone step. "Hadn't you better look for bricks? When we've got rid of those, you can put in the seedlings, once I've got some beds ready and sunk the holes."

It was only proper for one who saw himself as a helper to follow

一方,砖瓦的小块一一显露。力是何等地可贵,他潜藏着时,什么都不与相关,但是使用出来,可以使什么都变更。他工作了两点多钟。空地的六分之一翻松了,坐在阶上吸黄烟休息。

我的希望艳羡的心情,在他下第一耙的时候已欲迸溢而出,人生真实的愉快的滋味,这回我可要尝一尝了。他一停手,我急急地执着耙的柄,学着他那姿势和动作工作起来。但是那柄耙似乎不服从我的样子:我举他起来时,他在空中只是前后左右地摇晃;着地时他的四齿入土仅一寸光景;我再用力将他举起,平面结实的泥土上只有四个掘松的痕迹。我绝不灰心,这样总比以前松了些,我更下第二耙,第三耙……奇怪,那柄耙的重量为什么一回一回地增加!不到二十耙,我再也不能举起了。一缕焦烘烘的热从背脊散向全身,似乎每一个细胞都在燃烧着。呼吸是急促了,外面的空气钻入似地进我的鼻管,几乎容受不得。两手失了正常的知觉,还像执着那柄耙——虽然已放在地上——所以握不紧拳来。

福堂将烟管在石阶上敲去里面的烟灰,说道,"这个不是先生做得来的,你还是检砖瓦罢。去了砖瓦,待我先爬成几畦,打好了潭,你就可以下菜秧了。"

英汉对照
English-Chinese
中国文学宝库
Gems of Chinese Literature
现代文学系列
Modern Literature

his instructions, and indeed looking for bricks was labour too. And how sweet, how stirring were the words "you can put in the seedlings!" I bent myself to the unremitting task of picking up bricks with both hands and throwing them into the coarsely plaited bamboo skip. He continued his previous work, raising and bringing down the rake, the heavy, even sound of whose contact with the earth was for all the world like that of a machine.

Treading the soft soil, now cleared of bricks, my shoes sank in to their uppers as if into a goose-down carpet, and the scent of the soil wafting into my nostrils engendered a feeling of freshness and exhilaration. The cozily dormant earthworms, now turned up, burrowed in disorder towards the deep soil, only to stop short with their rear halves still exposed, and the wild chrysanthemums were mixed stem and leaf into the soil, the perfect green manure, victims now of "artificial selection." Time seemed not to move for me. Bereft of all contemplation and sentiment, I had become transformed. Strength was me, I was strength, a state of mind admitting only of an ineffable personal understanding.

Not until Futang stopped work and called to me "You can give it a rest now, sir," did I return to my normal state. Back aching, legs atremble and unsteady, brain shrouded in dizzying noise, I retreated to the front of the steps, leaned back against the door and sat to compose myself with closed eyes. I had never before experienced such a feeling of healthy exhaustion.

Two days later, twenty beds were planted. I had watched in admiration as Futang layed them out with no yardstick, just piling them lightly with the rake into rectangles, all of equal area, with

我既自认是他的副手,我应当服从他的指挥,况且检砖瓦一样是一种劳动。那句"就可以下菜秧"又何等地可喜,何等地足以勖勉我。我就佝偻着身子,两手不停地拾起砖瓦,投在粗竹丝编的大畚箕里。他继续他先前的工作,手里那柄耙一上一下,着地的声音沉重而调匀,竟像一架机器。

我踏在已检去砖瓦的松软的泥土上,鞋帮没了一半,似乎踏着鹅绒的毯子。泥土的气息一阵一阵透入鼻管,引起一种新鲜而快适的感觉。蚯蚓很安适地蛰伏着,这回经了翻动,他们只向泥土深处乱钻;但是到后半段身体还赤露着的时候,他们就不再钻了。菊科的野草连根带叶地杂在泥里,正好用作绿肥:他们现在是遭逢了"人为淘汰"了。

我不觉得时间在那里移换;我没有一切思虑和情绪。我化了,力就是我,我就是力。这等心境,只容体会,不可言说。

"先生,你可以歇歇了,"福堂停着工作在那里唤我,我才回复了平时的心境。腰部酸痛了,两腿战战的不能再站了,脑际也昏晕而作响。我便退到阶前,背靠着门坐下,闭着眼睛养神。这时我才感觉那从未感受的健康的疲倦。

两天之后,二十个畦都已下了菜秧。我看福堂造畦,心里很佩服他。他不用尺量,只将耙轻轻地爬剔,自然成了极正确的长方形的畦;而且各个畦的面积都相等呢。他又提起石潭槌来

英汉对照
English-Chinese
中国文学宝库
Gems of Chinese Literature
现代文学系列
Modern Literature

perfect natural accuracy, then dibbling the holes one by one, all exactly the same distance apart and exactly a hundred to a bed. Then came my part, the planting out. All this entailed was placing the seedlings in the holes and poking a little loose soil around the stems to cover them, but it was no light task for me, and as each bed was completed I fetched a bucket to water the seedlings, doubtless consumed with thirst after at least a day out of their native soil.

I stood in the ditch between the beds and gazed around me at the tender green leaves serried and supine upon them like an artist's sketch, an indescribable joy rising in me. What had I ever before achieved through toil? And now these greens would be nurtured by my toil. In two or three days, according to Futang, they would have absorbed sufficient water to resume their upright stance and would then with manure grow apace, their aspect daily altering.

There was no further strenuous work in the garden. The watering was done at dawn and dusk by Futang, who would at times squat between the beds to catch insects feeding on the leaves. The household chores were simple, and he was frequently free most of the day, when he would just sit on the porch smoking pipe after pipe, eternally shrouded in his air of melancholy and the plumes of smoke from his pipe and mouth.

Every day I went to look at the greens I had planted. Fifteen or sixteen days after bedding out, the leaf stems were still thin, and the leaves had not grown much, having moreover taken on a yellow hue, which made me doubt. "I expect it's because of the new

在畦上打成一个一个的潭,距离也无不相等,每畦恰是一百个。至于下秧是我的工作了:将菜秧放入潭里,拨些松泥掩没了根部,就完事了;但在我这不能算是轻易的事。插满了一畦,我又提一桶水来灌溉。那些菜秧自离母土,至少已经一天,应是饥渴了。

我站在畦间的沟里四望,嫩绿的叶一顺地偃在畦上,好似一幅图案画,心中起一种不可名言的快感。我以前几曾真将劳力成就过一件事物?现在那些菜,却受了我劳力的滋养了。据福堂说,隔上两三天,他们吸足了水,就能复原竖起来。此后加上粪肥,便轰地生长,每天要换一个样子呢。

菜园里更没有繁重的工作了。每天晨晚由福堂浇一回水,有时他蹲在畦间捉食叶的小虫。我家事务简单,他往往大半天闲着,于是只是坐在廊下吸烟,一管完了又一管,他那副幽郁的神情和烟管里嘴里缭绕的烟气总将他密密地笼罩住。

我天天去看手种的菜,距下秧的时候已是十五六天了,叶柄还是细细的,叶瓣也没有长大许多,更有呈露淡黄色的,这个很引起我的疑

land," Futang told me languidly. "Wait twenty days and you'll get three to the pound." As the sterling value of these words had fallen seventy percent a fortnight after the date of maturity had passed, I was somehow unswayed by his conviction. He had been fully aware on arrival that the land was new, and one with his experience of growing greens since childhood would scarcely be off by as much as two-thirds in reckoning the results of a planting. What then was the reason?

I scrutinized the leaves. Almost all had small holes. True, some had been discernible a few days before, but now they were denser and more widespread. On some, several had connected into cavities describing curves. In the depth of my sorrow I could not help upbraiding Futang. "You were just slipshod about the insects," I told him, "and the plants have been eaten to rags."

"It's not that easy, you know," he said, turning over a leaf with a forced smile only to see a black caterpillar drop down and searching for it. "Ah, here it is." He picked it out of the soil, tossed it underfoot and squashed it. Some disappeared as soon as they fell and had perforce to be abandoned to return to their ravening.

It would never have come to this, I thought, if he had spent his ample time on a slow, painstaking hunt; it was not as if he was a man unable to care properly for an acre or more. In his place I would have thought it, subjectively, a life of the most absorbing interest, where professional assiduity should appear an exclusive addiction. How could he prefer tobacco to farmwork and ignore all his professional duties, totally apathetic to the inroads on his stunted crop?

惑。福堂懒懒地向我说,"这个大约因为这里是生地的缘故。但二十天之后,三棵一斤总有的。"他这句话,超过豫料的成熟期有半个月,成色又打了三折,不由我不动摇对于他的坚信。这里是生地,他来时不是不晓得。他从小就种菜,根据他的经验推测种植的成绩,也不至相差到三分之二。究竟为了什么呢?

我细看叶瓣,几乎瓣瓣有小孔,前几天固然也有发见,但如今更是普遍而稠密了;有些瓣子上多孔通连,成为曲线描绘的大窟窿。我满腔的惋惜,不禁责备福堂道,"你捕虫太不留心了,菜竟被吃到这般地步。"

"这个不容易呀!"他勉强笑着,翻转一瓣叶子,就见一条黑色的幼虫坠下,他检寻了一会,"在这里了,"从泥上拾起那条虫,掷在脚下踏烂了。有时一坠下去就寻不见,只得舍了它,一会儿又在那里大吃了。

我想他时间尽多,慢慢地细细地捉虫,一定不至于此;又不是十亩八亩一个人照顾不周。以我主观的意见替他想,他过的是最有意思最有趣味的生活,就应当勤于他的职务,视为唯一的嗜好。何以他喜欢吸黄烟胜于农作?何以他绝不负职务上的责任,对于菜的不发育和被侵害又全无同情心呢?

英汉对照
English-Chinese
中国文学宝库
Gems of Chinese Literature
现代文学系列
Modern Literature

After many a surmise, I labelled him a "shirker." How could the results have been so poor unless his planting lacked a certain shrewdness of skill and his job meticulous attention in the doing? Yet what was the reason?

Futang was sitting smoking on the porch, as was his wont, when profiting from a spare moment I asked him about his family and was given the following account:

"We have two-thirds of an acre handed down from my grandfather, which I've been planting these twenty-odd years. He died when I was seven. It's not all that true what I've heard you say, sir, that there's a great savour to farming. At least, there is a savour to it, but it's bitter, more than I can say. Every night I dream it's over for me, and I won't be happy until that day comes.

"Farming all year round, there's one thought dogs me, and that's the rent. It has to be paid, of course it has. I need food and I need clothes and I wouldn't mind a good time or two, but I can't do that and pay the rent. It's no good. How can you manage all that with two-thirds of an acre?

"When I was nineteen we had a daughter. A stroke of luck, that was. The wife went out as a wet-nurse, which was as good as another acre. She's had six now, the second, third, fourth and fifth were all girls, and we farmed them out. The sixth was a boy. After he was born she wet-nursed as usual, and he was looked after by the eldest girl. She was always making porridge for him.

"He wasn't four months old when he got a touch of fever and cried all the time. I didn't understand why. I told the girl to hold him

我再四推想,断定他是"怠业"了。他于种植的技术,一定有许多不够精明之处;于他现在的职务,又一定没有做得周到完密;否则成绩何至于这么坏?但是为了什么呢?

福堂依他的老例,坐在廊下吸烟,我乘着没事,问他家里的状况。他就告诉我以下的话。

"我家里有四亩田,是爷传下来的。我种这四亩田,到今二十多年了。我八岁上爷就死了。我听你先生说,种田最有滋味,这话不大对。……滋味呢,固然有的,但是苦,苦到说不出!我夜夜做梦,梦见我不种田了。真有这一天,我才乐呢。

"我终年种田,只有一个念头刻刻迫着我,就是'还租'。租固然是应当还的,但我要吃,我要穿,我也想乐乐,一还租,那些就办不到了,没有了。只有四亩田,那里能料理这许多呢!

"我二十岁上生了个女儿,这是天帮我的,我妻就去当人家的乳母,伊一个人倒可抵六七亩田呢。伊到今共生了六胎,二三四五全是女,都送给人家养去,第六胎是个男。伊生了这个男孩,照例出去当乳母,由大女儿看守着他,时时调些米浆给他吃。

"他生了不满四个月,身上有些发烧,不住地啼哭。我不懂为什么,教大女儿好好抱着他,

英汉对照
English-Chinese
中国文学宝库
Gems of Chinese Literature
现代文学系列
Modern Literature

properly and give him more porridge. But he would never let up. There wasn't a moment's peace all night, and slowly it got lower and huskier, and after three days like that he died. By the time I'd gone into town to fetch his mother and she'd got back, his little eyes were shut tight...."

Futang had no more tragic words to relate his misfortune. Similar words, unencumbered by rhetoric, are often to be heard on the lips of misfortune. As I stared at the fallen leaves in the yard, a peculiar sadness hovered disconsolately with nowhere to settle.

Futang filled another pipe, drawing on it unlit as he continued:

"She changed after that. She scarcely came home, and then all she did was cry or pick on me. Not that you could blame her for that. She was as lost without the kid as I was, only who could I cry to or pick on?

"We married the eldest girl this spring, if you could call it a marriage, just seeing her to his house. Still, it was a weight off my shoulders at long last.

"Now there's just me.

"If you don't mind, sir, I'd like to stay on here. I'll get someone to take over my two-thirds of an acre which never yield much."

Now I understood. He detested working on the land, and I had put him back to his old line. That was the reason for the unexpected shirking.

My grasp of life had in fact been simple and shallow, and I had now been given greater confidence. Did our diametrically opposed appreciations of the same task raise me above Futang? Supposing our positions reversed, I should not have had his patience to endure

多给他吃些米浆。但是他的啼哭总不肯停,夜里也没一刻安静,声音慢慢地变得低而沙了。这么过了三天,他就死了。待我入城唤他母亲,伊到家时,他的小眼睛已闭得紧紧了……"

福堂不会将更哀伤的话讲述他的不幸了。但是足够了,这等没有修辞工夫的话,时时可以从不幸的人们口里听见,里面深深地含着普遍而摧心的悲哀,使我只是瞪视着庭中的落叶,一缕奇异而深刻的悲绪,徬徨惆怅,无有着处。

福堂再装上一管烟,却不燃着吸,继续说:

"伊从此变了个模样了。伊不常归家,到了家只是哭,和我吵闹。这也不能怪伊,伊和我一样地舍不得这个儿子。但是我向谁去哭,和谁去吵闹?

"今春将大女儿嫁了,实在算不得嫁,给人家领了去就是了。但我的肩上总算轻了些。

"家里只我一个人。

"先生,你若是不嫌我,我愿意长在这里,四亩种不得的田,我将转给他人去承种了。"

我才明白,他厌恶种田,我却仍使他做老本行,这便是不期然而然息业的缘故。

我所知于人生的,究竟简单而浅薄,于此更加自信。我和福堂做同一的事务,感受的滋味却绝对相反,我真高出于他么?倘若我和他易地以处,还没他这般忍耐,耐了二十年才决然舍

twenty years before resolving to be done with it. Had it not been superficial fantasy to consider that I had attained true happiness and recognized the core of life by the chance wielding of a rake and planting of a few greens?

From the shirking of the planter who detests planting, amplified to the shirking of the worker or teacher who detests working or teaching, we may infer formulaically that any practitioner of X who detests X will shirk it. How unfortunate and shameful that we should, upon our interminable path, ever and again be brought up short, fettered by unexpected shirking!

When there is nothing whatsoever detestable in X, this quality must reside in an entrammelling concomitance, the extirpation of which effects the cure.

The artistic life....

The remote but encroaching anxieties turned fleetingly like a windmill in my mind, persuading me that the so-called "present self" was an amalgam of sorrow, listlessness, vapidity and shame.

The greens in the garden were indeed out of the ground twenty days later, their thin leaves on stalks that could be bunched together in the fingers of one hand. They averaged four to the pound. The season's first offering was boiled up and tasted bitter.

I have ever since associated unpalatable fruit and vegetables or crudely-made utensils with the bitter greens from my garden, and then the remote but encroaching anxieties turn like a windmill in my mind.

February 6, 1921
Translated by Simon Johnstone

去呢。偶然当一柄耙,种几棵菜,就自以为得到了真实的愉快,认识了生命的真际,还不是些虚浮的幻想么?

从"种田的厌恶种田便致怠业",推衍出"作工或教书的厌恶作工或教书便致怠业",更可归纳成一个公式:"凡从事 X 的厌恶 X,便致怠业"。人们在无穷尽的道路中,频频被不期然而然的怠业羁绊住两条腿,不能迈步前进,是何等地不幸和可耻!

X 决无可以厌恶的地方,可厌恶的乃是纠缠着 X 的附生物。去掉这附生物,才是治病除根的法子。

艺术的生活……

那些空远而僭越的忧虑,一霎时在我心里风轮似地环转。我就觉这个所谓"现在的我",是个悲哀,怅惘,虚幻,惭愧……的集合体。

又隔了二十多天,园里的菜真离了土了,叶瓣是薄薄的,一手可以将叶柄捏拢来;平均四棵重一斤。煮熟了尝新,味道是苦的。

以后我吃味道不好的菜蔬和果子,或者遇见粗制的器物,就联想到我家园里的苦菜,同时那些空远而僭越的忧虑便在我心里风轮似地环转。

1921,2,6

英汉对照
English-Chinese
中国文学宝库
Gems of Chinese Literature
现代文学系列
Modern Literature

A Stroll at Dawn

The sun was rising as I crossed the fields drinking the lovely, peaceful scenes around. The trees by the village, all an enchanting grey, seemed to be afloat. They reminded me of my first impression of the West Lake in Hangzhou. That morning, early in summer, going out of Qiantang Gate and skirting a cliff, I suddenly had a view of the whole lake. The green hills enfolding it had a mysterious beauty which overwhelmed me, making me oblivious of everything else. It was an indescribable sensation, and mulling it over I have since realized that this was the most satisfying aesthetic experience of my whole life. Now the distant village trees, like green ranges of hills, made the same impression on me as had the West Lake, although then instead of walking through the countryside I was boating. I had been hankering after the West Lake, and here unexpectedly was a comforting substitute.

The wheat was all reaped. The peasants had ploughed the land and with their water-wheels were soaking it with river water ready for paddy. So the half-grown frogs had acquired new territory. The strident croaking from their slender throats blended in one cacophony. Most were squatting on clods of mud above the water, while some hopped from place to place, their heads in the air. Looking carefully one could see their white chests throbbing. When I passed close by they stopped croaking one after another and dived

晓 行

朝阳还没升高,我经过田野间,四望景物,非常秀丽且静穆。一带村树都作浅黛可爱的颜色,似乎正在浮动。我便忆起初见西湖时的情绪:那时是初夏的朝晨,出了钱塘门,经过了一带石壁,忽然间全湖在目。环湖的浅青的山色含有神秘而不可说的美,我只觉无可奈何,同时也遗忘了一切。这是一种不可描绘的情绪,过后思量,竟是我生享受美感的很满足的一回。现在那些远处的村树仿佛是连绵的青山,而我所得的印象又与初到西湖时相似,然则我不是野行,竟是在湖上荡桨了。我原有点渴忆西湖呢,不料无意间得到了替代的安慰。

田里的麦全已割去。农人将泥土翻转来,更车了河水进来浸润着,预备种稻。已成形而还不会长足的蛙就得了新的领土。他们狭小的喉咙里发出阔大而烦躁的声音,彼此应和,联成一片。他们大多蹲在高出水面的泥块上,或从此处跳到彼处;头部仰起,留心看去可以看见他们白色的胸部在那里鼓动。当我经过他们近旁的时候,他们顺次停止了鸣声,极轻便地没入水

A Stroll at Dawn

lightly into the water. Presently, when I receded, they set up a racket again behind my back.

The muddy path bore the footprints of people and cattle but not a blade of grass. On both sides though grew clumps of weeds, mostly of the grass family, bearing tiny multi-coloured flowers — not likely to be noticed except by insects. The flowers and leaves were pearled in the most delightful way with shining dewdrops. The faint smell of dung from the distance, so redolent of country life, negated my earlier notion that I was boating on the celebrated West Lake.

I reached a pond. The grass on its sides and the trees on the banks were reflected in the water, greener, fresher and lovelier than the plants themselves. The sun was not as yet shining on the pond. Its deep blue water was utterly still. In one corner floated duckweed, clusters of leaves supporting small flowers — these had not been out a few days ago I remembered. Tiddlers occasionally swam near the surface, setting up ripples or making the duckweed quiver.

Southeast of the pond stood a tumbledown cottage, a ditch running from its back to the pond. I strolled to the front. The single-panelled door was open, but a rickety table and some stools on the rough earthen floor were all I could see inside. The shutters by the door were raised, and a girl was standing under the window. The square front yard was the same size as the cottage. Paved with small rectangular bricks it served as a threshing-floor.

The girl's reddish hair was so sparse, she could only plait it into one small braid. Her face was very thin and sallow and there was a

中。不一会,我离他们较远,一片噪音又在我背后喧闹了。

　　印有人及家畜的足迹的泥路上竟没一棵草。两旁却丛生野草,大部分是禾本科的植物,开着各色的小花——除了昆虫恐怕再没有注意他们的了。细小而晶莹可爱的露珠附着在花和叶上,很有可玩的意趣。远处粪肥的气味微微地送入我的鼻管,充满着农田生活的感觉,使我否认先前的假想:我并不在清游雅玩的西湖上。

　　我走到一个池旁。岸滩的草和傍岸的树映入池中,倒影比本身绿得更鲜嫩,更可爱。这时候池面还没受日光的照耀,深蓝色的静定的池水满含着沉默。池面的一角浮着萍叶,数叶攒聚处蠢起些桂黄色的小花——记得前几天还没有呢。偶然有些小鱼游近水面,才起极轻微的波纹,或者使萍花略微颤动。

　　靠着池的东南岸是一所破旧的农舍,屋后有一个水埠通到池面。我信足走去,已到了那所屋舍的前面。一扇板门开着,里面只见些破的台凳和高低不平的泥地。门旁两扇板窗都撑起,一个女孩儿站在窗下。屋前一方地和屋的面积一样大,铺着长方的小砖,是他们的曝场。

　　那女孩儿有略带红色的头发,非常稀疏,仅能编成一条小辫子;面孔很瘦削,呈淡黄色;眼

blank look in her eyes. She stared at me as if at a suspicious stranger.

I had never been this way before. Seeing no path through the bean field ahead I asked her, "Can I get from here to the river?" This inquiry allayed her suspicions and she nodded. "Just cut right through." With a word of thanks I was walking on when she added, "But the bean leaves are covered with dew — it'll wet your clothes and shoes." "It doesn't matter," I answered as I parted the bean stalks and set off along a narrow furrow. Although I ignored her warning I was grateful for her concern for me — a stranger.

After crossing the bean field to the river bank, my shoes and the lower part of my clothes were sopping wet. The river was as blue and motionless as the pond, except for glints here and there caused by the current flowing unseen beneath. Some peasants were working on the other bank, looking dwarfed by the immensity of the fields. Soft serene sunshine lit up the soil as if giving boundless vitality to all creation. All matter — whether each bank, each plot of land or each hoe in a peasant's hands — seemed to have a life of its own.

I stood watching for a while, then walked on beside the river. Ahead two peasants were working a hand-operated water-wheel on the bank, each turning a handle to sluice water into the fields. Soon I came up with them. One was very tall and bronzed, his face wrinkled, with large eyes and a prominent nose. He looked as if in his forties. The other seemed little more than twenty and had the air of a student from the city. But although his skin was not too dark, his well-developed muscles showed that he was used to farm-

光作茫昧的瞪视。她见了我,只是对我看,仿佛我身上丛集着什么疑讶。

我不会走过这条路,看前面都种着豆,不见通路,疑是不能通过的了。便问她道,"从这里可以到那条河边么?"这个问询减损了她疑讶的神情的大部分,她点头道,"转过去就是。"我答应了一声,再往前走。她又说,"但是豆叶上全是露水,要沾湿你的衣裳和鞋。"我说,"不要紧,"就分开两边的豆茎,顺着很狭的田岸走去。我虽然没听她的话,心里却感激她对于我——她的不相识者——的好意。

走完了种豆的地方便到河岸,我的鞋和衣裳的下半截真湿了,河水和池水一样地深蓝和静定,但因潜隐的流动有几处发出光亮。对岸的田里有几个农人在那里工作,因田地的空旷显出他们的微小。和平而轻淡的阳光照到田面,就像对一切给与无限的生意,一条田岸,一方泥土,和农人手里的一柄锄头,都似乎物质里面含有内在的精神。

我站着望了一会,便沿着河走。在我的前路有两个农人在那里车水:一架手摇水车设在岸滩,他们俩各执一个柄摇动机关,引河水到田里。不多时我已到了他们俩跟前。一个农人非常高大,露出的皮肤全是酱一般的颜色;面部皱纹很多,有巨大的眼睛和鼻子。他约摸四十多岁。又一个是二十出头的年纪,面目很像城市间的读书人;皮肤也不至于深赤;但是他四肢的发达的肌肉可以证明他是久操农作的人。他们

英汉对照
English-Chinese
中国文学宝库
Gems of Chinese Literature
现代文学系列
Modern Literature

A Stroll at Dawn

ing. So engrossed in their work were both that neither spoke nor even glanced at the other. This is a fairly common phenomenon. Two carpenters sawing the same piece of timber, two tailors at one table, behave as if each were alone. The onlooker imagines that they must feel unbearably lonely. But being only an onlooker how can he judge whether they are lonely or not?

The water drawn up by the water-wheel flowed into the fields through a temporary ditch which crossed my path. Both sides of it were muddy. I was hitching up my clothes to step across when the elder of the peasants said with a smile, "Watch your step or you may slip." He stopped working as he spoke, and the young fellow followed suit. The creaking of the water-wheel broke off abruptly.

"It's all right, I can manage," I answered and sprang across the ditch. As I had never taken this path before, all the sights here were new to me, and I was intrigued by the way they worked the wheel. So, since it was still early, I halted here.

Seeing me safely across they went on with their work. The elder man looked at me and asked, "Are you from that school there, sir?"

"Yes."

"More than three hundred children, haven't you?"

"That's right, more than four hundred."

"Seem to have fun all right. Each time I pass your wall I hear them laughing and fooling about. Don't suppose they play truant, do they?"

"No, they don't." Presently I asked, "Was your wheat harvest good this year? There were no storms while it was ripening."

俩只顾工作,非但不交一语,并且不看一看共同操作的伴侣。这个情形无论到什么地方都可遇见,锯开一段木头的两个工匠,同一作台的两个裁缝,都是好像没有第二个人在他们旁边似的,旁人看着他们,就要想他们何以耐得这般寂寞。其实旁人不就是他们,究竟寂寞与否怎便能断定呢!

水车引起的水经过一条临时掘成的沟流到田里。那条沟横断我的前路,而且有好些湿泥塞在两旁。我提起了衣服,正要跨过那条沟,那个年长的农人笑着对我说,"须留心跨,防跌交。"他说时两手停了工作,那个年轻的也停了,繁喧的水车声便划然而止。

我说,"不妨事,我能跨,"身体略一腾跃,已过了小沟。我来这一条未尝走惯的路上觉得一切的景物都新鲜,看农人车水也有趣味,时光又很早,所以就停了脚步。

他们俩见我过了小沟,便继续他们的工作。那年长的看着我问道,"先生是在那边学堂里的么?"

"是的。"

"那里的学生不止二三百吧?"

"不错。四百有余。"

"那些学生真开心,我从你们墙外走过,只听见他们笑和闹。大约不会有逃学的了。"

"逃学的确然没有。"停了一会,我问他说,"今年的麦收成想还不差,结实的时候不曾有过大风雨呢。"

英汉对照
English-Chinese
中国文学宝库
Gems of Chinese Literature
现代文学系列
Modern Literature

A Stroll at Dawn

"Not bad at all, the best in the last five or six years."

"Will you be planting rice in this plot of yours now?"

"Yes." He pointed to a square seedling bed fifty paces away. "The seedlings there are already this tall. It's high time to transplant them."

I looked where he was pointing. The tender green seedlings in neat, orderly rows were like a square of green velvet. That natural green of theirs, a green never seen in paintings, was really enchanting.

He went on, "Once we have enough water in this field and have ploughed it, we can put in the seedlings. The afternoon of the day after tomorrow at the latest." His face lit up as he said this, with an ingenuous smile.

"You're in for some hard work," I observed. "You'll have to water and weed the fields every day, with the blazing sun grilling you too. Don't you find it tough?"

"Of course we don't have a soft life like you, but we don't find it hard either. You may think we do, but then we're used to it. Which of us villagers hasn't soaked his legs in the paddy fields? Which of us hasn't been baked in the sun? We've been used to it since we were kids, so who finds it tough?"

"You must love the crops you grow."

"Of course, they're our life. When we see them growing well, it puts fresh life into us. The year before last those pesky insects came to eat our paddy just as it was in flower. Made each stalk snap in two and wither. When we looked carefully, it was all because of those damned pests! Nothing we could do about it but

"今年很好,五六年没有这样的收成了。"

"现在你这块田预备种稻了?"

"是的,"他指着五十步外一方秧田说,"那里的秧已长得那么高,赶紧要插了。"

我望那方秧田,柔细而嫩绿的秧生得非常整齐,好似一方绿绒。那种绿是自然的色彩,决不能在画幅中看见,真足以迷醉人的心目。

他接着说,"我们在这田里车足了水,更犁松了泥土,就可以插秧。至迟到后天下午我们必得插秧。"他说时脸上有一种欣悦的神采,更伴着简朴真挚的微笑。

我说,"此后你们要辛苦了,添水拔草等工作你们天天要做,四无遮盖的猛烈的太阳又专和你们为难。你们以为这些是苦楚不是?"

"我们的日子自然不及你们那么舒服,但是也不见得苦楚。你们看我们以为苦楚,其实我们乡村里的人谁不会将两腿没在水里尽浸?谁不会将身体挺在阳光中尽晒?我们从小到大都是这样,管什么苦楚不苦楚?"

"你们一定爱你们田里种的东西。"

"那自然,那是我们的性命。我们看他们很顺遂地发达起来,就好比我们的性命更为坚固且长久。前年那些天杀的小虫来吃我们的稻:一块田里的稻都已开花,忽然每棵稻的中段都折了,茎也枯萎了。留心看去,都是那些天杀的在那里作恶!我们没有法想,只对着稻田叹

英汉对照
English-Chinese
中国文学宝库
Gems of Chinese Literature
现代文学系列
Modern Literature

wring our hands?!" At this recollection he spoke more gravely and slowly — a sure sign of anger among country folk.

"Why didn't you catch them? Weren't plenty of people sent from town to teach you how to guard against them and catch them?"

"How to guard against them, eh? We don't have much faith in that insecticide with the outlandish name. Lighting lamps in the evening and filling bowls with oil for them to drown in — that works all right. But everyone has to join in, and that can't be done. If only one or two families catch all the pests in their fields this way, when those in other people's fields have nothing left to eat they'll swarm over like refugees; so catching them is just a waste of time."

"The year before last was disastrous. Was last year better?"

"A bit." He laughed caustically. "But there's no killing them off! They've preyed on us for over ten years in a row, not leaving us one year in peace. Some years aren't quite as bad as others — that's all."

"Do the landlords reduce your rent?"

"They reckon they do." He laughed caustically again.

"By how much?"

"That depends. They're a crafty lot mostly. Maybe not all the crops are destroyed, but if most are hard hit they allow a ten per cent discount for the lot. Not so as to help those folk who've come through all right, but to make things even worse for those whose crops were wiped out. What they say is, 'this is the easiest way to calculate. How can we inspect every field to decide how much you should pay?' Some first raise the price of rice, then put up a no-

气!"他引起了以往的愤恨,语音便沉重且有停顿——这是乡村中人普通的愤恨的征象。

"你们为什么不捕捉?城里曾经派出许多人员教你们预防和捕捉的法子。"

"预防呢,我们不很相信那叫也叫不清楚的药料。晚上点了灯,盛了油,待他们来投死,确是个靠得住的法子,但是要大家一齐做才行——这怎么办得到呢?独有一两家这么做,自己田里的提完了,别家田里的吃到没得吃了,就难民一般地搬了来,还是个提如未捉。"

"前年的灾情真厉害。去年好些吧?"

"好些,"他冷笑着说,"但是总不能灭尽!他们作恶一连十几年,那一年不和我们为难,至多恶得轻些罢了。"

"田主减收你们的田租吧?"

"总算减短些,"他仍旧冷笑。

"减短多少呢?"

"不一定。他们中间很有几家专会用取巧的法子。他们所有的田不一定全受虫灾,但是被灾的多,便统打个九折收租。他们的意思并不是要没受灾害的得些好处,简直是使受灾的更受些灾害!然而他们有他们的说法,'惟有这样才便于计算;否则怎能一块一块田都看到,确定出应收的成数呢?'又有几家,他们先抛大了

英汉对照
English-Chinese
中国文学宝库
Gems of Chinese Literature
现代文学系列
Modern Literature

tice announcing a twenty-five per cent discount for everyone. People hearing this think their rent has been lowered and rush to be the first to pay. The landlords end up better off than ever — they're the only ones to gain."

"What discount did you get the year before last?"

"Me?" He yanked the wheel to vent his indignation. "Ten per cent of course! Do you know whose land this is, sir?"

"No."

"Shao Hezhi's. His house is east of your school, you should know him."

I thought of the man who went every day to the teahouse in that street and sat at a corner table. His cheeks were hollow; behind his spectacles his short-sighted eyes were grim; his forehead was often wrinkled because he kept brooding. All in all, there was a calculating look about him. The only other customer I ever saw him speak to was the bailiff with whom he worked out what his tenants owed him. This was all I knew of him, but still I had to answer, "Yes, I know him."

"Just think, tilling *his* land, of course I pay ninety per cent!"

"I don't know much about him. Is he strict over the payment?"

"I'll say he is!" He paused before adding, "All landlords are, only some are more vicious than others. Mr. Shao beats the lot for viciousness."

"In what way?"

"The figure he works out is like a rocky peak, there's no budging it. No matter how you beg him to cut it down a bit, nothing doing. If you owe him rent he sends the bailiff to fetch you, and sets

米价,却挂出牌子来说田租统打七五折。大家听了这一句,以为他们的租轻松些,便争先缴租给他们。到末了他们的收数独多,还是他们占了便宜。"

"前年你的田租打了几折?"

"我么?"他摇动水车格外用力,借此发泄他的不平,"自然是九折! 先生可知道我种的谁家的田?"

"不知道。"

"邵和之,他的家就在你们学校的东面,先生总该知道。"

我便想起常在沿街的茶馆里坐着的那个人。他每天坐在靠墙角的桌旁。瘦削的两颊向里低陷;短视的眼睛从眼镜里放出冷酷的光;额上常有皱纹,因为常在那里思虑;总之,他的面孔全部含着计算的意思。我不曾见他和别的茶客谈话,除了和催甲或差吏计议农人积欠的田租的数目。——我所知于他的只有这些,但总算是知道他的,便答应那农人道,"我知道。"

"你想,我种的田就是他的,自然是九折了!"

"我不很知道他的底细,他收租很厉害么?"

"厉害!"他停了一会,又说,"田主收租谁都厉害,手段硬些软些罢了。邵大爷是惯用硬功的大王。"

"怎见得呢?"

"他算出来的数目就好比石头的山,不能移动一分。任你向他诉说恳求,巴望他减短一点,他的头总不肯点一点。欠了他的租,他就派差

英汉对照
English-Chinese
中国文学宝库
Gems of Chinese Literature
现代文学系列
Modern Literature

a date on which you must pay up. Those eyes of his are so devilish, you daren't plead any more but agree and go home to think up ways and means, borrowing money or pawning whatever you have — anything rather than have to face those devilish eyes again."

They stopped and straightened up to look round and take a breather. A plop sounded from the river as if someone had thrown in a stone. "What was that?" I asked. Ripples spread slowly over the surface, disappearing when the largest reached the bank.

The youngster exclaimed, "Must have been a whopping big carp!" He kept his eyes on the water.

"That Mr. Shao," the elder man went on, his voice sounding louder now that the wheel had stopped. "He's hard as flint. None harder. Once he went by boat to Yang Family Village to the east to collect rent. A family was supposed to pay up that day, but couldn't scrape together the money. The man was so frantic when he saw the boat coming, like a fool he hid himself in the latrine. When the bailiff found only a woman at home, he knew her husband was hiding. He hunted round and dragged him out of the latrine. In desperation the man said, 'I've got the money, I'll pay in full today.' So the bailiff let go of him. Then off he rushed to throw himself into the river! All who saw set up a shout, and soon the whole village ran out. The man had already surfaced and sunk several times. Mr. Shao's boatman was afraid, if he drowned, the villagers would sink his boat, so he hurriedly cast off to get away. Know what Mr. Shao did? He stepped aboard and yelled to the boatman to stay put. He wasn't worried, not he! He bellowed to the villagers on the bank, 'Defaulting on rent is a crime! If he

吏来叫去，由他说一个日期，约定到那一天必须缴还。他那双眼睛真可怕，望着他怎敢再求，只有答应下来，回来想法子，借债当东西全都做到，只求不再看他那双可怕的眼睛。"

他们俩停了手，挺一挺腰，望着四围舒一舒气，预备休息一会。河面忽然有一个声音，好似谁投了一块砖石。我无意地自语道，"什么？"看河面时，水花慢慢地扩散开来，最大的一圈已碰着对岸而消灭了。

那年轻的农人用艳羡的语气说，"该是一尾好大的鲤鱼。"他说时注视着河面。

"那位邵大爷，"年长的农人向我说，因为水车停了，显出他声音的响亮，"他有一次真是石头一般地定心，叫人万学不来。他坐了船到东面杨家村里去收租。一家人家同他约了那一天的期，但是竟没法想，一个钱也弄不到。那个男子情急了，看见船摇进村，便发痴一般地避到屋后的茅厕里。差吏进门要人时，只见一个女人，知是避开了，略一搜寻，便从茅厕里把他拖了出来。那男子十分慌张，嘴里却说，'我已有了钱，今天统可还清。'差吏听说，自然放了手。那知那男子拔脚飞跑，竟往河里一跳！看见的人齐喊起来，一会儿村人都奔了出来。水里的人已冒了几冒，沉下去了。那时候邵大爷的舟子见将有人命交涉，恐怕被村人打沉了他的船，急急解缆想要逃走。你知那位邵大爷怎样？他跨上船头喝住舟子不许解缆。他的脸上毫没着急的意思，大声对岸上的人说，'欠租是何等重大的

英汉对照
English-Chinese
中国文学宝库
Gems of Chinese Literature
现代文学系列
Modern Literature

drowns, his wife will have to pay!' Everyone was worried stiff. They felt what he said was right, so how could they smash his boat? Instead they managed to rescue the man, and later he had to sell his last picul of rice to pay his rent — went short of food to clear his debt."

I was sickened by this account, and not just by the part that Shao had played either. Looking down at the river, no longer deep blue now that the sun had risen, I just grunted by way of comment.

"Working for a man like that, it pays to be civil and hand in your rent in good time." One hand on the water-wheel, he spoke as if from bitter experience.

"And how do you make out farming?" I asked, suspecting that he was under cruel pressure.

"I manage somehow, sir, thank you. Not just tilling these few *mu* of land. I have some other fields too which yield a couple of poor crops each year. That helps."

"Then you're not badly off." I felt relieved.

The water-wheel started turning again. The river water flowed slowly into the field. I should be starting my own work soon, not just watch other people working.

"We must have another talk some other day," I said before walking on.

Behind me the creaking of the water-wheel seemed to carry a distant voice, "Be seeing you."

June 11, 1921
Translated by Wenxue

罪名！他便溺死了，还是要向他女人算！'那时村人个个着急，听邵大爷的说法又觉得不错，那还有劲儿打他的船，只拚命将河里的人救了起来。后来那个男子还是卖掉了留着自己吃的一石米，还清了租，才算了结。"

我听了这一段叙述，心里起一种憎恨的情绪，但并不只为那个姓邵的。因此，我低头望着河水——那时已不是深蓝的颜色，因为太阳升高了，——不答说什么，只发出个"哦"的声音。

"种了这种人的田，客客气气早日还租就是便宜。"他一手撑在水车的木桩上，以很有经验的神情向我这么说。

"像你，种田过活，还过得去吧？"我想和我对面的人或者也曾受过严酷的逼迫，所以急切地问他。

"多谢先生，我还算过得去。单靠这几亩田是不济事的。我另有几亩烂田，一年两熟半，贴补我不少呢。"

"那就舒服了，"我如同身受那么安慰。

水车的机关又转动了，河水汩汩地流入田里。我想我的工作快要开始了，怎能只看着他人工作呢？我对那农人说，"他日再同你谈罢，"便向前走去。

水车的声音里带一个似乎很远的人语声——"改日再会"——在我的背后。

1921，6，11

英汉对照
English-Chinese
中国文学宝库
Gems of Chinese Literature
现代文学系列
Modern Literature

How Mr. Pan Weathered the Storm

1

The station was crowded with people, each of them preoccupied with his own problems and looking not quite his usual self. The porters, hands thrust into the pockets of their numbered uniforms, stood motionless as if they had fallen asleep on their feet. They knew they still had a long wait ahead; it was not yet time for the tips they were hoping to get so there was no point in looking energetic at this moment. The oppressive atmosphere made breathing somewhat difficult. It looked like rain. The lights which had been turned on for some time were dimmer than usual and made everything appear as if in a fog.

A notice on the blackboard announced that the incoming express from the west was going to be four hours late. This notice had been read and reread several hours ago and now, like those old, torn theatre bills left to flutter in the wind, could no longer draw a single glance from anyone. Since such notices had been posted for practically every incoming train this week, they had become the thing to be expected.

This train which had been on the mind of so many people finally appeared. The sombre station became a hive of activity. We shall

潘先生在难中

一

　　车站里挤满了人，各有各的心事，都现出异样的神色。脚夫的两手插在号衣的口袋里，睡着一般地站着；他们知道可以得到特别收入的时间离得还远，也犯不着老早放出精神来。空气沉闷得很，人们略微感到呼吸受压迫，大概快要下雨了。电灯亮了一会了，仿佛比平时昏黄一点，望去好像一切的人物都在雾里梦里。

　　揭示处的黑漆版上标明西来的快车须迟到四点钟。这个报告在几点钟以前早就教人家看熟了，现在便同风化了的戏单一样，没有一个人再望它一眼。像这种报告，在这一个礼拜里，几乎每天每趟的行车都有；大家也习以为当然了。

　　不知几多人心系着的来车居然到了，闷闷的一个车站就一变而为扰扰的境界。来客的安

英汉对照
English-Chinese
中国文学宝库
Gems of Chinese Literature
现代文学系列
Modern Literature

not go into the relief of the travellers who had reached their journey's end, the joy of those waiting for them, or the tips received by the porters. We are concerned only with a certain Mr. Pan who had come from a nearby small town, Rangli. Before the train chugged into the station, he had managed to arrange everything to his satisfaction: He was at the head of his small family, his right hand holding a black leather bag and his left leading his six-year-old son. The child's other hand held on to his eight-year-old brother who in turn held his mother's hand. Mr. Pan said he would not be able to take care of them all unless they held together like this. For with hands linked, they could wriggle through like a snake wherever they wanted to go. He told his family again and again to lock their hands tightly; they were not to let go whatever happened. Lest the others should forget, he kept swinging his left hand as a reminder to be passed down the line.

It was good of course to form a line, yet not without disadvantages too. As the rain slowed to a stop all the passengers with their luggage surged towards the door. In this exigency, the line formed by Mr. Pan and his family suffered for its length. Using his black leather bag to clear the way, he had pushed on vigorously with his chest and stomach till he was only two windows away from the door. But his six-year-old son was still four windows away, wedged tightly in between other passengers and the wooden seats. Arms stretching out in two directions and pulled vigorously from both ends, the child felt that his limbs would soon be torn off. "Oh, my arms, my arms!" he wailed in desperation.

The other passengers were not aware that there was a child

心,候客者的快意,以及脚夫的小小发财,我们且都不提。单讲一位从让里来的潘先生。他当火车没有驶进月台之先,早已安排得十分周妥:他领头,右手提着个黑漆皮包,左手牵着个七岁的孩子;七岁的孩子牵着他哥哥(今年九岁),哥哥又牵着他母亲。潘先生说人多照顾不齐,这么牵着,首尾一气,犹如一条蛇,什么地方都好钻了。他又屡次叮嘱,教大家握得紧紧,切勿放手;尚恐大家万一忘了,又屡次摇荡他的左手,意思是教把这警告打电报一般一站一站递过去。

首尾一气诚然不错,可是也不能全然没有弊病。火车将停时,所有的客人和东西都要涌向车门,潘先生一家的那条蛇就有点尾大不掉了。他用黑漆皮包做前锋,胸腹部用力向前抵,居然进展到距车门只两个窗洞的地位。但是他的七岁的孩子还在距车门四个窗洞的地方,被挤在好些客人和坐椅之间,一动不能动;两臂一前一后,伸得很长,前后的牵引力都很大,似乎快要把胳臂拉了去的样子。他急得直喊,"啊!我的胳臂!我的胳臂!"

英汉对照
English-Chinese
中国文学宝库
Gems of Chinese Literature
现代文学系列
Modern Literature

wedged in between their legs until his cries reached their ears. A closer look revealed that the family of four was linked in a long line with hands tightly locked.

"Let go at once," ordered one passenger. "Or else you'll be pulling the child apart."

"What's this! Why doesn't the man carry the child?" muttered another, his tone full of scorn, as he edged his own way towards the door.

"No," Mr. Pan disagreed with them. There were good reasons for holding on together. He realized, however, on second thought that not everyone was intelligent enough to see these reasons and it was a waste of breath to argue with them. But the six-year-old was still yelling, "My arms, my arms!" Since Mr. Pan could see no way either to advance or to turn back, he had to be the first to violate his own admonition and let go of the child's hand. "Keep your eyes on me, don't lose sight of me," he ordered, flustered and worried.

The train stopped with a clang and a jerk. A number of people shot out of the carriage door and Mr. Pan felt the pressure from in front suddenly relax but the pushing from behind gained in momentum so that his legs carried him forward without any effort on his part. He meant to turn to rally his small forces but finding that impossible merely shouted at the backs of the heads before him, "Follow close behind me! Follow me!"

Somehow or other he too shot out of the door. Turning round quickly, he saw that his wife and sons were not behind him; they were still squeezed in somewhere in the train. Waiting by the door seemed to him the best possible solution. Another hundred or so

一些客人听见了带哭的喊声,方才知道腰下挤着个孩子;留心一看,见他们四个人一串,手联手牵着。一个客人呵斥道,"赶快放手;要不然,把孩子拉做两半了!"

"怎么的,孩子不抱在手里!"又一个客人用鄙夷的声气自语,一方面他仍注意在攫得向前行进的机会。

"不,"潘先生心想他们的话不对,牵着自有牵着的妙用;再转一念,妙用岂是人人能够了解的,向他们辩白,也不过徒费唇舌,不如省些精神罢:就把以下的话咽了下去。而七岁的孩子还是"胳臂!胳臂!"喊着。潘先生前进后退都没有希望,只得自己失约,先放了手,随即惊惶地发命令道,"你们看着我!你们看着我!"

车轮一顿,在轨道上站定了;车门里弹出去似地跳下了许多人。潘先生觉得前头松动了些;但是后面的力量突然增加,他的脚作不得一点主,只得向前推移;要回转头来招呼自己的队伍,也不得自由,于是对着前面的人的后脑叫喊,"你们跟着我!你们跟着我!"

他居然从车门里被弹出来了。旋转身子一看,后面没有他的儿子同夫人。心知他们还挤在车中,守住车门老等总是稳当的办法。又下来了百多人,方才看见脚踏上人丛中现出七岁

英汉对照
English-Chinese
中国文学宝库
Gems of Chinese Literature
现代文学系列
Modern Literature

passengers alighted before the screwed-up, tearful face of his younger son appeared under the lamplight. Mr. Pan hurried up and, after being swept back several times by alighting passengers, picked up his son in his left arm and set him down on the platform. Another short wait and Mrs. Pan and the eight-year-old emerged. Panting heavily and uttering groans of pain, she turned her mournful gaze to her husband's face, like a child seeking consolation.

Mr. Pan was after all a man with some presence of mind. Now that his forces had been reassembled he issued another order, "We must link hands again. See what a crowd there is on the platform and look at that bottleneck at the exit. If we don't hold on together we're bound to lose each other."

The six-year-old had had enough. Hugging his father's legs, he said, "Carry me, daddy."

"You little nuisance!" Mr. Pan was exasperated, but he restrained himself and, stooping down, picked up the child. He told his older son to hold on to the tail of his long gown with one hand and on to Mrs. Pan with the other.

Never before had Mrs. Pan been through an ordeal like this. The prospect of an even greater crush was more than she could bear after the effort of getting off the train. "If I had known it was going to be like this," she grumbled, "I'd have stayed at home and waited for death rather than come out and be a refugee."

"What's the use of regretting?" Mr. Pan's annoyance was tinged with sympathy. "Now that we're here, why regret? Besides, at least we're safe here. Let's go now. Mind your steps!" And all four together, they staggered into the crowd.

的孩子的上半身,承着电灯光,面目作哭泣的形相。他走前去,几次被跳下来的客人冲回,才用左臂把孩子抱了下来。再等了一会,潘师母同九岁的孩子也下来了;她吁吁地呼着气,连喊,"哎唷,哎唷,"凄然的眼光相着潘先生的脸,似乎要求抚慰的孩子。

潘先生到底镇定,看见自己的队伍全下来了,重又发命令道,"我们仍旧像刚才一样联起来。你们看月台上的人这么多,收票处又挤得厉害,要不是联着,就走散了!"

七岁的孩子觉得害怕,拦住他的膝头说,"爸爸,抱。"

"没用的东西!"潘先生颇有点愤怒,但随即耐住,蹲下身子把孩子抱了起来。同时关照大的孩子拉着他的长衫的后幅,一手要紧紧牵着母亲,因为他自己两只手都不空了。

潘师母从来不曾受过这样的困累,好容易下了车,却还有可怕的拥挤在前头,不禁发怨道,"早知道这样子,宁可死在家里,再也不要逃难了!"

"悔什么!"潘先生一半发气,一半又觉得怜惜。"到了这里,懊悔也是没用。并且,性命到底安全了。走罢,当心脚下。"于是四个一串向人丛中蹒跚地移过去。

英汉对照
English-Chinese
中国文学宝库
Gems of Chinese Literature
现代文学系列
Modern Literature

How Mr. Pan Weathered the Storm

A frantic rush and Mr. Pan emerged as if from a dream through the narrow exit guarded by the ticket collector. Like a drop of water in a torrent, he had no alternative but to be swept along by the multitude around him, his feet barely touching the ground. In a moment he had cleared the wire fence of the railway station, stepped across the tramway and arrived on the cement pavement of the street outside. Turning round hurriedly, he saw countless faces pale in the lamplight and numerous bags and bundles rolling in his direction. Suddenly he realized that the little hand that had been clutching the tail of his long gown was no longer there; he had no idea when it had let go. An indescribable sorrow filled his heart and he automatically turned his head round. But there was no sign of his wife and son. He felt he had lost his family. The lights and figures round him began to swim as tears filled his eyes.

Fortunately the child in his arm had sharp eyes. "Mama, there she is," he pointed. He had spied and recognized the fringe over his mother's brows.

Mr. Pan was overjoyed. He first rubbed his eyes on the child's clothes before he looked in the direction pointed out for he hardly dared to believe the good news. After a slight search, he saw his wife darting left and right in the crowd, her hands held protectively round their older son. They were still on the other side of the tramway. "Ada!" he hailed and hurrying over brought them back to where he had been standing on the pavement. Putting down the six-year-old at last, he breathed a sigh of relief. "Now, all's well!" he said, mopping his face. Indeed all was well, for once they crossed

一阵的拥挤,潘先生像在梦里似的,出了收票处的隘口。他仿佛急流里的一滴水滴,没有回旋转侧的余地,只有顺着大众的势,脚不点地地走。一会儿已经出了车站的铁栅栏,跨过了电车轨道,来到水门汀的人行道上。慌忙地回转身来,只见数不清的给电灯光耀得发白的面孔以及数不清的提箱与包裹,一齐向自己这边涌来,忽然觉得长衫后幅上的小手没有了,不知什么时候放了的;心头怅惘到不可言说,只是无意识地把身子乱转。转了几回,一丝踪影也没有。家破人亡之感立时袭进他的心,禁不住渗出两滴眼泪来,望出去电灯人形都有点模糊了。

幸而抱着的孩子眼光敏锐,他瞥见母亲的疏疏的额发,便认识了,举起手来指点道,"妈妈,那边。"

潘先生一喜;但是还有点不大相信,眼睛凑近孩子的衣衫擦了擦,然后望去。搜寻了一会,果然看见他的夫人呆鼠一般在人丛中瞎撞,前面护着那大的孩子,他们还没跨过电车轨道呢。他便向前迎上去,连喊"阿大",把他们引到刚才站定的人行道上。于是放下手中的孩子,舒畅地吐一口气,一手抹着脸上的汗说,"现在好了!"的确好了,只要跨出那一道铁栅栏,就有人

英汉对照
English-Chinese
中国文学宝库
Gems of Chinese Literature
现代文学系列
Modern Literature

that wire fencing① they were insured against war, fire and robbery. Besides, he had found his lost son and wife. It was as if from the jaws of disaster he had rescued four lives and one black bag. All was well, indeed. Authoritatively, Mr. Pan shouted, "Rickshaw!" Several rickshaw men pulled up clamouring to know where he wanted to go. He raised his head slightly as if to add dignity to his words and waved two fingers, "Only two, we want only two." Then, having given the matter some thought, he continued, "Ten coppers. Who'll go to Fourth Avenue for ten coppers?" This ought to show them he knew his way around in Shanghai.

After a fairly long argument they got two rickshaws for twelve coppers apiece. Mrs. Pan got into one with the older boy and Mr. Pan climbed into the other with the younger child and the black bag.

The outstretched arm of an Indian policeman shouldering a gun blocked the way just as the rickshaw man straightened up to go. This fearful apparition made the child on Mr. Pan's knee hide his head in fright.

"There's nothing to be afraid of," said his father. "That's only an Indian policeman. Look at his handsome red turban. We have to come here because we don't have policemen like him at home. He'll use his gun to protect us. His beard is interesting, look at it, like that of the arhats in the temples."

The child was too frightened to look even at a beard like that of an arhat. Only when the clanging of a tram caught his attention did he peep out and find that a very brightly lit room had swept past in

---

① Meaning that they have entered the foreign settlement.

保险,什么兵火焚掠都遭逢不到;而已经散失的一妻一子,又幸运得很,一寻即着:岂不是四条性命,一个皮包,都从毁灭和危难之中捡了回来么?岂不是"现在好了"?

"黄包车!"潘先生很入调地喊。

车夫们听见了,一齐拉着车围拢来,问他到什么地方。

他稍微昂起了头,似乎增加了好几分威严,伸出两个指头扬着说,"只消两辆!两辆!"他想了一想,继续说,"十个铜子,四马路,去的就去!"这分明表示他是个"老上海"。

辩论了好一会,终于讲定十二个铜子一辆。潘师母带着大的孩子坐一辆,潘先生带着小的孩子同黑漆皮包坐一辆。

车夫刚要拔脚前奔,一个背枪的印度巡捕一条胳臂在前面一横,只得缩住了。小的孩子看这个人的形相可怕,不由得回过脸来,贴着父亲的胸际。

潘先生领悟了,连忙解释道,"不要害怕,那就是印度巡捕,你看他的红包头。我们因为本地没有他,所以要逃到这里来;他背着枪保护我们。他的胡子很好玩的,他可以看一看,同罗汉的胡子一个样子。"

孩子总觉得怕,便是同罗汉一样的胡子也不想看。直到听见当当的声音,才从侧边斜睨过去,只见很亮很亮的一个房间一闪就过去了;

英汉对照
English-Chinese
中国文学宝库
Gems of Chinese Literature
现代文学系列
Modern Literature

a flash. On the other side of the road were also brightly lit houses full of dazzling objects. He finally raised his face from his father's chest.

When they reached Fourth Avenue they asked for a room at half a dozen hotels all of which had a big sign with the words "House Full." One glance was enough to assure them that it was no use trying to coax the manager into letting them have a room because temporary beds had been set up even in the lounge. Obviously the hotels were really full. At last, at one hotel they were met by a clerk who drawled lazily, "Want a room?"

"Yes, we want a room. Have you got one?" A ray of hope shot through Mr. Pan making him feel he had reached haven.

"We do have one. The last occupant vacated it only a moment ago. He has rented a house for himself. If you had come a few minutes later, it would have been snapped up."

"Let us have that room." Mr. Pan put his younger son down and turned back to help his wife and older son alight. "We are in luck after all," he told them. "We've finally got a room," When it came to paying off the rickshaws he generously offered one copper more than the agreed fee. It was his belief that if you treated others well when luck was with you, your luck would continue. But the rickshaw men turned out to be very ungrateful. They declared that they had spent a great deal of time taking them from one hotel to another so Mr. Pan must pay them five coppers extra each. In the end, the hotel attendant came out to mediate and Mr. Pan parted with four extra coppers.

The room was on the ground floor. Besides a bed, a lamp, a

那边一家家都是花花灿灿的,都点得亮亮的,他于是不再贴着父亲的胸际。

到了四马路,一连问了八九家旅馆,都大大的写着"客满"的牌子;而且一望而知情商也没用,因为客堂里都搭起床铺,可知确实是住满了。最后到一家也标着"客满",但是一个伙计懒懒地开口道,"找房间么?"

"是找房间,这里还有么?"一缕安慰的心直透潘先生的周身,仿佛到了家似的。

"有是有一间,客人刚刚搬走,他自己租了房子了。你先生若是迟来一刻,说不定就没有了。"

"那一间就归我们住好了。"他放了小的孩子,回身去扶下夫人同大的孩子来,说,"我们总算运气好,居然有房间住了!"随即付车钱,慷慨地照原价加上一个铜子;他相信运气好的时候多给人一些好处,以后好运气会连续而来的。但是车夫偏不知足,说跟着他们回来回去走了这多时,非加上五个铜子不可。结果旅馆里的伙计出来调停,潘先生又多破费了四个铜子。

英汉对照
English-Chinese
中国文学宝库
Gems of Chinese Literature
现代文学系列
Modern Literature

table and two chairs, it contained nothing but smoke. When Mr. Pan took his family inside, his nostrils were immediately assailed by the pungent odour of fried fish mixed with the stink of urine. "What a foul smell!" Mr. Pan muttered with annoyance. From next door came the sizzling of food frying in hot oil, the kitchen was obviously only a wall away. However unpleasant the stench, it was better than getting shot at or sleeping without a roof, Mr. Pan decided, immediately feeling better. He settled himself comfortably in one of the chairs.

"Want some supper?" asked the hotel attendant putting down the black bag.

"I want ham soup with my rice," announced the younger child sucking his fingers.

His mother gave him a severe look. "Ham soup with rice indeed! We are refugees, lucky to have anything at all to eat. How can you ask for this or that!"

The older boy was no better than his brother. "Now that we're in Shanghai," he begged his father, "I want to try some European food."

Mrs. Pan was furious now. Rounding on her firstborn, she said scathingly, "The idea! You deserve to have nothing to eat. You should simply starve...."

Mr. Pan was embarrassed. "Children don't know what they're talking about," he said, trying to smooth things over. He told the attendant, "We had something on the train. Just bring us two orders of fried rice and eggs."

The waiter nodded in a noncommittal way and left. He had no

这房间就在楼下,有一张床,一盏电灯,一张桌子,两把椅子,此外就只有烟雾一般的一房间的空气。潘先生一家跟着茶房走进去时,立刻闻到刺鼻的油腥味,中间又混着阵阵的尿臭。潘先生不快地自语道,"讨厌的气味!"随即听见隔壁有食料投下油锅的声音,才知道那里是厨房。再一想时,气味虽讨厌,究比吃枪子睡露天好多了;也就觉得没有什么,舒舒泰泰地在一把椅子上坐下。

"用晚饭吧?"茶房放下皮包回头问。

"我要吃火腿汤淘饭,"小的孩子咬着指头说。

潘师母马上对他看个白眼,凛然说,"火腿汤淘饭!是逃难呢,有得吃就好了,还要这样那样点戏!"

大的孩子也不知道看看风色,央着潘先生说,"今天到上海了,你给我吃大菜。"

潘师母竟然发怒了,她回头呵斥道,"你们都是没有心肝的,只配什么也没得吃,活活地饿……"

潘先生有点儿窘,却作没事的样子说,"小孩子懂得什么。"便分付茶房道,"我们在路上吃了东西了,现在只消来两客蛋炒饭。"

英汉对照
English-Chinese
中国文学宝库
Gems of Chinese Literature
现代文学系列
Modern Literature

sooner got out of the door than Mr. Pan called him back. "Bring me a catty of Shaoxing wine and ten cents of smoked fish."

When the sound of the attendant's footsteps died away, Mr. Pan, looking relieved and uplifted, said to his wife, "Now we ought to relax a little and have a drink. Just think, we got away from a place fraught with danger to this haven where no harm can come to us. This is something to celebrate. Just now you two were lost and I had a hard time finding you. I was nearly frantic with worry. But A'er was sharp." Mr. Pan pulled his son closer and gently stroked his head. "He spied you at once and I was able to find you. That's another thing to celebrate. Everything's wonderful so let's relax and enjoy a few cups." Beaming with pleasure, he raised an imaginary cup to his lips.

His wife did not reply. She was thinking of home. True, they had packed their valuables away and deposited them for safe-keeping in a church, but there were still a number of things left in the house. She was not at all sure whether Wang, the maid, was reliable. She also wondered whether their poor neighbours knew that her whole family was away with only the maid to watch over the household. She wondered whether the maid would remember to close all the doors and windows at night. She also remembered her three fat hens in the backyard, the pair of trousers she was working on for her younger son, the bowl of braised duck in the kitchen.... These considerations, flashing through her mind, made her extremely uncomfortable. "I wonder what sort of mess they'll make of the place," she sighed.

A feeling of disappointment swept over the children. Vaguely they

茶房似答非答地一点头就走,刚出房门,潘先生又把他喊回来道,"带一斤绍兴,一毛钱熏鱼来。"

茶房的脚声听不见了,潘先生舒快地对潘师母道,"这一刻该得乐一乐,喝一杯了。你想,从兵祸凶险的地方,来到这绝无其事的境界,第一件可乐。刚才你们忽然离开了我,找了半天找不见,真把我急死了;倒是阿二乖觉(他说着,把阿二拖在身边,一手轻轻地拍着),他一眼便看见了你,于是我迎上来,这是第二件可乐。乐哉乐哉,陶陶酌一杯。"他作举杯就口的样子,迷迷地笑着。

潘师母不响,她正想着家里呢。细软的虽然已经带在皮包里,寄到教堂里去了,但是留下的东西究竟还不少。不知王妈到底可靠不可靠;又不知隔壁那家穷人家有没有知道他们一家都出来了,只剩个王妈在家里看守;又不知王妈睡觉时,会不会忘了关上一扇门或是一扇窗。她又想起院子里的三只母鸡,没有完工的阿二的裤子,厨房里的一碗白燠鸭……真同通了电一般,一刻之间,种种的事情都涌上心头,觉得异样地不舒服;便叹口气道,"不知弄到怎样呢!"

英汉对照
English-Chinese
中国文学宝库
Gems of Chinese Literature
现代文学系列
Modern Literature

65

sensed that this Shanghai where they had just arrived was not as interesting and fascinating as that Shanghai they had heard so much about from their parents.

Raindrops drifted in through the window. "It's really raining. Lucky it didn't start any earlier," cried Mr. Pan standing up to close the window. Suddenly he caught sight of the hotel notice on the wall which had been half hidden by the opened window. Remembering a most important thing, he fixed his eyes unblinkingly on the piece of paper.

"My, my! Two dollars, no less," was his startled cry and he turned round to look significantly into his wife's eyes, gasping at what he had discovered.

2

When the next day dawned, the hotel attendants were still curled up in deep slumber on a few benches put together in the hallway. The narrow skylight did not let in much light. Dim yellow lamps were still burning in several hotel rooms. But Mr. and Mrs. Pan were already talking things over. The two boys, hoping that today's Shanghai would turn out better than the Shanghai of yesterday, had been awake for some time. Their parents asked them to sleep a little longer so they were still in bed tickling each other.

"I think you'd better not go back," said Mrs. Pan, very worried. "How can you be sure what they say in the papers is true? Since we went through so much difficulty to get away, there's hardly any sense in your going back right away."

两个孩子都怀着失望的心情,茫昧地觉得这样的上海没有平时父母嘴里的上海来得好玩而有味。

疏疏的雨点从窗外洒进来,潘先生站起来说,"果真下雨了,幸亏在这时候下,"就把窗子关上。突然看见原先给窗子掩没的旅客须知单,他便想起一件顶紧要的事情,一眼不眨地直望那单子。

"不折不扣,两块!"他惊讶地喊。回转头时,眼珠瞪视着潘师母,一段舌头从嘴里伸了出来。

二

第二天早上,走廊中茶房们正蜷在几条长凳上熟睡,狭得只有一条的天井上面很少有晨光透下来,几许房间里的电灯还是昏黄地亮着。但是潘先生夫妇两个已经在那里谈话了;两个孩子希望今天的上海或许比昨晚的好一点,也醒了一会了,只因父母教他们再睡一会,所以还躺在床上,彼此呵痒为戏。

"我说你一定不要回去,"潘师母焦心地说。"这报上的话,知道它靠得住靠不住的。既然千难万难地逃了出来,那有立刻又回去的道理!"

英汉对照
English-Chinese
中国文学宝库
Gems of Chinese Literature
现代文学系列
Modern Literature

67

"Actually, I had some idea that this might happen. Director Gu was never one to let things go. 'Since there's no fighting here, the schools must naturally start as usual.' Yes, that sounds like him all right. I know this correspondent too. He happens to work in the Bureau of Education. So, there's no question about the authenticity of his report. I'll simply have to go back."

"Don't you know it's dangerous going back?" Mrs. Pan's tone was quite tragic. "Maybe in two or three days they'll be fighting in our parts. Suppose you went back and got the school started, do you think the students will come to school? Besides, even if the fighting doesn't spread to our parts, you'll have a good answer for the director of education if he wants to know why you didn't start school. You have only to ask him: What's more important, the school or human lives? He is not immortal himself, he could hardly blame you for not going back."

"You don't understand," said Mr. Pan with some contempt. "This is the kind of argument that only silly women like you, safe at home or in bed, can use. You don't expect me to go and say something like that? Now, don't try to stop me." His tone had become quite conciliatory. "For back I must go. There won't be the least danger. I know how to keep out of harm's way. Besides," Mr. Pan smiled at his own diplomacy, "weren't you worried just now about the things we left at home? Once I'm home I'll be able to keep an eye on them so you can stay here without worrying. When things settle down a bit I'll come promptly to fetch you and the boys home."

Mrs. Pan knew now there was absolutely no way to prevent her

"料是我早先也料到的。顾局长的脾气就是一点不肯马虎。'地方上又没有战事,学自然照常要开的,'这句话确然是他的声口。这个通信员我也认识,就是教育局里的职员,又那里会靠不住?回去是一定要回去的。"

"你要晓得,回去危险呢!"潘师母凄然地说。"说不定三天两天他们就会打到我们那地方去,你就是回去开学,有什么学生来念书?就是不打到我们那地方,将来教育局长怪你为什么不开学时,你也有话回答。你只要问他,到底性命要紧还是学堂要紧?他也是一条性命,想来决不会对你过不去。"

"你懂得什么!"潘先生颇怀着鄙薄的意思。"这种话只配躲在家里,伏在床角里,由你这种女人去说;你道我们也说得出口么!你切不要拦阻我(这时候他已转为抚慰的声调),回去是一定要回去的;但是包你没有一点危险,我自有保全自己的法子。而且(他自喜心思灵敏,微微笑着),你不是很不放心家里的东西么?我回去了,就可以自己照看,你也能定心定意住在这里了。等到时局平定了,我马上来接你们回去。"

英汉对照
English-Chinese
中国文学宝库
Gems of Chinese Literature
现代文学系列
Modern Literature

husband from going back. It would be nice to have him at home and keeping an eye on things but, in these uncertain times, once he left he would be like a pearl cast into the sea, she might never get him back. The sorrows of parting and fear of death overwhelmed her. Tears stung her eyelids and came so near to trickling out that she dared not even glance at her husband. It struck her at once that tears at this moment were a bad omen, nothing tragic had happened and she should not be weeping. Holding back her tears with an effort, more to comfort herself than in real earnest she said, "Then, just go back and see how things are. If the Bureau of Education doesn't say anything about starting the school according to schedule you just come right back, catching the afternoon train if you can and if not the early train the next morning. You see," here she could no longer restrain herself and one tear dropped on the back of her hand, to be hastily brushed away — "I worry about you so!"

Mr. Pan was feeling very vexed himself. Since the director of education wanted the schools to start as usual, he himself had no reason whatever to insist that they should remain closed. It followed naturally that he should go back. But how could he not worry about his family here? He noticed the look of gentle sorrow on his wife's face. It seemed heartless to leave a woman with two young children, so weak and helpless, without anyone to rely on. How could he be sure nothing untoward would happen to them. All this made him angry and disturbed. He was angry at those sending troops out to fight this army or that, angry at the director of education who talked about starting school without delay, angry at himself for not having a grown-up son who might have helped him out.

潘师母知道丈夫的回去是万无挽回的了。回去可以照看东西固然很好；但是风声这样紧，一去之后，犹如珠子抛在海里，谁保得定必能捞回来呢！生离死别的哀感涌上心头，她再不敢正眼看她的丈夫，眼泪早在眼角边偷偷地想跑出来了。她又立刻想起这个场面不大吉利，现在并没有什么不好的事情，怎么能凄惨地流起眼泪来。于是勉强忍住眼泪，聊作自慰的请求道，"那么你去看看情形，假使教育局长并没有照常开学这句话，要是还来得及，你就搭了今天下午的车来，不然，搭了明天的早车来。你要知道（她到底忍不住，一滴眼泪落在手背，立刻在衫子上擦去了），我不放心呢！"

　　潘先生心里也着实有点烦乱，局长的意思照常开学，自己万无主张暂缓开学之理，回去当然是天经地义，但是又怎么放得下这里！看他夫人这样的依依之情，断然一走，未免太没有恩义。又况一个女人两个孩子都是很懦弱的，一无依傍，寄住在外边，怎能断言决没有意外？他这样想时，不禁深深地发恨：恨这人那人调兵遣将，预备作战，恨教育局长主张照常开课，又恨自己没有个已经成年，可以帮助一臂的儿子。

英汉对照
English-Chinese
中国文学宝库
Gems of Chinese Literature
现代文学系列
Modern Literature

Nevertheless, he was not a woman, he had to look ahead. He knew that going back was the right thing to do. Forgetting his anger and without showing a trace of his inner disturbance, he nodded to show that he agreed with her. "If I find that the director has no intention of starting the schools, I'll do as you say and come back by the afternoon train," he said soothingly.

The children had overheard this last remark. The younger boy, his head half buried in the pillow, lisped babyishly, "I wanna go back too."

"Mama and daddy and I are going back and we'll leave you here all by yourself," teased the older boy, making a face.

The younger boy started to wail at the top of his voice, rubbing his eyes vigorously although there was not a single tear in them.

"You will both stay here with mama," said Mr. Pan raising his voice. "No more nonsense now. Get dressed and ready for breakfast." After a few more words with his wife, Mr. Pan set out for the station.

On the way, he heard passers-by commenting on the fact that trains were no longer running. "If the trains have stopped that settles the question for me. Even if they decide to fire me for staying away, I can't help it." The news gave him a let-down feeling. But if his luck held, it might prove no more than a rumour. To find out the true situation he was anxious that the rickshaw man should go faster.

His luck turned out to be good. There was no sign posted at the station saying that trains were suspended. On the blackboard a notice declared that the night train would be four hours late. It was

但是他究竟不比女人,他更从利害远近种种方面着想,觉得回去终于是天经地义。便把恼恨搁在一旁,脸上也不露一毫形色,顺着夫人的口气点头道,"假若打听明白局长并没有这个意思,依你的话,就搭了下午的车来。"

两个孩子约略听得回去和再来的话,小的就伏在床沿作娇道,"我也要回去。"

"我同爸爸妈妈回去,剩下你独个儿住在这里,"大的孩子扮着鬼脸说。

小的听着,便迫紧喉咙叫唤,作啼哭的腔调,小手擦着眉眼的部分,但眼睛里实在没有眼泪。

"你们都跟着妈妈留在这里,"潘先生提高了声音说。"再不许胡闹了,好好儿起来等吃早饭吧。"说罢,又嘱咐了潘师母几句,径出雇车,赶往车站。

模糊地听得行人在那里说铁路已断火车不开的话,潘先生想,"火车如果不开,倒死了我的心,就是立刻免职也只得由他了。"同时又觉得这消息很使他失望;又想他要是运气好,未必会逢到这等失望的事,那么行人的话也未必可靠。欲决此疑,只希望车夫三步并作一步跑。

他的运气果然不坏,赶到车站一看,并没有火车不开的通告;揭示处只标明夜车要迟四点钟才到,这时候还没到呢。买票处绝不拥挤,时

英汉对照
English-Chinese
中国文学宝库
Gems of Chinese Literature
现代文学系列
Modern Literature

still not in yet. The ticket window was far from crowded. From time to time one or two people stepped up to buy tickets. The crowd in the station was made up half of people awaiting travellers, half of spectators. Some carried cameras and were waiting to snap the bustle accompanying the arrival of the night train so that the pictures could be used in some future "History of Wars and Changes." The baggage room was filled with an assortment of bags and cases piled so high that they nearly touched the ceiling.

He felt both relieved and depressed. After a slight hesitation he bought himself a third-class ticket and boarded the train. The clear sunlight made the whole compartment bright but not hot. There were plenty of empty seats. Had he wanted to, he could have lain down. He thought, "This is unusual. If I were in a better mood this could have been a very pleasant trip."

The train was held up at various stops to give right of way to troop trains. By the time he got into Rangli, it was past three in the afternoon. Mr. Pan hurried home and found his gate tightly closed. The tension in his heart eased a little for this precaution was one thing he had tried very hard to impress on Wang, the maid, before he left.

He had to knock a number of times before the maid appeared. She exclaimed in surprise at sight of Mr. Pan, "Is that you back, sir? Is there no need to run away now?"

Mr. Pan muttered a vague answer as he rushed in and looked around. Then he unlocked the door to his room, strode in and examined it with care. No change. There was no change at all. Everything was as he had left it the day before. His heart which had been

时有一两个人前去买票。聚集在站中的人却不少,一半是候客的,一半是来看看的,也有带着照相器具的,专等夜车到时摄取车站拥挤的情形,好作《风云变幻史》的一页。行李房满满地堆着箱子铺盖,各色各样,几乎碰到铅皮的屋顶。

他心中似乎很安慰,又似乎有点儿怅惘,顿了一顿,终于前去买了一张三等票,就走入车厢里坐着。晴明的阳光照得一车通亮,可是不嫌燠热;座位很宽舒,勉强要躺躺也可以。他想,"这是难得逢到的。倘若心里没有事,真是一趟愉快的旅行呢。"

这趟车一路耽搁,听候军人的命令,等待兵车的通过。开到让里,已是下午三点过了。潘先生下了车,急忙赶到家,看见大门紧紧关着,心便一定,原来昨天再四叮嘱王妈的就是这一件。

扣了十几下,王妈方才把门开了。一见潘先生,出惊地说,"怎么,先生回来了! 不用逃难了么?"

潘先生含糊回答了她;奔进里面四周一看,便开了房门的锁,直闯进去上下左右打量着。没有变更,一点没有变更,什么都同昨天一样。

英汉对照
English-Chinese
中国文学宝库
Gems of Chinese Literature
现代文学系列
Modern Literature

palpitating relaxed somewhat but he was not yet fully assured. He locked the room again and turned to go. "See that the gate's properly locked," he told the maid.

The maid was very puzzled. Having closed the gate, she went in and began to wonder. The master and mistress must still be somewhere in town. Perhaps they were afraid she might want to go with them and had only pretended to run away to Shanghai. "Otherwise, why is the master back so soon? The mistress and the boys are not with him. Where can they be hiding themselves? But why didn't they want me with them? Of course, it's because they didn't have room for so many. They are probably in that red building belonging to the foreigner. Those soldiers are all in the know; they will not touch that red building even when they are fighting. Actually they could have told me the truth for I wouldn't have been keen on going even if they had asked me. I'm not a bit frightened. Even if fighting breaks out here, my burial costume has been ready a long time." She saw in her mind's eye the beautiful embroidered burial shoes presented to her by her niece and felt sure these would make the King of Hell treat her with respect when she went to the nether world. This reflection gave her a subtle pleasure which kept her mind off the question of where her master and mistress were.

Mr. Pan went to see the correspondent who was a member of the Bureau of Education to ask whether the director really intended the schools to start as usual. "But certainly," the man answered. "He also said some teachers were so busy getting themselves out of harm's way they quite neglected their duty. It just showed they were unworthy to work in the field of education and this was a good

于是他吊起的半个心放下来了。还有半个心没放下,便又锁上房门,回身出门;吩咐王妈道,"你照旧好好把门关上了。"

王妈摸不清头绪,关了门进去只是思索。她想主人们一定就住在本地,恐怕她也要跟去,所以骗她说逃到上海去。"不然,怎么先生又回来了?奶奶同两个孩子不同来,又躲在什么地方呢?但是,他们为什么不让我跟去?这自然嫌得人多了不好。——他们一定就住在那洋人的红房子里,那些兵都讲通的,打起仗来不打那红房子。——其实就是老实告诉我,要我跟去,我也不高兴去呢。我在这里一点也不怕;如果打仗打到这里来,反正我的老衣早就做好了。"她随即想起甥女儿送她的一双绣花鞋真好看,穿了那双鞋上西方,阎王一定另眼相看;于是她感到一种微妙的舒快,不再想主人究竟在那里的问题。

潘先生出门,就去访那当通信员的教育局职员,问他局长究竟有没有照常开学的意思。那人回答道,"怎么没有?他还说有些教员只顾逃难,不顾职务,这就是表示教育的事业不配他们干;乘此淘汰一下也是好处。"潘先生听了,

英汉对照
English-Chinese
中国文学宝库
Gems of Chinese Literature
现代文学系列
Modern Literature

chance to eliminate some of them." This announcement made Mr. Pan sit up to take notice. At once he congratulated himself on his wisdom in coming back from Shanghai. He made straight for the school, picked up a writing brush and drafted a circular to the parents of the students. War and fighting might be worrisome, he stated, but the education of young people was like food and clothing which could not be dispensed with for a single day. Now that the summer holidays were over, the school would start as usual. In the time of the great war in Europe, a net was spread in the air to prevent bombing so that teaching might continue uninterrupted. This kind of heroism, the notice went on, should not go unrivalled. It was to be hoped that the parents would understand, and in this spirit would send their children to school as if nothing had happened. All this was in the interest of both the school and the students and also for the honour of the town and the country.

After reading the draft three times, he was finally satisfied that there was nothing more he could add. When the director of education saw this circular the least to be expected was the remark, "He thinks like me." In a mood of complacency, Mr. Pan cut the stencil himself and mimeographed more than a hundred copies which he dispatched through the school janitor. Now that he had done his duty by his work he let his mind return to his private affairs. Since the school must start, he could hardly go to Shanghai again. But his wife and children would have a hard time all by themselves in the hotel. There was nothing he could do about that, he must just tell them to be careful and remain there without worrying. He used what ink there was left after drafting his circular to write a letter to his

仿佛觉得一凛；但又赞赏自己有主意，决定从上海回来到底是不错的。一口气奔到自己的学校里，提起笔来就起草送给学生家属的通告。通告中说兵乱虽然可虑，子弟的教育犹如布帛菽粟，是一天一刻不可废弃的，现在暑假期满，学校照常开学。从前欧洲大战的时候，人家天空里布着御防炸弹的网，下面学校里却依然在那里上课：这种非常的精神，我们应当不让他们专美于前。希望家长们能够体谅这一层意思，若无其事地依旧把子弟送来：这不仅是家庭和学校的益处，也是地方和国家的荣誉。

他起好草稿，往复看了三遍，觉得再没有可以增损，局长看见了，至少也得说一声"先得我心"。便得意地誊上蜡纸，又自己动手印刷了百多张，派校役向一个个学生家里送去。公事算是完毕了，开始想到私事：既要开学，上海是去不成了，他们母子三个住在旅馆里怎么挨得下去！但也没有办法，惟有教他们一切留意，安心住着。于是蘸着刚才的残墨写寄与夫人的信。

英汉对照
English-Chinese
中国文学宝库
Gems of Chinese Literature
现代文学系列
Modern Literature

wife.

The next day in the tea-house he got authentic news that the railway was cut. His heart sank. Somehow, his beloved wife and two sons seemed to have drifted away on the wind to a distant land, out of his reach. In a sad state of mind, he strolled to the school where the janitor reported on his mission the day before. "When I took the circular around I found more than twenty households with doors tightly locked and no one round to answer my knocking. I had to slip the circular in through a slit in the door. About thirty households had only servants at home; the masters had run away to Shanghai taking their children with them, of course. No one knew when they'd be back for school. The rest all took the circular but a few said since they were not sure how long they'd be alive the question of schooling had better wait for the time being."

"I see," said Mr. Pan, his mind not on these matters at all but troubled by gloomier thoughts. After a cigarette, he reached a decision. He went to the branch office of the Red Cross Society.

He proclaimed himself willing to become a member of the Red Cross and paid his fees. He said his school had fairly spacious premises and he wanted the Red Cross to use it as a home for women refugees in case of emergency. Such a charitable offer was of course warmly accepted. Besides, Mr. Pan was a well-known and respected figure in the town. The branch office gave him a Red Cross banner to be hoisted up at the school entrance and a Red Cross badge to show that he was a member of that organization.

Mr. Pan held the flag and badge in his hands as if they were a talisman, a guarantee of life and security. A mysterious sense of

下一天,他从茶馆里得到确实的信息,铁路真个不通了。他心头突然一沉,似乎觉得最亲热的一妻两儿忽地乘风飘去,飘得很远,几乎至于渺茫。没精没采地踱到学校里,校役回报昨天的使命道,"昨天出去送通告,有二十多家关上了大门,打也打不开,只好从门缝里塞进去。有三十多家只有佣人在家里,主人逃到上海去了,孩子当然跟了去,不一定几时才能回来念书。其余的都说知道了;有的又说性命还保不定安全,读书的事再说罢。"

"哦,知道了。"潘先生并不留心在这些上边,更深的忧虑正萦绕在他的心头。他抽完了一支烟卷以后,应走的路途决定了,便赶到红十字会分会的办事处。

他缴纳会费愿做会员;又宣称自己的学校房屋还宽敞,愿意作为妇女收容所,到万一的时候收容妇女。这是慈善的举措,当然受热诚的欢迎,更兼潘先生本来是体面的大家知道的人物。办事处就给他红十字的旗子,好在学校门前张起来;又给他红十字的徽章,标明他是红十字会的一员。

潘先生接旗子和徽章在手,像捧着救命的神符,心头起一种神秘的快慰。"现在什么都安

英汉对照
English-Chinese
中国文学宝库
Gems of Chinese Literature
现代文学系列
Modern Literature

satisfaction stole into his heart. "Everything is safe now. But...." He turned back to the man in the branch office with a smile. "Give me an extra banner and a few more badges, will you?" His reason was that the school had a back door and the badge was so small he might easily lose it so it was better to have a few to spare.

"This isn't something you can eat," said the Red Cross man jokingly, "and you can hardly use it as a plaything! Even if you take more than one badge, you're still only a member, so why ask for more than one?" But in the end he gave Mr. Pan a few spare ones to make him happy.

Both Red Cross banners were soon fluttering in the light breeze of early autumn but neither of them was near the school's back entrance. The second banner had been placed over Mr. Pan's own door. One Red Cross badge glittered with the solemn light of charity on Mr. Pan's lapel, giving its wearer a new kind of courage. As for the rest, these were kept with care, wrapped in paper, in the pocket of Mr. Pan's shirt. "One is for her," he thought, "one is for Ada and the other for the little one." Although they were still in distant Shanghai, out of his reach, the badges were a sort of double insurance for their safety which should give them a new courage too.

3

The two armies opened fire at Bizhuang.

Very few households in Rangli kept their doors open; the shops naturally all remained closed. Soldiers marched past in the streets

全了!但是……"想到这里,便笑向办事处的职员道,"多给我一面旗,几个徽章罢。"他的理由是学校还有个侧门,也得张一面旗,而徽章这东西太小巧,恐怕偶尔遗失了,不如多备几个在那里。

办事员同他说笑话,这东西又不好吃的,拿着玩也没有什么意思,多拿几个也只作一个会员,不如不要多拿罢。但是终于依他的话给了他。

两面红十字旗立刻在新秋的轻风中招展,可是学校的侧门上并没有旗,原来移到潘先生家的大门上去了。一个红十字徽章早已缀上潘先生的衣襟,闪耀着慈善庄严的光,给与潘先生一种新的勇气。其余几个呢,重重包裹,藏在潘先生贴身小衫的一个口袋里。他想,"一个是她的,一个是阿大的,一个是阿二的。"虽然他们远处在那渺茫难接的上海,但是仿佛给他们加保了一重险,他们也就各各增加一种新的勇气。

三

碧庄地方两军开火了。

让里的人家很少有开门的,店铺自然不用说,路上时时有兵士经过。他们快要开拔到前

frequently. They would soon be going to the front and felt that they were endowed with the highest authority; nothing was of any account in their eyes. They could trample whatever they liked underfoot. This was how the press-gang started. To prevent those forced into the army from running away, the conscripts were bound and marched along in a line with soldiers escorting them. Thus it came about that people were afraid of going out on the streets. When it was absolutely necessary to leave their houses, they went by small paths and byways. Even people, like Mr. Pan, who were armed with Red Cross badges, were rather wary and dared not strut about openly. The streets of Rangli seemed quiet and very desolate.

For several days now, the Shanghai papers had not come. The local army headquarters, however, sometimes posted battle news which usually said that the enemy had been routed and our troops had advanced several *li*. When a fresh bulletin appeared on the street corner, a small group would gather slowly to read it carefully. They were not altogether convinced by what they read for they felt there were many things unsaid. They would disperse with a feeling of foreboding, their brows still tightly knit.

Mr. Pan had been downcast for the last few days. He worried most about his absent wife and children of whom he had no news. It seemed he might never be able to get in touch with them again. And then there was the question of his own safety. "It's only a march of a hundred *li* or so from Bizhuang. Although the Red Cross badge may serve some purpose, nobody ever wrote me a guarantee, so who can I ask for compensation if it turns out to be useless after all? Bullets, shells, robbers and fire are no laughing matter. I'll have to

方去，觉得最高的权威附灵在自己身上，什么东西都不在眼里，只要高兴提起脚来踩，都可以踩做泥团踩做粉。这就来了拉夫的事情：恐怕被拉的人乘隙脱逃，便用长绳一个联一个拴着胳臂，几个弟兄在前，几个弟兄在后，一串一患牵着走。因此，大家对于出门这件事都觉得危惧，万不得已时，也只从小巷僻路走，甚至佩着红十字徽章如潘先生之辈，也不免怀着戒心，不敢大模大样地踱来踱去。于是让里的街道见得又清静又宽阔了。

上海的报纸好几天没来。本地的军事机关却常常有前方的战报公布出来，无非是些"敌军大败，我军进展若干里"的话。街头巷口贴出一张新鲜的战报时，也有些人慢慢聚集拢来，注目看着。但大家看罢以后依然不能定心，好似这布告背后还有许多话没说出来，于是怅怅地各自散了，眉头照旧皱着。

这几天潘先生无聊极了。最难堪的，自然是妻儿远离，而且消息不通，而且似乎有永远难通的朕兆。次之的便是自身的问题，"碧庄冲过来只一百多里路，这徽章虽说有用处，可是没有人写过笔据，万一没有用，又向谁去说话？——枪子炮弹劫掠放火都是真家伙，不是耍的，要底要

英汉对照
English-Chinese
中国文学宝库
Gems of Chinese Literature
现代文学系列
Modern Literature

make more inquiries and find some other means to ensure my safety." So he asked here and there for news about the front and was sure there was a grain of truth in whatever news he got that was different from the current rumour. He then calculated its effect on his own interest. The sight of anyone rushing along the street with a look of panic would startle him for he was sure the man had learned some reliable but fearful news. Only the fact the man was a complete stranger prevented Mr. Pan from accosting and questioning him.

The Red Cross sent people to the front to look after the wounded; Some of them came back frequently in army transports. The Red Cross was naturally the most reliable source of news. Although Mr. Pan belonged to the Red Cross he did not often go there for news for he was ashamed to admit his fear in public. Nevertheless, the Red Cross was a source of reliable information and it would be foolish to ask for news elsewhere. The result was Mr. Pan went at dusk every day to the house of Wu, a man who worked in the Red Cross office. Wu would tell him there was no news or that this side was doing all right at the front, after which Mr. Pan would go home with a sigh of relief.

One evening Mr. Pan went again to Wu's house. He had to wait a long time before Wu came back.

"Nothing new, eh?" asked Mr. Pan eagerly. "According to the bulletin, we launched a general offensive yesterday."

"Bad," said Wu looking worried and toying with his moustache.

"What?!" Mr. Pan's heart skipped a beat and he felt trapped.

As if afraid of being overheard, Wu answered in a low voice,

多打听多走门路才行。"他于是这里那里探听前方的消息,只要这消息与外间传说的不同,便觉得真实的成分越多,即根据着盘算对于自身的利害。街上如其有一个人神色仓皇急忙行走时,他便突地一惊,以为这个人一定探得确实而又可怕的消息了;只因与他不相识,"什么!"一声就在喉际咽住了。

红十字会派人在前方办理救护的事情,常有人搭着兵车回来,要打听消息自然最可靠了。潘先生虽然是个会员,却不常到办事处去探听,以为这样就是对公众表示胆怯,很不好意思。然而红十字会究竟是可以得到真消息的机关,舍此他求未免有点傻,于是每天傍晚到姓吴的办事员家里去打听。姓吴的告诉他没有什么,或者说前方抵住在那里,他才透了口气回家。

这一天傍晚,潘先生又到姓吴的家里,等了好久,姓吴的才从外面走进来。

"没有什么吧?"潘先生急切地问。"照布告上说,昨天正向对方总攻击呢。"

"不行,"姓吴的忧愁地说;但随即咽住了,捻着唇边仅有的几根二三分长的髭须。

"什么!"潘先生心头突地跳起来,周身有一种拘牵不自由的感觉。

英汉对照
English-Chinese
中国文学宝库
Gems of Chinese Literature
现代文学系列
Modern Literature

"The reliable news is that Zheng'an, a town eight *li* from Bizhuang, fell to the other side this morning."

Mr. Pan uttered one desperate cry, paused for a second or so and turned to leave, muttering as he went, "I'm going."

The street lamps seemed particularly dim that evening, Mr. Pan felt as if he were being chased from behind. Frightened and worried, he stumbled home as quickly as he could and told the maid, "You lock the doors and go to sleep, I'll be busy tonight and will not come back for the night." He saw there was an old padded silk gown in the wardrobe; they had forgotten to pack it in the suitcases which had been deposited for safekeeping. It would be a pity to lose it. There were also a few of the boys' lined cotton tunics. A close scrutiny showed that they were still wearable. There was also an old silk skirt which his wife would probably be loath to part with. He tied them all together and went out with his bundle.

"Rickshaw! The red building in Fuxing Lane. Ten cents."

"Whoever heard of ten cents?" drawled the rickshaw man. "How many rickshaws are out these days! Who would be out here risking his life for a few cents unless he needed them to keep alive? Thirty cents. Take it or leave it."

"Thirty cents then." Mr. Pan hurried over and stepped into the rickshaw. "But you must also do as I ask, go faster."

"Hey, Mr. Pan, where are you going?" a colleague by the name of Huang saw him and called out.

"Ur, Mr ... over there...." Mr. Pan in his panic was not quite sure who had spoken to him. Suddenly he realized it would be a waste of breath to answer for the rickshaw was going too fast to allow

姓吴的悄悄地回答,似乎防着人家偷听了去的样子,"确实的消息,正安(距碧庄八里的一个镇)今天早上失守了!"

"啊!"潘先生发狂似地喊出来。顿了一顿,回身就走,一壁说道,"我回去了!"

路上的电灯似乎特别昏暗,背后又仿佛有人追赶着的样子,惴惴地,歪斜的急步赶到了家,叮嘱王妈道,"你关着门安睡好了,我今夜有事,不回来住了。"他看见衣橱里有一件绉纱的旧棉袍,当时没收拾在寄出去的箱子里,丢了也可惜;又有孩子的几件布夹衫,仔细看时还可以穿穿;又有潘师母的一条旧绸裙,她不一定舍得便不要它:便胡乱包在一起,提着出门。

"车!车!福星街红房子,一毛钱。"

"那里有一毛钱的?"车夫懒懒地说。"你看这几天路上有几辆车?不是拚死寻饭吃的,早就躲起来了。随你要不要,三毛钱。"

"就是三毛钱,"潘先生迎上去,跨上脚踏坐稳了,"你也得依着我,跑得快一点!"

"潘先生,你到那里去?"一个姓黄的同业在途中瞥见了他,站定了问。

"哦,先生,到那边……"潘先生失措地回答,也不辨问他的是谁;忽然想起回答那人简直

英汉对照
English-Chinese
中国文学宝库
Gems of Chinese Literature
现代文学系列
Modern Literature

the other to chase after him to demand an answer. He swallowed the rest of his words.

The red building was full of people most of whom had moved in ten days ago. Children cried and people talked, lights were lit in many rooms so that there was even an atmosphere of cheer and bustle. "There is no vacant room here," his host told Mr. Pan. "But since all your things are here I can hardly turn you away. Just now, several others arrived unexpectedly too, and as I could not refuse them I've put them in a side room ordinarily used as a kitchen. I'll go and see if they couldn't take in one more."

"Oh, yes, surely they can take in one more." Mr. Pan felt comforted. "Besides, at a time like this, I don't intend to sleep through the night; a place to sit would be just fine."

When he stepped into the side room, his bundle on one arm, he thought at first that all this fear and panic were giving him hallucinations. He closed his eyes and opened them again but what he saw did not change. There, sitting by the window with a thick moustache twitching over his upper lip as he talked to someone opposite him, was no other than the director of the Bureau of Education.

Mr. Pan hesitated, the foot that had stepped over the threshold wavered; he meant to withdraw but thought better of it. The director had seen him too. "Ah, Mr. Pan, there you are," said he, smiling to cover his embarrassment. "Come in and sit down." When the host realized that they were acquainted he withdrew to attend to his own business.

"So you're here too, director. Can you accommodate one more in this room?"

是多事——车轮滚得绝快,那人决不会赶上来再问,——便缩住了。

红房子里早已住满了人,大都是十天以前就搬来的,儿啼人语,灯火这边那边亮着,颇有点热闹的气象。主人翁见面之后,说,"这里实在没有余屋了。但是先生的东西都寄在这里,也不好拒绝。刚才有几位匆忙地赶来,也因不好拒绝,权且把一间做厨房的厢房让他们安顿。现在去同他们商量,总可以多插你先生一个。"

"商量商量总可以,"潘先生到了家似地安慰。"何况在这样时候。我也不预备睡觉,随便坐坐就得了。"

他提着包裹跨进厢房的当儿,以为自己受惊太厉害了,眼睛生了翳,因而引起错觉;但是闭一闭眼睛再睁开来时,所见依然如前,这靠窗坐着,在那里同对面的人谈话,上唇翘起两笔浓须的,不就是教育局长?

他顿时踌躇起来,已跨进去的一只脚想要缩出来,又似乎不大好。那局长也望见了他,尴尬的脸上故作笑容说,"潘先生,你来了,进来坐坐。"主人翁听了,知道他们是相识的,转身自去。

"局长先在这里了,还方便吧,再容一个人?"

英汉对照
English-Chinese
中国文学宝库
Gems of Chinese Literature
现代文学系列
Modern Literature

"There's only the three of us here, of course we can. We brought along a mat so we could take turns lying down a bit. Good thing it's not too cold yet."

Mr. Pan felt that the director was extremely affable that night, not at all his usual stern and dignified self. Forgetting his restraint, he strode in. "Then allow me to come in and keep you three company for the night."

The room was far from spacious. A middle-aged man with glasses sat on a mat spread on the floor. There was a look of fatigue on his face but he showed no inclination for sleep. The stove and pots and pans were placed against one wall. Near the window stood three chairs in a row; the director occupied one, the director's cousin, a young man in his twenties with sleek hair, another, the third one was empty. In one corner were an osier suitcase and three bundles — probably the three men's luggage. The few things were enough to clutter up the room, there was hardly any vacant space left. The coat of dust on the electric bulb made everything in the room hazy.

Mr. Pan put his bundle down with those of the others. He took the vacant seat, with an air of apology. After the director had introduced him to his companions, he asked, "Have you also heard the news about Zheng'an?"

"Yes. With Zheng'an lost, Bizhuang is in great danger."

"Our side must have been careless along the southern route, the loss of Zheng'an is a sign of this. It's the easiest thing for the other side to steal up to Bizhuang from Zheng'an. At this very moment they may have got in. If so, I dare not think what will happen here!"

"我们只三个人,当然还可以容你。我们带着席子;好在天气不很凉,可以轮流躺着歇歇。"

潘先生觉得今晚上局长特别可亲,全不像平日那副庄严的神态,便忘形地直跨进去说,"那么不客气,就要陪三位先生过一夜了。"

这厢房不很宽阔。地上铺着一张席子,一个戴眼镜的中年人坐在上面,略微有疲倦的神色,但绝无欲睡的意思。锅灶等东西贴着一壁。靠窗一排摆着三只凳子,局长坐一只,头发梳得很光的二十多岁的人,局长的表弟,坐一只,一只空着。那边的墙角有一只柳条箱,三个衣包,大概就是三位先生带来的。仅仅这些,房间里已没有空地了。电灯的光本来很弱,又蒙上了一层灰尘,照得房间里的人物都昏黯模糊。

潘先生也把衣包放在那边的墙角,与三位的东西合伙。回过来谦逊地坐上那只空凳子。局长给他介绍了自己的同伴,随说,"你也听到了正安的消息么?"

"是呀,正安。正安失守,碧庄未必靠得住呢。"

"大概这方面对于南路很疏忽,正安失守,便是明证。那方面从正安袭取碧庄是最便当的,说不定此刻已被他们得手了。要是这样,不堪设想!"

英汉对照
English-Chinese
中国文学宝库
Gems of Chinese Literature
现代文学系列
Modern Literature

"If so, chaos will reign."

"But Commander Du on this side isn't a fool, you know, he's noted for strategy. He's probably foreseen all this and has plans to forestall the other side. Maybe he'll turn the tables at this juncture and take up the offensive, attacking the enemy in its lair."

"If that happens there'll be an end to hostilities and that'll be great. We, in the field of education, can then start school and carry on as usual."

The director promptly became conscious of his dignity at the mention of the word "education." Twisting his thick moustache, he said with a sigh, "This fighting has certainly caused a loss to students of different ages, to say nothing of other people." He forgot his cramped and uncomfortable position in the tiny room and felt as if he were back again in the dignified office of the Bureau of Education.

"Commander Zhu of the other side is really hateful," said the middle-aged man on the mat with some indignation. "Why must he resist when this side attacked? He's bound to be defeated. If he'd been smart and offered no resistance, all this fighting would not have occurred."

"He's a fool," the director's cousin agreed. "He won't give up till the end. And in the meanwhile we have to suffer cooped up in this small, dark room!" His tone was not serious.

Mr. Pan's thoughts went to his wife and children in Shanghai. He wondered if they were all right, if they had kept out of trouble. Were they asleep at this moment? Since he could not feel them near him and his imagination conjured up only a very hazy picture, he

"要是这样,这里非糜烂不可!"

"但是,这方面的杜统帅不是庸碌无能的人,他是著名善于用兵的,大约见得到这一层,总有方法抵挡得住。也许就此反守为攻,势如破竹,直捣那方面的巢穴呢。"

"若能这样,战事便收场了,那就好了!——我们办学的就可以开起学来,照常进行。"

局长一听到办学,立刻感到自己的尊严,捻着浓须叹道,"别的不要讲,这一场战争,大大小小的学生吃亏不小呢!"他把坐在这间小厢房里的局促不舒的感觉忘了,仿佛堂皇地坐在教育局的办公室里。

坐在席子上的中年人仰起头来含恨似地说,"那方面的朱统帅实在可恶!这方面打过去,他抵抗些什么,——他没有不终于吃败仗的。他若肯漂亮点儿让了,战事早就没有了。"

"他是傻子,"局长的表弟顺着说,"不到尽头不肯死心的。只是连累了我们,这当儿坐在这又暗又窄的房间里。"他带着玩笑的神气。

潘先生却想念起远在上海的妻儿来了。他不知道他们可安好,不知道他们出了什么乱子没有,不知道他们此刻睡了不曾,抓既抓不到,

felt that the fighting had injured him more than any of the others. He let his eyes rest mournfully on the little courtyard outside the window and stayed silent.

But then his thoughts turned to the terrible news he had heard from Wu and the threat of danger to follow. "I wonder what is really happening!" he exclaimed.

"Hard to say!" The director spoke knowingly. "In war, everything depends on making use of the right moment. The tide may turn any time and things may not happen as we thought. Perhaps at this very moment... we...." He smiled at the middle-aged man.

All the others in the room, the man on the mat, the director's cousin and Mr. Pan caught the significance of his smile. Assured that they were safe enough where they were, they also smiled with satisfaction.

The little yard overgrown with weeds provided a comfortable haven for mosquitoes and small insects of all descriptions. The lamp in the room drew the insects in swarms and the four frightened men had a bad time of it. Midges attacked their faces; a sudden sting from a particularly venomous mosquito kept making one or the other jump. From time to time they stopped talking to listen with trepidation for the sound of shooting or the clamour of frightened people. Sleep was out of the question, of course. They merely took turns lying down a bit as the director had predicted.

Mr. Pan's eyes were bloodshot the next morning and he shivered with cold. Longing to know how things were outside he slipped out all alone. The streets looked the same as on ordinary mornings. A few stray dogs, tails up, sniffed cheerily here and there. A man

想像也极模糊;因而想自己的被累要算最深重了,凄然望着窗外的小院子默不作声。

"不知道到底怎么样呢!"他又转而想到那个可怕的消息以及意料所及的危险,不自主地吐露了这一句。

"难说,"局长表示富有经验的样子说。"用兵全在趁一个机,机是刻刻变化的,也许竟不为我们的所料,此刻已……所以我们……"他对着中年人一笑。

中年人,局长的表弟同潘先生三个已经领会局长这一笑的意味;大家想坐在这地方总不至于有什么,也各安慰地一笑。

小院子里长满了草,是蚊虫同各种小虫的安适的国土。厢房里灯光亮着,虫子齐飞了进来。四位怀着惊恐的先生就够受用了;扑头扑面的全是那些小东西,蚊虫突然一针,痛得直跳起来。又时时停语侧耳,惶惶地听外边有没有枪声或人众的喧哗。睡眠当然是无望了,只实做了局长所说的轮流躺着歇歇。

下一天清晨,潘先生的眼球上添了几缕红丝;风吹过来,觉得身上很凉。他急欲知道外面的情形,独个儿闪出红房子的大门。路上同平时的早晨一样,街犬竖起了尾巴高兴地这头那

英汉对照
English-Chinese
中国文学宝库
Gems of Chinese Literature
现代文学系列
Modern Literature

with drowsy eyes walked past now and then. Mr. Pan turned a corner, still he neither saw nor heard anything unusual. He could hardly suppress a smile at the recollection of his own panic the night before, but on second thoughts he felt there was really nothing funny about it. Better, after all, to be overcautious than take unnecessary risks.

Three weeks or so later, the fighting came to an end. People wagged their heads and assured each other, "Now, things'll be all right. As long as there's no fighting, we'll be safe." Mr. Pan, though, was not quite happy for the trains were still not running and he could not fetch his wife and children back from Shanghai. There had been two letters, both very brief, which, instead of making him feel better, only made him miss them more. He was annoyed with himself for being such a poor prophet. He could very well have saved all that extra expense of taking his family away to Shanghai, and then he need not have led this lonely bachelor's life for several weeks.

Realizing that the Bureau of Education would soon be considering the question of starting school, he went there for news. As soon as he stepped into the reception room he noticed several clerks busy cutting up large strips of paper and grinding fresh ink. It looked as if they were getting ready for some festivity.

"Here's Mr. Pan, just the man we want," cried one. "You write beautifully in the Yan style. This is just the job for you."

"Yes, indeed, Mr. Pan is the only one who can do calligraphy of this size well," chimed in the rest.

"Write what? I'm completely at sea about what's going on."

头望,偶尔走过一两个睡眼惺忪的人。他走过去,转入又一条街,也听不见什么特别的风声。回想昨夜的匆忙情形,不禁心里好笑。但是再一转念,又觉得实在并无可笑,小心一点总比冒险好。

　　二十余天之后,战事停止了。大众点头自慰道,"这就好了! 只要不打仗,什么都平安了!"但是潘先生还不大满意,铁路还没通,不能就把避居上海的妻儿接回来。信是来过两封了,但简略得很,比不看更教他想念。他又恨自己到底没有先见之明;不然,这一笔冤枉的逃难费可以省下,又免得几十天的孤单。

　　他知道教育局里一定要提到开学的事情了,便前去打听。跨进招待室,看见局里的几个职员在那里裁纸磨墨,像是办喜事的样子。

　　一个职员喊道,"巧得很,潘先生来了! 你写得一手好颜字,这个差使就请你当了吧。"

　　"这么大的字,非得潘先生写不可,"其余几个人附和着。

英汉对照
English-Chinese
中国文学宝库
Gems of Chinese Literature
现代文学系列
Modern Literature

"We are getting ready to welcome the triumphant return of Commander Du. Four festooned archways are to be erected at the railway station to welcome Commander Du's train. We need to write inscriptions for the four archways."

"Who am I to write for such an important event?"

"We all agree you're the best man!" "You mustn't be modest," came the cry from all sides as a writing brush was thrust into Mr. Pan's hands.

Mr. Pan was quite overwhelmed. He took the writing brush and dipped it in the ink. After a pensive silence, he wrote, "His Deeds Surpass All Others" and on the second strip of paper, "His Might Sweeps the Southeast." On the third piece of paper he wrote, "Virtue and Benevolence So Bountiful." But as his brush formed the word "bountiful," he had a vision of press-gangs, exploding shells, houses in flame, raped women, pale-faced refugees and rotting corpses.

"This epithet shows the people's heartfelt gratitude!" cried one of the men watching, with a sigh of admiration. "The writing is more beautiful too."

"I wonder what he'll find to match this epithet," commented another man.

November 27, 1924
Translated by Tang Sheng

"写什么东西？我完全茫然。"

"我们这里正筹备欢迎杜统帅凯旋的事务。车站的两头要搭起四个彩牌坊，让杜统帅的花车在中间通过。现在要写的就是牌坊上的几个字。"

"我那里配写这上边的字？"

"当仁不让，""一致推举，"几个人一哄地说；笔杆便送到潘先生手里。

潘先生觉得这当儿很有点意味，接了笔便在墨盆里蘸墨汁。凝想一下，提起笔来在蜡笺上一并排写"功高岳牧"四个大字。第二张写的是"威镇东南"。又写第三张，是"德隆恩溥"。——他写到"溥"字，仿佛看见许多影片，拉夫，开炮，焚烧房屋，奸淫妇人，菜色的男女，腐烂的死尸，在眼前一闪。

旁边看写字的一个人赞叹说，"这一句更见恳切。字也越来越好了。"

"看他对上一句什么，"又一个说。

1924，11，27。

英汉对照
English-Chinese
中国文学宝库
Gems of Chinese Literature
现代文学系列
Modern Literature

The Package

The gentle jolting of the bus made him feel as comfortable as if a barber were massaging his back. Drowsiness was like a cap slipped over his head, and everything flashing before him blurred. He realized vaguely that the whiffs of scent drifting past his nostrils emanated from the bobbed-haired figure in a long gown who was staring out of the window, but he couldn't be troubled to look at her more closely, and felt no regret when the scent dissipated.

The bus suddenly lurched and rocked as if crossing some furrows, but then came to a stop. The passengers sighed, relieved that the tiring journey was over, then scrambled towards the door through which only one person at a time could pass. As this jostling held everyone up, they started exclaiming scathingly, "Steady on!" "What's the hurry?"

He was one of the last to stand up. As he neared the door, that bobbed-haired, long-gowned figure who seemed to be in a hurry leaned one hand on the doorway to steady herself. He halted instinctively to let her out first, and glanced casually at the smooth, rounded neck between the bobbed hair and the collar of her gown.... His thoughts started wandering.

"What's that?"

After he alighted this was the question asked by a man in black who had materialized before him. Over his black serge gown he

一包东西

公共汽车软和地震荡着,他觉得很舒适,犹如让理发匠捶着背似地,微微的倦意笼罩他的头顶和前额,在眼前晃动的一切都不大有明显的轮廓。一阵阵的香气拂过他的鼻端,他模糊地想,这是从那个望着窗外的短发长袍的躯体上飘过来的;但也没有心思移准眼光去看她个仔细,对于香气的消散也不以为可惜。

车身突然跳跃似地动荡,好像车轮正滚过几道土埂,但随即停住了。乘客都微微嘘气,仿佛庆幸那厌倦的旅程已经完毕,便争先挤出那个不容两个身躯并行的车门。争先的结果是大家不得先,于是,"慢慢来呀!""要紧什么的!"大家吐出这些略觉薄情的语句。

他站起来比较迟;走近车门,那短发长袍的形象似乎带点儿匆忙的姿势,伸出一只手扶住那门框。他本能地停住脚,让她先出门下去;无意间瞥见短发之下袍领之上的一段脖子,圆圆的,腻腻的……一时想得非常玄远。

"什么东西?"

下了车以后,显现在他面前这样问的是个全身玄色的汉子;玄色呢的长袍加上玄色花缎

英汉对照
English-Chinese
中国文学宝库
Gems of Chinese Literature
现代文学系列
Modern Literature

had a sleeveless black brocade jacket, and his broad-brimmed hat was black too. There was something very crude about his bronzed fleshy face. One could see at a glance that he was a secret agent. He was questioning someone with a package under one arm, prodding it with thick fingers on which flashed several gold rings.

This galvanized him into recollecting the package in his own hand. He realized the danger he was in. His earlier nonchalance and drowsiness fled, leaving him as terrified as a mouse confronting a cat. He forbade himself to look at that fellow in black, as if this would make him invisible to the latter; but his refractory eyes would dart that way, and he saw that the man had let the other passenger go and his upraised eyes now seemed to be probing into the package in his own hands.

"I'm done for!" Thinking this he instinctively whirled around. But people were milling about through the heavy traffic, and how could he get away? Those baleful black eyes had already fixed on his package!

"Run for it...." he thought hazily, and threw himself into a decrepit old rickshaw. As he was pulled away he could hear his heart pounding.

Actually he had no idea what that package contained. While waiting for the bus, staring raptly at the carvings on a four-storey building, someone had patted him suddenly on the back. Turning, he saw his good friend Old Li. Old Li told him he wasn't going back at once on account of some business and asked him to take this package and keep it until he could fetch it. It wasn't heavy or troublesome, just the size of a dozen journals, so no amount of

的屈襟背心,宽檐的帽子也是玄色的;紫褐色的脸,胖胖的,眉目间颇带粗俗的气分。那汉子是个侦探,可以一望而知,其时正在查问一个人挟着的包裹,在包裹周围按着捏着的粗大的手指上,黄澄澄的,套着几个金戒指。

电掣似地,他立刻省悟自己手里拿着一包东西,现在的境地已经十分危险。刚才那恬适的甚至于朦胧的心情完全消散了,只是老鼠见了猫似地警觉且震栗。他故意制止眼睛不要去望那玄色的汉子,仿佛这样也就不会给那汉子看见;可是不顺从的眼睛偏要溜过去,却见那汉子已经放走了挟包裹的人,眼光略微抬起来,似乎正射在自己手里的一包东西上。

"不好!"他这样想时,不自主地旋了一转。虽然来往的人那样纷扰,车辆那样繁密,但是有什么法子可以躲避呢?那双乌光光的凶狠的眼睛已经盯住这包东西了!

"逃——"他突然又模糊地想,连忙跨上一辆破旧的人力车。当身体被载着向前移动时,他听见腔子里心脏突突跳动的声音。

那一包是什么东西,他自己也不知道。在等候公共汽车的时候,悠悠望着四层洋楼的雕饰正在出神,忽然有人拍他的肩背。回头一看,是熟朋友老李。老李说还有点事不就回去,一包东西费神先带走,等会儿自己去取。并不重,也不累赘,不过十本杂志那样的一包;就是剖开

英汉对照
English-Chinese
中国文学宝库
Gems of Chinese Literature
现代文学系列
Modern Literature

soul-searching could have shown him the least reason to refuse this commission. By the time he was seated in the bus, one hand holding the package, he felt as calm as if nothing at all had happened.

But that rasping "What's that?" and that surly figure in black convinced him what the package contained just as surely as if he had opened it to look. He had known quite well for years what Old Li was up to: he was not afraid of the forces of reaction and was charging boldly ahead to unmask their ugly faces and rip out their vicious guts. What else could he be carrying but plans for downing those devils or indictments of their crimes? On those squares of thick paper must be printed a prostrate corpse, a fearful sight weltering in blood — the most recent victim of the reactionaries. And below undoubtedly would be the caption, "He died for the people! Another enemy atrocity!"

Past him flashed the coloured signboards of shops on both sides. His mind was befogged as if from a hangover. And he felt chilled from head to foot right to the marrow of his bones, as if his whole being had shrunk there in acute discomfort. He tried to dismiss the idea, but it kept stabbing at his heart like a needle. "Is that fellow in black trailing me? Is he after me?" He could have ascertained this by looking round, but his neck seemed as stiff as a ramrod, and he believed that if he turned his head he would find himself looking up the black barrel of a revolver!

"I really don't deserve to be arrested. Old Li now, he's chosen his course, so he can't complain if he gets put away. But why should someone like me, someone innocent, be involved? Still...."

Unconsciously he hunched up his shoulders as if a black arm

心来,也决不会发见一丝儿不愿代带的意思。待上了车坐下,一只手按住那包东西,非常自然,好像并没有拿什么。

但当听见那声怪刺耳的"什么东西!"又望见那不感愉快的玄色的形象时,他自信已经知道是一包什么东西了,像解开来看一样清楚。年来老李干的什么事业是知道得很清楚的,他不怕恶魔的锋利的爪牙,勇敢地冲上前去,要撕下它们的凶恶的脸皮,要拉断它们的狠毒的心肠。他手里携带的东西,还有别的么?不是制服恶魔的方略,便是它们的罪状的宣告书。现在这一包,方方的,是坚实的纸张,那一定印着个横倒的难看的尸体,胸口有模糊的一滩;就是新近被恶魔残害的一个。而且,无疑地,下面一定印着警切的题语:"为人们牺牲的!请看恶魔的猖狂!"

两旁店家一扇扇彩色的招牌在眼角拂过,觉得头里很昏乱,像带着宿醉。而且周身发冷,不在肌肤而在骨子里,仿佛身躯尽在那里缩拢来,很不好过。待要不想,偏又一针一针似地刺着心头,"那玄色的家伙在背后吧?那玄色的家伙在背后吧?"这只要回头一看就能解决,但是脖子差不多僵硬了;而且相信一回头就得对准一个深深的乌黑的小管子!

"被他带去,未免不上算。像老李,他愿意那么干,被带了去也没有什么怨的。而我……我倘若……不是累及无辜么?但是……"

英汉对照
English-Chinese
中国文学宝库
Gems of Chinese Literature
现代文学系列
Modern Literature

were reaching for his neck and a powerful hand were about to clamp down on his head. After that, third degree ... then he'd wallow in mud and faeces, his blood sucked by parasites of every kind, his cell-mates bearded robbers with matted hair.... Weighed down with heavy chains he'd have to drag a great roller over a stony road which cut his feet ... or else he'd get a bullet through his head!

As all before him turned black, he simply gritted his teeth and closed his eyes.

"Ah! To end like this before I'm even thirty! It goes against the grain. I want to live on!... Though it may not count as aiming very high, I did want to make a success of that school of mine; I wanted to see my students amount to something. But now, when I've just got going, am I to be cut off like this?" He felt so embittered, his head began to whirl.

For what seemed quite a while the rickshaw jolted forward, but no powerful hand clamped down on his head. He opened his eyes a crack. He saw the skirt of his lined gown covering his thighs and hanging down over his knees. Sticking out beneath the hem was that paper package.

"Ah, the package!" When he had scrambled helter-skelter on to the rickshaw, how could he have put it on the foot-board like that with no attempt at concealment? This passed his understanding. And he now saw that one side of the package had at some stage been ripped open, so that passers-by could easily see the contents.

"That fellow must have seen the print of a prostrate corpse!" But he dared not stoop down to adjust the wrapping-paper. All he

他这么想,脖子自然而然又缩紧些。他仿佛觉得那玄色的胳膊正在伸近来,一只粗大的手马上要盖到头顶上来了;随后就是惨酷的拷问——躺在溲溺浸渍的泥地里……让各种小虫吸全身的血……与蓬头长胡子的强盗作伴……重而硬的链条缠住身体……拖动大石滚碾平那刺脚底痛的石子路……或者是"砰"!

他眼前一阵黑暗,索性咬紧牙关,闭上眼睛。

"啊!没到三十的生命,就这样完了么!我不愿意!我要活下去!……虽然算不得什么大志愿,我那个学校总要把它搞得像个样儿;那些学生,也要看看他们将来的眉目。然而,现在,还只是刚刚起头呢,难道就不容我活下去了么!"他凄然心酸,往下就想不大清楚了。

似乎有了好一会儿,身体依然一颠一侧地前进,而那只粗大的手还不曾盖上头顶来;眼睛便又张开一线来。看见的是自己的夹袍的前幅,盖在大腿上,沿着膝盖直垂下去;在下缘的前面,露出那个纸包。

"啊,这个包!"刚才匆促上车,怎么就把它摆在脚踏上,一点儿遮掩也没有,他自己想不明白了。而且,他发见那个包的一面,不知什么时候给弄破了,破纸向外翘起,当然旁人可以很清楚地看见内容。

"印着的横倒的尸体一定让那家伙看见了!"但是他绝不敢俯下身子把包纸整理好,只

英汉对照
English-Chinese
中国文学宝库
Gems of Chinese Literature
现代文学系列
Modern Literature

could do was furtively shove the package further in with his heels, and softly spread the skirt of his gown over it. At the same time he looked up as if nonchalantly at the faded number printed on the back of the rickshaw puller's jacket. When presently he lowered his anxious eyes for another glance, he saw that he hadn't fixed things properly. Though the front of the package was hidden, the sides were still visible.

"Caught red-handed, how can you clear yourself? At very least you'll be charged as an agitator!" He actually shivered, his heels clamped against the package, as if eager to break the front of the seat and hide it underneath.

"Old Li now, he's chosen his course, so he can't complain if he gets put away. But why should someone like me, someone innocent, be involved?" His thoughts were back on the old track.

But at once he felt rather ashamed. "I may be innocent; but has Old Li done anything wrong?" He thought of the various forms the diehards took and their various machinations. Red blood and raging flames, gaunt figures and dead faces flashed through his mind like a film. "This is absurd! To tolerate those devils is an insult to decent people. Old Li's cause should be the cause of us all. I should follow his example."

"But I have my own work to do." His mind turned to education. "I'm teaching young people not to lapse into bad ways, and that's very important too, besides being more basic. As for the other, I'm not up to it. They have fierce agents and absolute power, whereas I have nothing. Only a fool tries to smash a stone with an egg." These reflections rid him of his sense of shame, and he

能行窃似地用脚跟把那个包勾进一点儿,又轻轻理直夹袍的前幅把它掩没;同时抬起眼光来,故作无事似地,看那车夫号衣背上模糊了的数目字。一会儿,不放心地垂下眼光再去偷看,却见并没有弄妥贴,前面固然掩没了,旁侧还是露出来。

"真凭实据在手里,还能抵赖什么,至少办个煽动的罪名!"他简直有点儿发抖了;脚跟用力抵住那个包,似乎要抵破了车座的竖板,把它藏到坐垫底下去。

"像老李,他愿意那么干,被带了去也没有什么怨的。而我……我……不是累及无辜么?"他重又想到老路上去。

然而立刻觉得有些惭愧了,"我是无辜;老李那么干,难道就是有罪么?"于是想起恶魔的种种形相,种种作为;红血与烈火,饥容与死脸,急速地电影似地都在脑子里闪过。"这太岂有此理!假如宽恕了恶魔,就是侮蔑了人们。老李的事业,正是人人该做的事业。我也该去做同样的事业!"

"然而,我自有我的事业在,"他一转念就想到教育。"我是教人不要堕入魔道,也非常重要,而且尤为根本。至于那个,我的力量太微弱了。它们有锋利的爪牙,我有什么呢?它们有无上的威力,我有什么呢?用鸡蛋同石头去碰,到底不是聪明人干的事。"想着,也就无所谓惭

英汉对照
English-Chinese
中国文学宝库
Gems of Chinese Literature
现代文学系列
Modern Literature

couldn't help feeling a certain contempt for Old Li's foolhardiness. While as for Old Li asking him to carry such dangerous materials, that really put his back up.

"Which way?" the rickshaw puller turned to ask as they approached a crossroad. In the gathering dusk the distant pedestrians and traffic were dark blurred shadows.

"Turn left," he answered automatically. That was the way to his school. Had he stopped to think he would have hesitated.

"Is that fellow trailing me?... Surely he can't be. This cream felt hat of mine is so distinctive he'd be bound to recognize it, couldn't mistake it. I meant originally to wear my old hat, what made me put this on instead?... Shall I take it off?... Better not. If I did, he'd certainly rush over, his black revolver aimed at the back of my head.... Raise the rickshaw hood?... No good either. It's obviously not raining, so why put up the hood? That would just show him I've panicked.... Ah, I'm done for."

"In one or two seconds maybe, or a minute or so later, whenever that brute feels like it he can call to me to halt. Of course I'd go with him. How could I resist?" He had a mental picture of tomorrow's big newspaper headline, "Capture of a Distributor of Subversive Journals" with his name underneath. Tens of thousands of readers would discuss the matter, some sighing, "Too bad, a brave, high-minded man!" Others would jeer, "Bah, what did he hope to achieve!" Others would swear, "Fine, these pests should be wiped out!" But which of them would be right? What distressed him most was the thought of his colleagues and students reacting in the same way to the news, but all of them agreeing that they had

愧:对于老李那种不聪明的蛮干,未免有些鄙夷的意思;而老李要托他带那种危险东西,尤属大可痛恨。

"往那里走?"车夫回转头来。前边是叉路了,暮色渐浓,远处的行人和车辆都成一团团的黑影。

"往左,"他随口说了。那是回学校去的道路,假如他仔细想了,决不会这样绝不踌躇的。

"那家伙不在后头了吧?——不会的,不会的。我这一顶米色呢帽很触目,他认定了米色呢帽,再也不会错失。……本来想戴那项旧帽子出来的,怎么又戴了这一顶!……脱去了吧?……不好,米色呢帽这么一晃动,那家伙一定奔过来把乌黑的小管子指着我的后脑勺。……把车篷拉了起来吧?……也不好,明明不下雨,为什么拉起车篷来?不是告诉人家我在胆怯么?……啊,简直没办法!"

"或是一秒钟两秒钟里头,或是再迟半分钟一分钟,只要那家伙高兴,马上可以叫住我。我当然跟着他走。难道还能抵抗么?"他仿佛已经看见明天的情形了:报上刊载着大号字的题目"捕获运输危险刊物的",下面就是自己的名字。成千成万的读者纷纷议论着,有的嗟叹说,"可惜,有志气的人!"有的讥讽说,"嗤,蚊虫想负山!"有的痛骂说,"好呀,这班东西要捉个干净!"但是,他们说对了那一项呢?尤其痛心的是学校里的同事和学生看见了,也会同样地嗟叹或者讥讽,或者痛骂,而大家一致的一句话是

never expected this of their head.... Of course this would be the end of the school: no one would collect funds now or take charge. His colleagues would go their different ways while the students would be fetched home by their families. Two years' preparation and over six months of implementing his programme had all come to nothing! Even if he were lucky enough to clear himself, he couldn't run the school any longer. He'd have to hide his face and beat a retreat. Visualizing all this, he felt his life had ended. Ahead was nothing but black emptiness.

But the thought of third degree and wallowing in the mud with parasites sucking his blood and robbers for cell-mates goaded him into tacking about in search of a better way out. "When they question me, of course I'll tell them nothing. If they ask who will vouch for me I'll refer them to Old Mr. Wang — they should believe him. The school will be notified at once, and they can approach the educational association. I'll send a telegram to my elder brother, and the provincial governor should be able to help. But will they let me communicate with outside? Not if the crime is considered serious. What then?" He sighed again in dismay, in his mind a vague recollection of how the prisoners in one of Tolstoy's stories communicated with each other by tapping the walls of their cells.

"Here we are!" he thought, at the sight of the familiar electric light with a white porcelain shade at the school gate. For a second he hesitated: his first idea was not to go in, as that would show the agent where he lived. But since he had let the rickshaw pull him here and the brute had trailed him, he must know anyway. The best thing would be to leave the package in the rickshaw when he

"不料校长先生……"学校前途自然不堪设想了,款没人筹,一切事务没人总管,同事便各自分散,学生当然由家属领回去了。两年的筹划,半年有余的实施,完全付于流水!……就是事情幸而能辨白,学校也不能办了。岂但学校,简直社会上一切活动都不能参加。偶然站在人前,只要听见低低的一声"他是吃过一场官司的",还能不掩了脸逃走么?——他看到这些情形,觉得自己已到生命的尽头,前面是漫黑的一大团空虚。

但是惨酷的拷问,躺在泥地里,让小虫吸血,与强盗作伴等等激刺着他,使他改换方向,去寻一条漫着青光的生路。"他们问我,我当然不知情。他们问谁可作证,我就把王老先生说出来,他们该相信了吧。立刻通知学校里,叫他们去找教育会也行。打个电报给老大,省长方面想来也可以有路子。——不过,他们许我同外面通信么?如其说案情重大,概不许通信,又怎么办呢?"他又怅然了,轻轻地叹一口气,同时朦胧地想到托尔斯泰一篇小说里犯人相互敲墙壁通信的法子。

"到学校了!"他看见相熟的一盏白瓷罩电灯在前面发亮,这样想。在极短的时间里,却反复地踌躇:起初想不要进去,进去了给那家伙认识了所在是不好的。然而尽让车夫拖着跑,那家伙始终跟在后头,同样是个给他看住。最好的办法是把那包东西留在车里,自己走进学校。

英汉对照
English-Chinese
中国文学宝库
Gems of Chinese Literature
现代文学系列
Modern Literature

went in. But the fellow knew quite well who had hired the rickshaw, and could easily track him down.

In any case, the rickshaw had now reached the school gate. In a daze, screwing up more courage than ever before, he called, "Stop!" The rickshaw puller set his rickshaw down. He stuffed some coppers into his hands, and snatching up the package scuttled through the school gate.

"Meisheng, go out and see if anyone's asking for me. If so, say I'm out."

Meisheng in bewilderment gave a dubious smile and started off slowly.

"Hurry up! I'm not here, tell him that!" Going into his own room, he hastily hid the package behind a case under his bed. He then sat down, resting his head on his hands, breathing hard, his heart still thumping.

Some time passed but Meisheng didn't come back. He could hear him fanning the stove on which he heated water.

"Meisheng!" he called repressively. "Has anyone been asking for me outside?"

Meisheng's thin face appeared in the doorway. "I went to the gate just now and saw some people...."

"Ah!"

"But they were just passers-by. No one asked for you, sir."

"Oh." He felt like exploding but thought better of it. Of course his mind was more at rest, yet he still seemed caught in a web which he could not unravel. He stood up and paced the room a few times, then leaned against the window to look at the brightening

但是那家伙明明看清车是谁坐来的,只要一搜查,人赃还是在他手里。

车辆不管什么,已经滚到校门前了。莫名其妙地,他使出生平未有的勇气说"停!"车夫放下车柄,他塞一把铜子在车夫手心里,急忙提起那纸包刺猬似地冲进学校的门。

"梅生,外边去看有没有人问起我。如果有,说我不在这里。"

梅生莫名所以,疑怪的笑意在口角边一嘻,慢慢地退出去。

"快去!不在这里,说我不在这里!"他走进自己的房间,慌忙地把手里的纸包藏在床底下箱子背后。坐定下来,两手支着头喘气;心头依然突突地跳。

梅生去了一会儿,没有来回话,却听他拍拍拍地在那里扇水炉子了。

"梅生!"他用敛抑的声气叫唤。"外边有没有人问起我?"

梅生的瘦脸显露在房门口了,"刚才门口去看,人是有的……"

"啊!"

"不过都是来往的人,没有走来问起先生的。"

"哦!"他想发作,不知道为什么又缩住了。心里自然安舒些儿,但总还是给几条细麻绳缠住了肚肠似地,不能释然。站起来转了几个圈子,又靠窗望了一会儿新月将上发亮的天,便回

The Package

sky where the new moon was rising. Turning back to his bed he took out the paper package from behind the case and with curiosity mixed with apprehension placed it respectfully on his desk.

"Ha — so that's what it is!" he exclaimed, having tugged out a sheet. On the paper was printed a portrait of an old lady with a kindly face, deeply lined yet in no way desiccated or haggard. Turning to the back he saw an obituary notice, and under "your mourning grandson" was Old Li's name.

After overcoming an indefinable sensation he looked up at his own reflection in the mirror on the wall. His face was flushed red, his eyes were bright.

Sheepishly he lowered his head.

November 30, 1926
Translated by Wenxue

到床前取出箱子背后的纸包,带着又好奇又害怕的心绪,郑重地放在桌子上。

"嘻——这个东西!"他用力抽出一张来看时说。纸面印着一位老太太的半身像,面貌很慈祥,皱纹虽多,却没有干枯憔悴之意。翻过来看是讣告,"降服孙"下面印着老李的名字。

一阵微妙的心情消逝之后,他抬起头来,看见映在墙上一面镜子里的自己的脸,涨得红红地,眼角里发亮。

他觉得不好意思,又低下头来了。

1926, 11, 30

英汉对照
English-Chinese
中国文学宝库
Gems of Chinese Literature
现代文学系列
Modern Literature

Night

In a lane not too clean and neat there was a two-storey house with one room downstairs and one upstairs. All the furniture in the downstairs room was in a blur as if the dim yellowish paraffin lamp on the table had darkened the room instead of giving it light. Beside the table sat an elderly woman with a child about two in her arms. There was nothing unusual about the woman's features. Though her forehead was wrinkled, she did not look old or feeble. Only her reddened eyes were a little strange, staring fixedly from their deep sockets at the child's face. She looked sad and lost, noting how the colour had faded from the little boy's cheeks and how weak he was after his recent shock.

Of late the child had cried as much as six months ago when he was being weaned. He would burst out crying abruptly just as if someone had hit him. Once he started he would go on endlessly, like cicadas chirping in summer. The woman tried her best to soothe him, recalling all the phrases she had used to comfort babies in her younger days, but all to little avail; perhaps the child found them too outlandish or old-fashioned. Only after he had exhausted himself by sobbing would his eyelids begin to flutter until finally they closed altogether.

Tonight the woman felt relieved because, for a change, the child had not started crying. If he should go to sleep like that, wouldn't

夜

　　一条不很整洁的里里,一幢一楼一底的屋内,桌上的煤油灯发出黄晕的光,照得所有的器物模糊,惨淡,好像反而加浓了阴黯。桌旁坐着个老妇人,手里抱着一个大约不过两周岁的孩子。那老妇人的状貌没有什么特点,额上虽然已画上好几条皱纹,还不见得怎么衰老。只是她的眼睛有点儿怪,深陷的眼眶里,红筋连连牵牵的,发亮;放大的瞳子注视着孩子的脸,定定的,凄然失神。她想孩子因为受着突然的打击,红润的颜色已转成苍白,肌肉也宽松不少了。

　　近来,那孩子特别爱哭,犹如半年前刚断奶的时候。仿佛给谁骤然打了一下,不知怎么一来就拉开喉咙直叫。叫开了头便难得停,好比大暑天的蝉。老妇人于是百般抚慰,把自己年轻时抚慰孩子的语句一一背了出来。可是不大见效,似乎孩子嫌那些语句太古旧又太拙劣了。直到他自己没了力,一面呜咽,一面让眼皮一会儿开一会儿闭而终于阖拢,才算收场。

　　今晚那老妇人却似乎感觉特别安慰;时候到了,孩子的哭还不见开场,假如就这样倦下来

英汉对照
English-Chinese
中国文学宝库
Gems of Chinese Literature
现代文学系列
Modern Literature

it be a rare quiet night? But on the other hand, she was wondering uneasily what news her younger brother would bring back, what he had learned of her poor darling who had been in her thoughts day and night.

These evenings had been torture to her, apart from the child's crying, for she seemed to see so many shadowy pictures in the dim lamplight. First here, now there, she could have sworn she glimpsed pools of bright red blood! As cars sped by or heavy trucks thundered steadily past outside, she seemed to see the two of them in a car with heavy clanking chains on their wrists and ankles. When footsteps — heavy or light, slow or quick — passed by her door, she was afraid the police had come for her and the baby. The ringing of her neighbour's doorbell set her heart throbbing. Already of the age when one sleeps little, she could not fall asleep at all now for terror. When she went to bed she dared not light the lamp for fear the light upstairs would attract attention and cause trouble. Besides, she preferred to see nothing, to be in sheer darkness. But no! The flickering shadows appeared just the same: the red pool like the setting sun even seemed to be spreading. All she could do was to hug the child who often sobbed in his dreams....

She kept gazing at the child. Weak and stricken, she did not know which way to turn. The future loomed before her like a sea of mist which surely hid wild beasts of pitfalls. And her only companion in danger was this small child. She was virtually alone. She dreaded to think more and, wanting something better to do, she asked the child, "Big Baby, precious, what's your surname?"

睡着,岂不是难得的安静的一晚。然而在另一方面,她又感觉特别不安;不知道快要回来的阿弟将怎么说,不知道几天来醒里梦里系念着的可怜的宝贝到底有没有着落。

晚上,在她,这几天真不好过。除了孩子的啼哭,黄晕的灯火里,她仿佛看见隐隐闪闪的好些形象。有时又仿佛看见鲜红的一摊,在这里或是那里——那是血!里外,汽车奔驰而过,笨重的运货车的铁轮有韵律地响着,她就仿佛看见一辆汽车载着被捆绑的两个,他们手足上是累赘而击触有声的镣铐。门首时时有轻重徐疾的脚步声经过,她总觉得害怕,以为或者就是来找她和孩子的。邻家的门环一声响,那更使她心头突地一跳。本来已届少眠年龄的她,这样提心吊胆地细尝恐怖的味道,就一刻也不得入梦。睡时,灯是不敢点的,她怕楼上的灯光招惹是非,也希冀眼前干净些,完全一片黑。然而没有用,隐隐闪闪的那些形象还是显现,鲜红的一摊还是落山的太阳一般似乎尽在那里扩大开来。于是,只得紧紧地抱住梦里时而呜咽的孩子……

这时候,她注视着孩子,在她衰弱而创伤的脑里,涌现着雾海似的迷茫的未来。往那方走才是道路呢? 她丝毫不能辨认。怕有些猛兽或者陷阱隐在雾海里吧? 她想那是十分之九会有的。而伴同前去冒险的,只有这方才学话的孩子;简直等于自己孤零零一个。她不敢再想,无聊地问孩子,"大男乖的,你姓什么?"

英汉对照
English-Chinese
中国文学宝库
Gems of Chinese Literature
现代文学系列
Modern Literature

"Zhang," he replied. Not knowing what a surname means, a child simply repeats what he is told just as he is taught to say papa and mama.

"No, no," the woman scolded him mildly, a little worried because he had not learned his new lesson well. "Don't say that, nobody's surname is Zhang. Listen, Big Baby's surname is Sun. Remember, Sun, Sun...."

"Sun," the child did not insist but repeated after her in his babyish tone, looking up into her face.

She shut her eyes tightly twice. Her tears had nearly run dry but she felt close to sobbing. "That's right. Sun, Sun. Now again, what is your surname?"

"Sun," repeated the little boy mischievously, reaching out for the green jade hairpin in her hair.

"Good, Big Baby's a dear!" She held the child tightly, her face brushing against his cotton shirt. "Whoever asks you, your surname is Sun, Sun...." Her voice, tinged with sadness, died away.

The child, his arms pinioned, was unable to reach the hairpin. Suddenly he burst out crying, struggling with all his might, tears streaming down his face.

She knew what this meant — the normal routine had started, no chance of a quiet evening! In a very gentle voice she crooned, "Big Baby, precious, don't cry!... A nice doll's coming to see Big Baby.... She's in a red sedan-chair ... in a pretty carriage...."

The little boy as usual paid no heed but cried even louder. "I

"张，"大男随口回答。孩子在尚未了解姓的意义的时候，自己的姓往往被教练成口头的熟语，同叫爹爹妈妈一样地习惯。

"不！不！"老妇人轻轻呵斥。她想他的新功课还没练熟，有点儿发愁，只得重行矫正他说，"不要瞎说，那个姓张！我教你，大男姓孙。记着，孙，孙……"

"孙，"大男并不坚持，仰起脸来看老妇人的脸，就这样学着说，发音带十二分的稚气。

老妇人的眼睛重重地闭了两闭；她的泪泉差不多枯竭了，眼睛闭两闭就表示心头一阵酸，周身经验到哭泣时的一切感觉。"不错，姓孙，孙。再来问你，大男姓什么？"

"孙，"大男玩皮地学舌，同时伸手想去取老妇人头上那翡翠簪儿。

"乖的，大男乖的。"老妇人把大男紧紧抱住，脸贴着他的花洋布衫。"不管那个问你，你说姓孙，你说姓孙……"声音渐渐凄咽了。

大男的胳臂给老妇人抱住，不能取那翡翠簪儿，"哇——"突然哭起来了。小身躯死命地挣扎，泪水淌得满脸。

老妇人知道每晚的常课又开头了，安然而过已成梦想，便故意做出柔和的声音哄他道："大男乖的……不要哭呀……花团团来看大男了……坐着红轿子来了……坐着花马车来了……"

大男照例不理睬，喉咙却张得更大了，"哇——妈妈呀——妈妈呀——"

英汉对照
English-Chinese
中国文学宝库
Gems of Chinese Literature
现代文学系列
Modern Literature

want ... my mam...."

More distressed and frightened than ever, the woman felt his cries were piercing her heart like sharp needles and worried lest the neighbours hear through the thin walls and become suspicious. But it was not easy to appease him. Fully aware that what she was saying was no use, still she repeated again and again in a trembling voice, "Mama will be back soon." At that the child only cried louder, opening wide his tearful eyes and looking around for his mother.

She stood up and started pacing the floor, holding the child in her arms. Her slow, heavy steps showed her age. She paced to and fro, reciting those outlandish, old-fashioned expressions meant to soothe a child. The furniture in the room seemed to be vibrating with the child's crying, the wick of the lamp seemed to be expanding, expanding ... and ah, a pool of blood! She shut her weary eyes, not daring to look again. Although the child's cries were piercing her ears, she felt she was alone on a strange mountain; in surroundings so weird that her blood was turning cold.

Tap, tap, somebody was knocking at the door. At the same time the scabby brown dog across the lane started barking. She started, then recognized the familiar knock. Her younger brother had come back. She hurried to open the door.

The door had barely opened a crack when in slipped the man outside. Swiftly and softly he turned back to close the door as if shutting out something that was after him.

"Well?" asked the woman eagerly in a low voice. She wished she could see into his heart, to share all he knew.

这样的哭最使老妇人又伤心又害怕。伤心的是一声就像一针，针针刺着自己的心。害怕的是单墙薄壁，左右邻舍留心一听就会起疑念。然而治他的哭却不容易；一句明知无效的"妈妈就会来的"战兢兢地说了再说，只使他哭得更响些，而且张大了水汪汪的眼睛四望，看妈妈从那里来。

　　老妇人于是站起来踱步，让大男躺在臂弯里；从她那动作的滞钝以及步履的沉重，又见得她确实有点衰老了。她来回地踱着，背诵那些又古旧又拙劣的抚慰孩子的语句。屋内的器物仿佛跟着哭声的震荡而晃动起来，灯焰似乎在化得大，化得大——啊，一摊血！她闭上疲劳的眼，不敢再看。耳际虽有孩子撕裂似的哭声，却如同在神怪的空山里一样，幽寂得使血都变冷。

　　搭，搭，外面有叩门声，同时，躺在跨街楼底下的那条癞黄狗汪汪地叫起来。她吓得一跳，但随即省悟这声音极熟，一定是阿弟回来了，便匆遽地走去开门。

　　门才开一道缝，外面的人便闪了进来；连忙，轻轻地，转身把门关上，好像提防别的什么东西也乘势掩了进来。

Her brother walked in, glancing around and taking a seat, gasping. He looked like a merchant of about forty, fine wrinkles around his narrow eyes making it seem as if he were always smiling. His nose was not big either. Sweat glimmered on his forehead, yet he was shivering. The child's crying reminded him of a few water-chestnuts he had in his porkert. He took them out and handed them to the child, saying, "Eat these! Don't cry!"

Tired already and attracted by the water-chestnuts, the child took them and fell to nibbling them between sobs. Only then did the woman sit down again by the table.

"Well, I saw what I went for," said her brother faintly. Hand on forehead, he looked crestfallen and exhausted.

"You did?" The woman's eyes were dilated, her heart racked by a feeling stronger than grief.

"Yes, just now."

Only fear prevented the woman from dragging him out to show her. She uttered a cry of despair.

"Sister, nowadays there is hardly a good-hearted person to be found. But the fellow I met today, he is a good sort." Her brother stuck up one thumb in admiration.

"The one you went to look for?"

"That's right. I found him, at a small tea-house. I approached him in a friendly way, saying there were these two people he probably remembered. Now they were finished, but I begged him to have a heart and show me their coffins." He knitted his brows, making the wrinkles around his eyes more conspicuous, scratched his head and pursed his lips to show that it had not been easy. "At

"怎么样?"老妇人悄然地焦急地问。她恨不得阿弟挖一颗心给她看,让她一下子知道他所知道的一切。

阿弟走进屋内,向四下看了一周,便一屁股坐下来,张开口腔喘气。是四十左右商人模样的人,眼睛颇细,四围刻着纤细的皱纹形成永久的笑意,鼻子也不大,额上渍着汗水发亮,但是他正感觉一阵阵寒冷呢。他见大男啼哭,想起袋子里的几个荸荠,便掏出来授给他,"你吃荸荠,,不要哭吧。"

大男原也倦了,几个荸荠又多少有点引诱力,便伸出两只小手接了,一面抽咽一面咬荸荠。这才让老妇人仍得坐在桌旁。

"唉!总算看见了。"阿弟摸着额角,颓然,像完全消失了力气。

"看见了?"老妇人的眼睛张得可怕地大,心头是一种超乎悲痛的麻麻辣辣的况味。

"才看见了来。"

老妇人几乎要拉了阿弟便引她跑出去看,但恐怖心告诉她不应该这样卤莽,只得怅然地"喔!"

"阿姊,你说世界上没有一个好人,是不是?其实也不一定,像今天遇见的那个弟兄,他就是个好人。"他感服地竖起右手的大拇指。

"就是你去找他的那一个不是?"

"是呀。我找着了他,在一家小茶馆里。我好言好语同他说,有这样这样两个人,想来该有数。现在,人是完了,求他的恩典,大慈大悲,指点我去认一认他们的棺材。"他眉头一皱,原有的眼睛四围的皱纹见得更为显著,同时摇头咂

英汉对照
English-Chinese
中国文学宝库
Gems of Chinese Literature
现代文学系列
Modern Literature

first he paid little attention to me, just told me to forget it. So many people were finished, male and female, in long gowns or in short coats, how could he remember any two of them? Anyway, it was forbidden to see the coffins, he said. But as I had found the fellow, I would not give up. I tried again, telling him how sad their case was, a husband and wife, the woman leaving an old mother and a baby crying for mama day in and day out in its grandmother's arms.... I begged him to take pity on the old and the young.... In fact, I did everything I could short of kowtowing to him."

The woman listened, sadly casting down her eyes to watch the child who was falling asleep. The water-chestnuts had dropped on to her lap.

"My pleading moved him," her brother continued in a proud tone, a genuine smile appearing for one brief instant on his seemingly eternally smiling face. "After all, everybody is human. Appeal to someone as a fellow man and he's bound to be touched. He stopped holding aloof, thought for a while and sighed. 'There was a couple like that. Naturally, everyone is dear to his parents. Since you made it out such a sad case, I'll show you the place. But why should a young married couple do such things instead of leading a quiet life?' I told him I didn't know. We merchants couldn't understand those scholars. Probably...."

The woman heaved a sigh from the depth of her aching heart. Like her brother, she did not know the mind of her daughter and son-in-law either. But of one thing she was certain: they did not belong to the same category as those prisoners with ferocious looks

嘴,表示进行并不顺利。"他却不大理睬,说别麻烦吧,完了的人也多得很,男的,女的,穿长衫的,披短褂的,谁记得清这样两个,那样两个;况且棺材是不让去认的。我既然找着了他,那里肯放手。我又朝他说了,我说这两个人怎样可怜,是夫妻两个,女的有年老的娘,他们的孩子天天在外婆手里啼哭,叫着妈妈,妈妈……请他看老的小的面上发点慈悲心……唉!不用说吧,总之什么都说了,只少跪下来对他叩头。"

老妇人听着,凄然垂下眼光看手中的孩子;孩子朦胧欲睡了,几个荸荠已落在她的袖弯里。

"这一番话却动了他的心,"阿弟带着矜夸的声调继续说;永久作笑意的脸上浮现真实的笑,但立刻就收敛了。"这叫人情人情,只要是人,跟他讲情,没有讲不通的:他不像开头那样讲官话了,想了想叹口气说,'人是有这样两个的。谁不是爷娘的心肝骨肉!听你说得伤心,就给你指点了吧。不过好好儿夫妻两个,为什么不安分过日子,却去干那些勾当!'我说这可不大明白,我们生意人不懂他们念书人的心思,大概是——"

"嘘——"老妇人舒一口气,她感觉心胸被压得太紧结了。她同阿弟一样不懂女儿女婿的心思,但她清楚地知道,他们同脸生横肉声带杀

131

and rough voices. Not the same category, yet the same fate, why? Recently she had been pondering this painful problem but she could not solve it. Nobody was there to give her an answer either.

"He told me to meet him at six o'clock at a street corner. I of course thanked him again and again and went to the appointed place ahead of time to wait for him. After six he turned up, in ordinary civilian clothes. He led me to the fields, talking to me as we walked. Ah...."

He stopped, afraid of what came next. The fearful, ugly recollections refused to be brushed aside. But could his sister bear to hear? Perhaps she would faint.... The two of them had walked towards the open country.... There was no street light, no moon and no stars in the sky, the oppressive darkness weighed heavily upon them. The black shadows of distant trees and nearby buildings in the deathly silence seemed like monsters forming ranks. Occasionally two or three fireflies floated up and down as if ghosts were blinking their eyes with joy as they danced! The dogs' barking and the automobiles' honking in the distance sounded as if they came from beyond the horizon. But the faint droning in the air emanated from scores of small ephemeral insects. It had rained in the morning and the ground was muddy and slippery. He stumbled along in the dark. The other, a cigarette between his lips, said slowly, "They seemed kindly folk. They came to this place full of indignation yet they still looked kindly. Each eyed the other, then both lowered their heads, as if they wanted to say something yet could not. You know, that is the type we are afraid of. We don't mind fighting, we can raise our guns and open fire. I suppose you

气的那些囚徒决不是一类人。不是一类人为什么得到同样的结果？这是她近来时刻想起,老想不通,以致非常苦闷的问题。可是没有人给她解答。

"他约我六点钟在某路转角等他。我自然千恩万谢,那里还敢怠慢,提早就到那里去等着。六点过他果真来了,换了平常人的衣服。他引着我向野外走,一路同我谈。啊——"

他停住了。他不敢回想;然而那些见闻偏同无赖汉一般撩拨着他,叫他不得不回想。他想如果照样说出来,太伤阿姊的心了,说不定她会昏厥不省人事。——两个人向野外走。没有路灯。天上也没有星月,是闷郁得像要压到头顶上来的黑暗。远处树木和建筑物的黑影动也不动,像怪物摆着阵势。偶或有两三点萤火飘起又落下,这不是鬼在跳舞,快活得眨眼么？狗吠声同汽车的呜呜声远得几乎渺茫,好像在天末的那边。却有微细的嘶嘶声在空中流荡,那是些才得到生命的小虫子。早上还下雨,湿泥地不容易走,又看不清,好几回险些儿跌倒。那弟兄唇边粘着支烟卷,一壁吸烟一壁幽幽地说,"他们两个都和善,到这儿满脸的气愤,可还是透着和善。他们你看我,我看你,看了几眼就低头,想说话又说不上。你知道,这样的家伙我们就怕。我们不怕打仗,抬起枪来一阵地扳机关,

英汉对照
English-Chinese
中国文学宝库
Gems of Chinese Literature
现代文学系列
Modern Literature

could, too, provided you were strong enough to carry a gun. Before you is the enemy, whether you hit him or not, you don't know what he looks like. But if someone is bound and placed before you so that you see even his hair and eyebrows clearly, then it is hard to pull the trigger! After all, he's a human being. It's especially hard with those kindly ones, who look delicate enough to fall at a breath. That day the one given the job backed away several times and then — orders are orders! — tightly knitting his brows he fired. For some reason he missed. The man was hit in the arm and he writhed in pain. The woman, seeing that, screamed like mad. To tell you frankly I felt so bad that I turned away. Three more shots and the thing was finished. The two of them were covered with blood." As he listened, holding his breath, his legs grew numb and he hardly dared move for fear he might tread on a skeleton. So he followed closely, his chest almost brushing against the other man's back.

The woman saw that her brother was in a sort of trance, his small eyes bulging, scratching his head. She knew there must be something more. "What did he say?" she asked. "Did he see the end?"

The "end" was something which had been on her mind for days and nights. But she could not picture it to herself. Guns she had seen on the shoulders of soldiers and policemen. Was that dark glistening tube the thing which had finished her daughter and son-in-law? No, she could not believe it! She could see the young couple as clearly as in life. In what way did they deserve to be shot? She could not understand. How did the blood flow from their

我想你也该会,就只怕你抬不动枪。敌人在前面呀,打中的,打不中的,你都不知道他们面长面短。若说人是捆好在前面,一根头发一根眉毛都看得清楚,要动手,那就怕。没有别的,到底明明白白是一个人呀。尤其是那些和善得很的,又加上瘦骨伶仃,吹口气就会跌倒似的,那简直干不了。那一天,我们那个弟兄,上头的命令呀,退缩了好几回,才皱着眉头,砰的一响放出去。那知道这就差了准儿,中在男的胳膊上。他痛得一阵挣扎。女的好像发了狂,直叫起来。老实说,我心里维受了,回转头不想再看。又是三响,才算结果了,两个染了满身红。"那弟兄这样叙述,他听得似乎气都透不来了;两腿僵僵的提起了不敢放下,仿佛踏下去就会触着个骷髅。然而总得要走,只好紧紧跟随那弟兄的步子,前胸差不多贴着他的背。

老妇人见阿弟瞪着细眼凝想,同时搔着头皮,知道有下文,愕然问,"他谈些什么? 他看见他们那个的么?"

他们怎样"那个"的,这问题,她也想了好几天好几夜了,但终于苦闷。枪,看见过的,兵和警察背在背上,是乌亮的一根管子。难道结果女儿女婿的就是那东西么? 她不信。女儿女婿的形象,真是画都画得出。那一处地方该吃枪弹呢? 她不能想像。血,怎样从他们身体里流

英汉对照
English-Chinese
中国文学宝库
Gems of Chinese Literature
现代文学系列
Modern Literature

bodies? How did their breath cease and vanish into thin air? There was something so dreamlike and unreal about this that she sometimes felt her daughter and son-in-law had not been "done for." One day the door would open to their familiar knock and the dear young pair would come in, full of life, shoulder to shoulder. But this feeling was equally dreamlike and unreal.

"He didn't see the end," her brother hastened to reply. "He said the man was very generous giving away his clothes. That's how he got the pair of foreign-style trousers he had on."

"A light grey pair, made last August," murmured the woman, gazing at the lamplight, screwing up her eyes.

"I couldn't see clearly because it was dark and the ground was slippery. Several times I nearly fell. If I hadn't been wearing shoes with leather soles, my feet would have been soaked. We came to a spot and he said that was the place. I looked around. There were a dozen or so big dark trees under which were some dead white coffins." The brother lowered his head, and his bald spot glimmered in the lamplight. He had not the heart to tell her his sensation when he was told to look for coffins "numbers 17 and 18." Words would fail him to describe it. He had felt that all kinds of corpses — some frowning or gritting their teeth, some with shoulders or breasts shot through, some with broken noses or limbs — were about to kick off the coffin lids and dash at him. He was almost paralysed with horror. His guide struck several matches and said, "Look here, 17 and 18." The white coffin lids showed dimly in the match light. At first they looked like creeping snakes, but when he could fix his eyes on them, they stopped moving and he

出来？气,怎样消散消散而终于断绝？这些都模糊之极,像个朦胧的梦。因此,她有时感觉到女儿女婿实在并没有"那个",会有一天,搭,搭,搭,叩门声是他们特别的调子,开进来,是肩并肩的活泼可爱的两个。但只是这么感觉到而已,而且也有点模糊,像个朦胧的梦。

"他没看见,"阿弟连忙躲闪。"他说那男的很慷慨,几件衣服都送了人,他得到一条外国裤子,身上穿的就是。"

"那是淡灰色的,去年八月里做的,"老妇人眯着眼凝视着灯火说。

"这没看清,因为天黑,野外没有灯。湿泥地真难走,好几回险些儿滑跌;幸亏是皮底鞋,不然一定湿透。走到一处,他说到了。他仔细地看,十来棵大黑树站在那边,树下一条一条死白的东西就是棺材。"阿弟低下头来了,微秃的额顶在灯光里发亮。受了那弟兄"十七号,十八号,你去认一认吧？"的指示而向那些棺材走去时的心情,他不敢说,也不能说。种种可怕的尸体,皱着眉咬着牙的,裂了肩穿了胸的,鼻子开花的,腿膀成段的,仿佛就将踢开棺材板一齐撞到他身上来。心情是超过了恐惧而几乎麻木了。还是那弟兄划着几根火柴提醒他说,"这就是,你看,十七,十八,"他才迷惘地向小火光所指的白板面看。起初似乎是蠕蠕而动的蛇样的东西,定睛再看,这才不动了,是墨笔写的十七,

英汉对照
English-Chinese
中国文学宝库
Gems of Chinese Literature
现代文学系列
Modern Literature

saw the two Arabic numbers, 17 and 18, written with a Chinese brush. "I've come to see you, niece!" he invoked her under his breath, praying that she would not follow him. Then he quickly fled back to the path. But this was not suitable for his sister's ears. He continued, "That fellow said the numbers were written on the coffins, and he remembered clearly their numbers were 17 and 18. We searched through the coffins one by one till we found them, one straight and one lying crosswise. I recognized the numbers on the coffins."

"Seventeen! Eighteen!" cried the woman in spite of herself, pale in anguish, her eyes shining with tears. Just as on that night when someone had slipped in to break the awful news, she felt aghast, stunned and cold, her mind a blank, with a strange sinking sensation. No more would she hear their familiar knock or see the dear young couple come in, full of life, shoulder to shoulder. They were gone beyond recall. Numbers 17 and 18 — there was evidence solid as iron! Hatred blazed from her empty heart, a fierce glint came into her eyes. "I could kill them!"

Seeing his sister in such a state, the brother turned away listlessly and said with a sigh, "I saw that the coffins were passable, not too thin...." Obviously just a well-intentioned lie. All of a sudden, for no reason at all, he was gripped by a wild suspicion: What if that man had remembered the wrong numbers? It was not likely. Still the suspicion kept gnawing at his heart like a poisonous serpent.

"Listen!" the woman told him, gritting her teeth and trembling violently. The sleeping baby stretched as if he were waking up but

那一边,十八,两个外国号码。"甥女儿,我看你来了,"他默默祝祷,望她不要跟了来,连忙逃回小路。——这些不说吧,他想定了,继续说,"他说棺材上都写着号码,他记得清楚,十七十八两号是他们俩。我们逐一认去,认到了,一横一竖放着,上面外国号码十七十八我识得。"

"十七,十八!"老妇人忘其所以地喊出来,脸色凄惨,眼眶里亮着仅有的泪。她重行经验那天晚上那个人幽幽悄悄来报告恶消息时的况味;惊吓,悲伤,晕眩,寒冷,种种搅和在一起,使她感觉心头异样空虚,身体也似乎飘飘浮浮的,一点不倚着什么。她知道搭,搭,搭,叩门声是他们特别的调子,开进来,是肩并肩的活泼可爱的两个,这种事情绝对不会有的了。已被收起了,号码十七,十八,这是铁一般的真凭实据!一阵忿恨的烈焰在她空虚的心里直冒起来,泪膜底下的眼珠闪着猛兽似的光芒,"那辈该死的东西!"

阿弟看阿姊这样,没精没采回转头,叹着说,"我看棺材还好的,板不算薄。"——分明是句善意的谎话。不知道怎么,阿弟忽然起了不可遏的疑念,那弟兄不要记错了号码吧。再想总不至于,但这疑念仍然毒蛇般钻他的心。

"我告诉你,"老妇人咬着牙说,身体索索地震动。睡着的孩子胳臂张动,似乎要醒来,结果

英汉对照
English-Chinese
中国文学宝库
Gems of Chinese Literature
现代文学系列
Modern Literature

simply turned over. Smoothing his cotton shirt, she continued, "I'm past caring! I don't mind whether I die tomorrow or this instant. I'm so old and my fate is hard." She went on between sobs, "The year that your brother-in-law died your niece was only five. Bringing her up wasn't easy for me, a poor widow all on my own. When she married a handsome, educated man, I was happy. I was happy when she gave birth to a son, a lively lovable boy." Her right hand unconsciously caressed the child's head. "The two were both teachers, doing their jobs gladly, loving and respecting each other. So much the better: that made me all the happier. But now what's become of them — 17 and 18! It's as if the sky had fallen suddenly, it's terrifying! What did they do? They were my daughter and son-in-law. I have a right to know. But I was told not to ask. Even you, you told me not to ask, saying that asking would bode no good.... What was there to be afraid of? I was Yingchuan's mother, Zhang was my son-in-law. I'll shout through the streets and see who dares do anything to me!" Her whole being burning with anger, she had raised her voice by the end in passionate protest for no longer was she afraid. Patting the child's back, she cried, "Who says your name is Sun? Our Big Baby's surname is Zhang, Zhang! If only I could kill those fiends, to take revenge for my young daughter and son-in-law!"

Dazed and frightened by this outburst, her brother strained his ears to hear if there was any sound outside. Then he muttered feebly, "Why, why, what does it matter to say his surname is Sun? Ah, there's something I forgot." He fumbled in his pocket, remembering the piece of crumpled paper the man had handed to him

翻了个身。老妇人一面理平孩子的花洋布衫，继续说，"我不想什么了，明天死好，立刻死也好。这样的年纪，这样的命！"以下转为郁抑的低诉。"你姊夫去世那年，你甥女儿还只五岁。把她养大来，像像样样成个人，在孤苦的我，不是容易的事啊！她嫁了，女婿是个清秀的人，我喜欢。她生儿子了，是个聪明活泼的孩子（她右手下意识地抚摩孩子的头顶），我喜欢。他们俩高高兴兴当教员，和和爱爱互相对待，我更喜欢，因为这样才像人样儿。唉！像人样儿的却成十七，十八！真是突地天坍下来，骇得我魂都散了。为什么呢？是我的女儿，我的女婿呀，总得让我知道。却说不必问了。就是你，也说不必问了，问没有好处。——怕什么呢！我是映川的娘，姓张的是我的女婿，我要到街上去喊，看有谁把我怎样！"忿恨的火差不多燃烧着她全身，说到后段，语声转成哀厉而响亮，再不存丝毫顾忌。她拍着孩子的背，又说，"说什么姓孙，我们大男姓张，姓张！啊！我只恨没有本领处置那辈该死的东西，给年青的女儿女婿报仇！"

阿弟听呆了，怀着莫可名状的恐惧，侧耳听了听外面有无声息，勉勉强强地说，"这何必，这何必，就说姓孙又有什么关系？——喔，我想起了，"他伸手掏衣袋。他记起刚才在黑暗的途中，那弟兄给他一团折皱的硬纸，说是那男的托

英汉对照
English-Chinese
中国文学宝库
Gems of Chinese Literature
现代文学系列
Modern Literature

in the dark on the road, saying that he had been asked to deliver it to the young couple's family, but he had slipped it in the pocket of the trousers and nearly forgotten it. As if it were something monstrous, the brother hesitated at first to accept. But he had to let it be put in his palm and, loosely crumpling it, he thrust it into his pocket like a thief, feeling more alarmed than ever.

"They've left a note!" he said, copper coins tinkling in his pocket.

"Ah, a note!" The woman straightened up in high tension. Expectation fervent as is felt by a woman running to open the door for her beloved took possession of her for a moment.

Though it was less than ten days since she was cut off from her daughter and son-in-law, she felt she had not seen their smiles or heard their voices for years. Now this note would tell her everything about them, answer all her questions, and link her heart to theirs. Naturally it meant the whole world to her in that instant.

The note was produced. It was a torn cigarette packet with several finger-prints and a burnt spot on it. On the inner side was scrawled a message in pencil.

Screwing up his small eyes and holding the note near the paraffin lamp, the brother read aloud, "'We are dying with no regret. Don't grieve over us.' What strange talk! Dying with no regret! 'Please take good care of Big Baby, we shall live in him!' Well, they want you to take good care of Big Baby, because he's them; if Big Baby is all right, it is as good as if they were alive themselves. But this business of 'no regret' is really queer, queer!"

"Let me see it!" The woman snatched the note and fixed her

他想法送与亲人的,忘了,一直留在外国裤子袋里。他的手软软地不敢便接,好像遇见了怪秘的魔物;又不好不接,便用手心去承受,松松地捏着,偷窃似地赶忙往衣袋里一塞。于是,本来惴惴的心又加增老大的不自在。

"他们留着字条呢!"他说着,衣袋里有铜元触击的声音。

"啊!字条!"老妇人身体一挺,周身的神经都拉得十分紧张。一种热望(自己切念的人在门外叩门,急忙迎出去时怀着的那种热望)一忽儿完全占领了她。不接触女儿女婿的声音笑貌,虽只十天还不到,似乎已隔绝了不知几多年。现在这字条将诉说他们的一切,解答她的种种疑问,使她与他们心心相通,那自然成了她目前整个的世界。

字条拿出来了,是撕破了的一个联珠牌卷烟匣子,印着好几个指印,又有一处焦痕,反面写着八分潦草的一行铅笔字。

阿弟凝着细眼凑近煤油灯念那字条。"'儿等今死,无所恨,请勿念。'嗐!这个话才叫怪。没了命,倒说没有什么恨!'恳求善视大男,大男即儿等也。'他们的意思,没有别的,求你好好看养大男;说大男就是他们,大男好,就等于他们没死。只这'无所恨'真是怪,真是怪!"

"拿来我看,"老妇人伸手攫取那字条,定睛

英汉对照
English-Chinese
中国文学宝库
Gems of Chinese Literature
现代文学系列
Modern Literature

eyes on it like an intent reader ready to devour a favourite book although actually she was illiterate.

It was very still in the room. The child's deep breathing was hardly audible.

Though illiterate, the woman understood that note. Not just the words, but the meaning hidden inside. For the first time she saw into the mind of her daughter and son-in-law. A new strength flowed through her whole being and her heart felt lighter. The furniture in the lamplight looked as quiet as usual. Outside she could hear nothing except distant singing accompanied by a fiddle played by an adept hand.

"Big Baby, my darling, go upstairs and sleep." She stood up and made for the stairs, her lips touching the little boy's head, the note pressed against his breast. Her tired eyes were glowing with maternal love, her steps were lighter than before. She had courageously made up her mind to take up a mother's responsibilities once again.

The child, jogged awake, without opening his eyes screwed up his little face and cried, "Mam...."

November 4, 1927
Translated by Zhang Su

直望,像嗜好读书的人想把书完全吞下去那样地专注。但是她并不识字。

室内十分静寂;小孩的鼾声微细到几乎听不见。

虽然不识字,她看明白那字条了。岂但看明白,并且参透了里头的意义,懂得了向来不懂得的女儿女婿的心思。就仿佛有一股新的生活力周布全身,心中也觉得充实了好些。睁眼四看,一些器物同平时一样,静处在灯光里。侧耳听外面,没有别的,有远处送来的唱戏声,和着圆熟的胡琴。

"大男,我的心肝,楼上去睡吧。"她站起来朝楼梯走,嘴唇贴着孩子的头顶,字条按在孩子的胸口,憔悴的眼透出母性的热光,脚步比先前轻快。她已决定勇敢地再担负一回母亲的责任了。

"哇——"孩子给颠醒了,并不睁开眼,皱着小眉心直叫,"妈妈呀——"

1927,11,4

英汉对照
English-Chinese
中国文学宝库
Gems of Chinese Literature
现代文学系列
Modern Literature

A Trainee

There was no way I could stay on after two years of junior middle school, so I left. It was not easy to find a job, and I did not argue with a few bowls of rice a day and a bed at night. Then, God knows for what reason, I got the sack.

Mother was forever knitting her brow, and Father's sighs were more alarmingly melancholy than the hoot of an owl. Even with Uncle Zhang's letter explaining that it was not my fault at all, the thought of Mother's brow and Father's sighs is discouraging enough without their tighter knots and deeper melancholy now. How can I go back and face them?

They laid Father off this spring. How could the peasants keep up with the rent when they were living off boilded sweet potatoes and wild plants? And how can one afford a book-keeper when one can't collect the rent?

An out-of-work book-keeper's son is worse off than a rickshaw man's son, frozen stiff like a fly in the west wind as soon as the money stops coming in and quite definitely unable to finish junior middle school.

"The fees are paid for this term," Father sighed, "so you might as well go. Next term is out of the question, though. You can't go to school when we don't even know how we're going to eat, now can you?"

一个练习生

初中读了两年,没法读下去了,就停了学。好容易找到个职业,以为每天几碗饭到晚一张铺总不成问题的了。谁知道为了偶然的缘故,就被斥退出来。

妈妈的眉心一向打着结。爸爸的叹气声比猫头鹰叫还要幽沉可怕。我虽然拿着张伯伯的信,他替我说明这并不是我的错处;可是想想那眉心,想想那叹气声,就够气馁的了,何况往后结要打得更紧,气要叹得更幽沉。我怎么敢回去见他们呢!

今年春天,爸爸被那人家辞退了。农民连饭都没得吃,只好吃一点野菜煮番薯,那里还缴得出什么租?那人家收不到租,那里还请得起什么管账先生?失业的管账先生的儿子比黄包车夫的儿子都不如,钱的来路一断绝,就像西风里的苍蝇一样冻僵了,还那里读得成什么初级中学?

爸爸叹着气说:"这一学期的学费是交付了,你还是读你的书去。下一学期可不用提了,我们的饭都不知道在那里,还读什么书!"

英汉对照
English-Chinese
中国文学宝库
Gems of Chinese Literature
现代文学系列
Modern Literature

Mother bent her head wordlessly, wrinkled her brow and pasted her matchboxes like a forlorn shadow. Her hands moved mechanically, picking up the thin wood, folding it and wrapping it in yellow paper printed with black to make a small, rectangular box, which she tossed into the bamboo-spill basket beside her as it was finished. This brought in thirty-nine cents a thousand. She could paste up to two thousand a day, making seventy-eight cents altogether.

I felt very bad about not being able to continue at school the next term, though thinking it through I could not have said why. Was I happy at school? I had really never felt so. Forcing oneself to memorize arid facts and write exercises like items in an account book; tests every week and examinations every term which amounted to so many unpaid debts: where was the fun in this? Was I miserable at leaving? If so, it was a very ordinary misery. Three students had left after the first term because they could not keep up, and the third and fourth terms each began with fewer for the same reason. Of the original class of fifty only thirty-five now remained. If this was misery it was no greater than that of the earlier leavers, and if they could take it, why could not I?

For all that, I applied myself diligently to my lessons after Father's warning. It was like eating sugarcane. You chomp away at first, but you bite slower and you chew slower when there are only one or two sections left, grudging every drop of wasted juice. Diligence at last taught me to savour the most arid things as I bit and chewed my way through history, geography, even the ultimate headache of arithmetic. Apart from the exercises to be handed in

妈妈不声不响,低着头,皱着眉心,糊她的自来火盒儿,像一个孤苦的影子。她两只手机械似地运动着:拿起一张薄木片,照它的折痕折起来,把那黄地墨印的小纸张箍上去,就成一个长方小盒儿,随即丢在身旁的篾篮里。这种工作的代价是三十九个铜子一千。她每天至多糊两千,可以收进七十八铜子。

下一学期不得读书了,我觉得非常难过。可是仔细想想,又说不清为什么要难过。读书算是快乐的事情吗?我实在没有感到什么快乐。硬要记住一些枯燥无味的东西,硬要写下一些账目一样的笔记;每月一小考,一学期一大考,好比永远还不清的债务。那里来的快乐?不得读书算是痛苦的事情吗?这种痛苦实在也平常得很。第一学期过去后,就有三个同学因为力量不够停了学。第三学期第四学期开学的时候都少了人,原因相同。起初全班五十个人,到现在只剩三十五个了。即使是痛苦,至多和那些先走的同学所感到的一样,他们能忍受,我为什么不能忍受呢?

虽然这么说,自从听了爸爸的警告,我却在功课上真个用起心来。好比吃甘蔗,开头只是乱嚼一顿,直到吃剩一节两节了,才慢慢地咬,慢慢地咀嚼,舍不得糟蹋一滴蔗汁。用心的结果,枯燥无味的东西变得新鲜甜美了;历史有咬嚼,地理有咬嚼,甚至最叫人头痛的算学也有咬嚼。除了应该交给先生批阅的笔记以外,我还写了一些学习笔记,把自己想到的一切记在里头。

英汉对照
English-Chinese
中国文学宝库
Gems of Chinese Literature
现代文学系列
Modern Literature

A Trainee

for correction, I wrote up study notes full of my own thoughts.

The time comes, alas, when you get to the last section of sugar-cane, and tarry as you will over each mouthful, it is gone before you can bat an eyelid. The end of the fourth term, in other words, left me without another drop of scholastic syrup. I cast a regretful eye over each master and pupil, gave my classroom place and the sports apparatus in the playground an infatuated caress and slipped away from school.

"Say what you will, it's no good," sighed Father. "You've got to get out, get out and do something. Never mind wages, the main thing is to get someone else's food inside you. Having you eating at home...." He stopped, looking askance at Mother as her hands moved mechanically, their backs beaded with sweat.

I wanted to get out, I wanted to get out and do something, but I was at a total loss where to go and what to do.

Nor was I alone. Father was at a total loss too. He would enlist the help of any friend or relative he met, always in much the same words: "I hate to trouble you, but if you could think of anything for my boy. Anything, shop apprentice, factory apprentice, just as long as he gets some food inside him." Anything. He had absolutely nothing in sight, just endless expanses of mist rolling across the heavens before his eyes.

Some replied encouragingly: "I know of a silk shop where I could ask." "The broker at the Deda Pawnshop's a friend of mine. I don't know if he takes on apprentices or not." "These days manual labour's where the prospects are. I'll make enquiries for you at the Lihua Ironworks." Such words were like boats rowed up to a

可惜甘蔗吃到末一节了,任你慢慢地咬,慢慢地咀嚼,一眨眼就到了吃完的时节。这就是说,第四学期读完了,我再不能在学校里多尝一滴蔗汁了。我不作一声,对每一个先生和同学恋恋不舍地看了一眼,把教室里我的座头以及运动场上的运动器械痴痴迷迷地抚摩了一阵,就此溜出了学校。

爸爸叹着气说:"这样总不对啊!你得出去,出去做一点事情。薪水且不必说,最要紧的是人家的饭填饱你的肚皮。家里的饭是……"他停住了,眼睛斜过去,看着妈妈机械似地运动的两只手,手背上缀满了汗珠。

我愿意出去,我愿意出去做一点事情。可是到那里去呢,做什么事情呢,我却完全茫然。

岂但我,就是爸爸也完全茫然。他遇见亲戚或是朋友少不得向他们请托,总是这么几句话:"费您的心,替我的孩子想想法子!商店里的学徒也好,工厂里的学徒也好,无论什么都好,只要让他填饱肚皮。"无论什么都好,其实就是漫无目标;他的眼前也只见白茫茫的一天大雾。

有几个人的回答很动听:"我认识一家绸缎铺子,可以去问一声。""德大当铺的当手是我的朋友,不知道他那里收不收学徒。""现在这时代,劳动做工是堂而皇之的了,我替你向利华铁工厂打听打听吧。"这几句话好像直向将要沉没的海船划过来的小舢板,载着一个巨大无比的希望——出死入生的希望。

sinking ship, laden with immense hope, the hope of life in the jaws of death.

But before many days had passed the boats had capsized and the immense hope had sunk to the ocean floor. The silk shop was laying off and cutting wages and could not think of taking on apprentices. The owner of the Deda Pawnshop had been trying for ages without success to wind up the business and could barely cope with the mess he was in, let alone feed more mouths. The Lihua Ironworks had bulk batches of contemporary furniture stacked in its depot with no takers and scant call for apprentices when half its skilled workers were idle.

In spite of seeing our boats founder, we were still craning our necks, casting about for some vessel of hope, were it only a strand of seaweed. Every day Father and I borrowed a paper and devoured every last inch of advertising space, poring again and again over every request for salesman, opening for assistant teacher, position as family tutor and seeking of editor-translator. But I had none of the qualifications. The sheets of advertisements might have been so much blank paper for all their use to us. One day an advertisement stabbed my eyes as with shafts of light. "Apprentices taken" and "junior middle school graduate or equivalent" were the two strongest of the shafts. I shut my eyes and, when the dizzying radiance had passed, perused the text. It turned out to be a Shanghai publisher wanting eight trainees.

"Or equivalent, or equivalent...." I read out, heaven knows how many times, and decided to give it a try.

Father read it just once. "If you have the equivalent," he said,

但是过不了几天,小舢板打翻了,巨大无比的希望沉到了海底。绸缎铺子正在裁员减薪,谈不到收学徒。德大当铺的主人久已想收场,可是收不了,在那里勉强支持残局,再不愿多添吃口。利华铁工厂制造了大批的摩登家具,陈列在发行所里没有人过问,熟练的工人大半歇了手,再招学徒做什么?

虽然看见小舢板打翻,还是伸长脖子四望,搜寻载着希望的东西,那怕是一根水草也好。爸爸和我每天借报来看,所有登载广告的地方不肯漏掉一个字。征求推销员的,招请助理教员的,延聘家庭教师的,物色编译人才的,都使我们眼巴巴地看了再看。可是样样不合格;几大张的广告对于我们宛如白纸。

一天,一条广告好像射着光芒似地直刺我的眼睛。"招收练习生","初中毕业或同等程度",这就是两道强烈的光芒。我闭一闭眼睛,待一阵眩耀过后,才细看全文。原来是上海一家书局登的,招收练习生八名。

"同等程度,同等程度……"我念了不知多少遍,想去试它一试。

英汉对照
English-Chinese
中国文学宝库
Gems of Chinese Literature
现代文学系列
Modern Literature

"of course you must give it a try. We must wait on opportunity, you know: it won't wait on us."

So, as the advertisement said, I copied out my latest essay, wrote samples of Chinese and Englist handwriting and sent them off to the firm along with a half-length photograph and a letter recounting my education and family background.

They replied. "Regret no replies to unqualified": well, as I had got a reply, I must be qualified and could go on to the next hurdle, an interview in Shanghai. This of course was good news and even smoothed a few wrinkles from Mother's brow. Still, we were far from being carefree wanderers who could hop on a train whenever we wanted to go. After many entreaties we borrowed something from the next-door neighbours and some more from those on the other side, which put us back two days before we eventually squeezed into a fourth-class train which crawled like a centipede. Another two days and we would have missed the date for the interview and need not have gone.

We oozed with sweat in the crowded fourth-class train and got covered with red bites in the small inn on Zhejiang Road. We did not care. Father just asked worriedly: "Think you can handle it, do you? Don't let the opportunity slip: they're hard to come by." What was I to say? I could not interview myself. How did I know whether I could handle it? I could only answer him: "All I can do is try my hardest." I did not get to sleep that night. Father tossed and turned too with many a melancholy sigh.

When we went round for the interview next day, there were some forty others sitting with me, six or seven much older, their mouths

爸爸可只看了一遍,他说:"既有同等程度的话,当然去试它一试。机会是不来伺候我们的,只有我们去伺候机会呀。"

于是依着广告上的话,誊了最近的一篇作文,写了汉文的英文的两张习字,又写了一封信,叙述自己的学历和家况,连同一张半身相片寄给那家书局。

回信来了。"不合格者恕不作复",得了回信算是合了格,可以去碰第二重机会——到上海去受试验。这当然是好消息,连妈妈的眉心也似乎抹掉了几条皱纹。可是我们不比无愁的游客,什么时候想动身就可以跨上火车;我们是说了许多的恳情话,向东家借一点,向西家借一点,实足拖延了两天工夫,才得挤上蜒蚰那样爬行的四等车。如果再拖延一天的话,试验的日期就错过了,也不用动身了。

在四等车里被挤得臭汗直淌,在浙江路的小客栈里被叮得满身是红疙瘩,我们都觉得不在乎。爸爸只是不放心地说:"你自问有把握吗,你?这是个难得的机会,不要把它放过了!"我怎么说呢?我没法试验我自己,那里知道有没有把握?我只能回答爸爸说:"我尽我的力量做去就是了。"当夜我没睡熟。爸爸也老是翻身,还时时幽沉地叹一声气。

第二天跑去受试验,看见同我坐在一起的有四十几个,其中七八个年纪比我大得多,嘴唇

英汉对照
English-Chinese
中国文学宝库
Gems of Chinese Literature
现代文学系列
Modern Literature

already moustachioed around with black. Surely with forty turning up for a mere eight places, success for one meant disappointment for five. And those seven or eight with the black moustaches must have twice the schooling and experience I had with my two years of junior middle school. These necessarily daunting thoughts left me as weak and bereft of strength as in the season when the chinaberries blossom.

Only when I immersed myself in the questions was this mood gradually dispelled. They were not as bad as an end-of-term exam, with all subjects apart from English, Chinese and arithmetic lumped together in a "general knowledge assessment" and only twenty questions to be ringed if you thought they were right and crossed if you thought they were wrong. I handed my script in among the first ten and went on to the oral. A gentleman with a full, black beard sat in a room like a face-reader, his slick eyeballs taking in my forehead, my eyes, my nose — his gaze, in fact, traveling over my entire body. Most disconcerted, I could only bow my head and look at my shoes. After a space of four or five minutes he began in a tone devoid of feeling to ask about my schooling and family. I replied as I had in my letter, against which he checked my answers, holding up my half-length photograph to compare it with the life and finally leafing through my script at a leisurely pace. This done, he said, with no more feeling than before: "Very well. Go next door for the physical."

I could not quite believe my ears, but he had clearly told me to go for the physical, which surely meant that I qualified to be taken on. Had I written such a good script, or did he approve of my

周围已经生了黑黑的胡须,招收的名额才八个,这里却来了四十几个,不是说一个人得意,必得有五个人失望吗?又有那生了黑黑的胡须的七八个,他们的学识和经验该比我这个初中二年生高超一倍吧。我这样想,不由得胆怯起来,好像逢到楝树花开的时节,周身软软地没有一丝力气。

直到把心思钻进试题里去,这种胆怯的情绪才渐渐忘怀。这并不比学期考试困难,除开"英""国""算",所有科目合并为"常识测验",只有二十个试题,认为对的,画个圈儿,认为不对,打个叉叉。我是前十名交卷,接着就是"口试"。一位满腮帮生着黑胡须的先生坐在一间屋子里,好像个相面先生,眼珠子骨溜溜的,相我的前额,相我的眼睛,相我的鼻子……总之,我的全身都给他的眼光游历遍了。我窘得很,只好低下头来看自己的鞋。大约经过了四五分钟,他开始用毫无感情的声调问我的学历和家况。我依照先前写的那封信回答了。他就检出我那封信来核对,竖起我的半身相片来和实体比照,最后才慢吞吞地翻看我的卷子。看完之后,他依然毫无感情地说:"好了,你到隔壁房间里检查身体去。"

我有点不相信我的耳朵,可是他明明教我检查身体去,这不是有了被录取的资格吗?是我的卷子做得实在好,还是我的相貌合了他的

英汉对照
English-Chinese
中国文学宝库
Gems of Chinese Literature
现代文学系列
Modern Literature

physiognomy? Who knew? Whatever the reason, I actually qualified! The doctor who listened to my heart must have found it beating very hard indeed.

I handed the form which the doctor filled in to the gentleman with the black beard, who looked at it, passed me a printed sheet and said, betraying a threadlike smile: "You have passed. This contains all the procedures for acceptance." And suppressing the threadlike smile, he indicated that I should leave and called in the next waiting outside the door.

I should never have read the "instructions for acceptance." But I did, and my elated heart quite stopped beating. "Surety sixty dollars." "Find a reliable Shanghai shopkeeper's guarantee." "Those who do not present themselves for work one week after acceptance will be summarily passed over in favour of the reserve pool." Was it possible? How could my unemployed father and matchbox-pasting mother raise that huge sum? And if they did not, I would of course "not present myself for work one week after acceptance" and be "summarily passed over." It had been like a pleasant dream from which one awakes only to see the stony face of disillusion.

"I passed," I said dispiritedly to Father, who was waiting in the hospitality room, "but...." And I passed him the "instructions for acceptance."

"You, you passed!... What? Sixty dollars surety? A trainee doest't handle cash, surely? What do they want surety for? And a reliable Shanghai shopkeeper's guarantee! What of? Are trainees liable to go in for banditry or kidnapping or something?" Father

意,可不知道。不知道有什么关系,我有了被录取的资格是真的!那位医生在听心音的时候,一定觉察我的心脏跳得特别厉害。

我把医生所填写的表格交给那位黑胡须先生,他看了看,递给我一张印刷品,这才透露一丝儿笑意说:"你考上了。进局的手续都写在这上头!"一丝儿笑意立刻消失,他示意叫我出去,又唤进候在门外的另一个。

啊,那张"进局须知"不看犹可,一看之后,我的兴奋的心脏简直停止了跳动!"保证金六十元。""在上海觅殷实铺保。""录取后一星期不到,随即除名,由备生递补。"这是可能的吗?一个失业的爸爸,一个糊自来火盒儿的妈妈,怎么担负得起这笔巨大的数目!担负不起,当然是"录取后一星期不到",当然是"随即除名"。这就同做了一声欢喜梦一样,醒来时还不是看见个绝望的铁脸!

爸爸等候在书局的会客室里,我有气没力地对他说:"我考上了。不过……"我递给他那张"进局须知"。

"你,你考上了!……什么,六十块保证金!难道练习生就得经手银钱,要保证金干吗?……还要在上海觅殷实铺保!保什么呢?难道练习生会当土匪,会干绑票?"爸爸的感情激动

英汉对照
English-Chinese
中国文学宝库
Gems of Chinese Literature
现代文学系列
Modern Literature

began to get carried away, fixing his vein-meshed eyes on the empty flower vase as if it was the firm's chief advocate and calling it rigorously to account.

After a while he closed his eyes in atypical resignation. "These are their rules, and if we don't play by them they'll dismiss you, so what can we say? It would mean a wasted journey, a wild goose chase pure and simple."

The most gifted of authors could not have described what I went through mentally in the fourth-class train home. Father not only sighed but knitted his brow in imitation of Mother. Neither of us said a word to the other the whole way.

The day after our return, Father all at once brought out *Verses of a Chaste Suicide*. "This is our only heirloom," he said to me, "and by rights we shouldn't part with it. It goes hard, even for your bread. If anyone fancies it enough to buy it, that's your surety taken care of. It's the last chance, and we've got to take it. Whether it works or not is up to our luck."

The Chaste Suicide was my ancestress ten or more generations back, born at the beginning of the Qing Dynasty, who had on her husband's death written eight suicide poems and ended her life by swallowing gold. This volume had become a family treasure, handed down from generation to generation, and had introductions and postscripts by twenty people or more, Wangs and Baos and Zhangs and Yus. It was said to be good writing, well versified and well copied out. It was not lightly shown, but those who saw it invariably clicked their tongues, exclaiming "Wonderful! Wonderful!"

Father lit incense and candles, placed the *Verses* reverently in

极了,网满红筋的眼睛瞪着那没插花的红花瓶,仿佛那花瓶就是书局的主持人,爸爸对它提出了严重的质问。

一会儿他又变得异常颓丧,闭上眼睛说:"这是他们的章程,不依章程做,他们就把你除名,有什么可说呢!我们白跑一趟,偷鸡不着蚀把粞,就是了!"

回家的四等车里,我的心头尝着怎样的滋味,只怕最出色的文学家也描摹不来。爸爸不但叹气,而且学着妈妈的样,把眉心皱得紧紧。一路上彼此都不说一句话。

回家的第二天早上,爸爸忽然把"节妇绝命诗卷"取出来,对我说:"我们只有这一件祖传的东西,依理是不该拿出去的。现在为了你的饭碗,也顾不得了。如果有人看中它,买了去,你的保证金就有着落。这是末了的机会,总得去碰一碰,碰得着碰不着却要看我们的运道了。"

那节妇是我的十几代的祖母,生当清朝初年,丈夫死了,她写下绝命诗八首,吞金自尽。她那诗卷就成为我家世世相传的宝贝:上边有姓王的姓包的姓张的姓俞的二十多人的题跋,据说都是好书法,好诗词,好文章。那卷子轻易不给人家看,看见的人总是啧啧连声地说:"了不起!了不起!"

英汉对照
English-Chinese
中国文学宝库
Gems of Chinese Literature
现代文学系列
Modern Literature

their midst, knelt and kowtowed, praying silently the while, evidently begging the forgiveness of his ancestors. The sight of his prostrate form and nodding head brought an involuntary pang to my heart and tears to my cheeks.

He returned from the tea-house that afternoon with the *Verses* still in his hand. Some tea-house worthies, he said, had agreed that while the notes were really not bad, the text, being after all suicide poems, was too unlucky for anyone to want to spend money on. Only one, he added, had professed not to care and would have made a deal if Father had been willing to let it go for fifty dollars. "I said 'Give me a hundred. There are notes by over twenty writers, all good hands. Under five dollars on average.' Do you know what he said? 'You've got to realize the times we live in. This is 1935; people are destitute. Who's going to spend money on things like calligraphy and painting when nobody gets enough to eat? You won't let it go for fifty? Fine: I'm glad to save the money, and you can keep your family heirloom!' He made me so angry I brought it back home."

"Couldn't you have raised him ten or twenty?" asked Mother meekly. "You shouldn't have got angry. You could have bargained with him properly. You've lost one man, and it may not be easy to find another."

"Bargained with him properly?" Father pressed his hand to his chest as if swallowing unpleasant medicine. "What do you mean by bargain, beg him outright, beg him for more because the book's not worth a penny more than he condescends to give? Fine. Tomorrow I'll swallow my pride and beg, swallow my pride and beg." He

爸爸点起了香烛,把诗卷供在正中,就跪下来叩头。一面叩头,一面默默地祷告。想来是恳求祖宗原宥他吧。我看着他的拜伏的身躯以及连连点动的脑袋,不由得一阵心酸,淌下了眼泪。

那天下午,他从茶馆里回来,诗卷依然在他手里。他说茶馆里的一些法家看过了,都说题跋倒不坏,不过本身是绝命诗,不大吉利,谁愿意花了钱来买它。他又说只有一个人以为不在乎,如果五十块钱肯脱手的话,那就立刻成交。"我说,一百块钱吧;这上边有二十多家的题跋,家家是好手,平均起来,五块钱一家还不到呢。你知道他怎么说?他说:'你得知道此刻是什么年代!此刻是民国二十四年,民穷财尽,大家连肚子都吃不饱,谁还肯花了钱来买字呀画呀这些东西!五十块钱不肯脱手吗?好,我乐得省了钱,你也保住了你家传的宝贝!'我听得生气,就把原件带了回来。"

妈妈低声低气地说:"再加十块二十块不行吗?你不要生气,你可以好好地同他商量。错过了这个人,再寻第二个只怕不容易了。"

"好好地同他商量吗?"爸爸咽下一口苦药似地按住了胸膛。"什么商量,干脆说恳求得了,恳求他多给一点!东西是一个钱也不值的,所有的钱全是他的施与!好,明天老着脸去恳求,老着脸去恳求!"他的气愤似乎消散了;他显

looked dreadfully weak, with his anger now seemingly dispelled, like a man quite paralysed, and I sensed within me how bitter and how intense was his struggle to give his son a chance in life.

He begged, and to our surprise the man agreed to go up ten dollars. *The Verses of a Chaste Suicide*, handed down for over ten generations, changed owners in a day. We had made the exact amount of the surety. Mother stopped her mechanical working and half happily, half sadly starched and washed my clothes and sorted my bedding. She also took out four Yuan Shikai dollars — God knows when she had tucked them away — and passed them to Father with a trembling hand saying: "Here are four dollars I've had scraped together. Take them. They'll go towards the journey."

That had solved the surety problem, but where was the shopkeeper's guarantee to come from? Once in Shanghai, we went to see if Uncle Zhang could think of anything. He had been at school with Father and was a salesman for a rubber boot factory.

"The boss doesn't usually stand guarantor," he said, "but I sublet from a shoe shop and I get on quite well with them. At least, I shouldn't think they'd refuse if I asked them to stamp a guarantee."

The scheme succeeded. With the shoe shop's seal affixed crooked on the guarantee form we hurried to the publishers. Furnished now with surety and guarantee, I was of course a qualified trainee. The moment they were handed to the man in charge, a look of pride appeared on Father's face, as if to say: "You made it hard, but not too hard for me. There they all are, see?"

The man in charge laid the banknotes on the desk and looked

得非常软弱,仿佛全身都瘫痪了似的。从这上边,我深深体会到他为了儿子的命运努力挣扎的苦心。

恳求的结果,那人居然答应加十块钱。传了十几代的"节妇绝命诗卷"一旦换了主人。到手的正好是保证金的数目。妈妈于是停了她那机械的工作,又像欢喜又像忧愁地替我浆洗衣服,整理铺盖。她还取出不知道什么时候藏起来的四块"袁世凯"交给爸爸,手索索地抖着,说:"我拢总藏着四块钱,你们拿去作盘费用吧。"

保证金的问题固然解决了,"铺保"却还没有着落,我们一到上海就去找张伯伯,托他想法。张伯伯是爸爸幼年的同学,在一家橡胶鞋厂当推销员。

张伯伯说:"公司厂家是照例不给人家作保的。我的二房东是一家鞋铺,同我还和好,托他们盖个图章作个保,想来不至于拒绝。"

张伯伯的谋干果然成功了,那家鞋铺的书柬图章歪斜地印在保单上面。我们这就赶到书局。保证金,店铺的保单,一样都不缺少,自然是合格的练习生了。在交付给管事员的当儿,爸爸脸上露出一点傲然的神色,仿佛表示这么个意思:"你们的题目尽管难,可是难不倒我,你看,都有在这里了!"

那管事员把钞票放在桌子上,先看保单。

英汉对照
English-Chinese
中国文学宝库
Gems of Chinese Literature
现代文学系列
Modern Literature

first at the guarantee. "Ah, a shoe shop. Could you take a seat while we send someone to check?"

It would check, all right. It was no forgery. Uncle Zhang's shoe shop had been quite clear. They would back us up.

Who would have thought that when the man in charge heard the report he would shake his head and say: "It won't do. A ten-foot frontage. No assistants and only two apprentices. Could you find another? The instructions for acceptance state explicitly a reliable shopkeeper's guarantee. Please note the word 'reliable.'"

"And if we can't find another?" said Father angrily. "What then?"

"Keep looking! Quite simply, this shoe shop will not do. These are our regulations, which you break if you cannot transfer."

Father snatched up the banknotes from the desk, grabbed me by the arm and decamped. "We can't break their regulations, so we'll just have to look elsewhere. When we've done that and found nothing, then you'll come home with me."

As before, we went to Uncle Zhang and entreated him to find us another reliable shop to stamp my papers. He rushed about for a whole day before dashing into the inn, his face pouring with sweat, to say he had found a coffin-maker's through a friend, which had agreed to affix its correspondence seal only when Uncle Zhang had promised them a written pledge.

The coffin-maker's, surprisingly, was deemed to possess the qualifications of reliability. A further form was taken to be stamped with its oxhorn seal and delivered to the man in charge at the publisher's. The banknotes were counted out correctly, sixty

"喔,是一家鞋铺。请你们坐一会儿,我们要派人去调查一下。"

调查就调查好了。我们并没作假,张伯伯向那家鞋铺说得清清楚楚的,问到他们当然承认。

谁料那管事员听了调查报告之后,却摇着头对我们说:"不行。一开间门面。伙计都没有,只有两个徒弟。请你们换一家吧。'进店须知'上边写得明白,要殷实铺保,'殷实'两个字必须注意!"

"我们找不到别一家,便怎样?"爸爸愤愤地说。

"找不到也得找,总之这一家鞋铺不行!我们的章程如此,不能迁就你们破坏了章程?"

爸爸抓桌子上的钞票,拉住我的胳膊转身就跑。"他们的章程破坏不得,只有另外去找了。找不到的时候,你同我一起回家去!"

仍旧烦劳张伯伯,恳求他特别帮忙,另外找一家殷实店铺给盖个圆章。张伯伯奔走了一天工夫,才满头大汗地跑到客栈里来,说找到一家棺材铺了,是一个朋友给介绍的。张伯伯答应出一封保证信,那棺材铺才肯盖书柬图章。

棺材铺居然被认为具有"殷实"的资格。于是重取一张保单,盖上他们那牛角质图章,交给书局管事员。钞票也点过了,不错,十二张五元

英汉对照
English-Chinese
中国文学宝库
Gems of Chinese Literature
现代文学系列
Modern Literature

dollars in notes of five, and at last I signed the deed of apprenticeship. My gaze raced over articles ⅰ), ⅱ), ⅲ), ⅳ) and all the rest without really taking them in. Uncle Zhang undertook to be my sponsor in Shanghai and filled in name, place of birth, age, occupation and postal address on the form as my father's proxy to the firm.

With the formalities duly completed I became a regular trainee in the firm. Father, who was to catch the two-o'clock train home, brought my bedding and trunk round to the publisher's but would not settle in a chair. "Well, at last you've found somewhere that'll feed you," he said, sweating and panting. "You're well off here. I've nothing to say to you but this: it's hard, very hard!"

His spent form receded out of sight round a bend in the road. I strode heavily up the publisher's steps, mumbling "hard, very hard" right up until the gentleman with the black beard assigned me my work.

It had been hard enough to get, and it would be easy to lose, very easy.

Yesterday was December 24th, an ordinary day. I scrambled down from my top bunk as usual, dressed and folded the quilt. Who was to know that I would not be sleeping in that bed that night?

Being in the stock department, I went out first thing to pick up a consignment of paper and was just passing the Continental Stores on Nanjing Road when I heard a sudden detonation, of uncertain origin but sharp and intense, accompanied by a horde of people welling out of the Stores, the sound of their running stirring up a

票，一共六十块钱。我才亲自填写"练习生习业契约"。上边"一""二""三""四"的条文很多，我的眼光跑了一下马，却没有看清楚什么。张伯伯还有任务，他作为我在上海的管护人，姓名，籍贯，年龄，职业，通信处，都填上了表格；对于书局，他是我爸爸的代表。

手续完全办妥，我是书局里的正式练习生了。爸爸要赶两点钟的火车回去，他把我的铺盖衣箱送到书局之后，坐也不坐，一面擦汗一面喘气地说："你总算有个吃饭地方了，好好地在这里吧！我没有什么对你说的，只有一个字，难！……唉，真是难！"

一会儿他的精疲力尽的背影在马路的拐弯处消失了。我提着沉重的脚步跨上书局的阶石，"难！真是难！"直咀嚼到那位黑胡须先生给我分配工作的时候。

得到它是这样难，失掉它却很容易，唉，简直太容易了！

昨天是十二月二十四日，一个平平常常的日子。早上，我从双层床的上层爬下来，跟每天一样，穿衣服，折棉被。谁知道当天晚上就不容我睡在那张床上！

我隶属于进货部，为了提取一批纸张，一早跑出去。经过南京路大陆商场，忽然听得一阵边炮的声音，不知从那里来的，爽脆，紧张。同时大陆商场涌出大批的人，人声脚步声搅起了

wild hissing like that of the sea. In an instant I was hemmed in by bodies. Fervid faces met me wherever I looked. White papers fluttered riotously in the air. Grabbing one, I read on it in extra-large type "Down with the thievery of imperialism!"

I understood. The citizens of Shanghai were now taking up the work begun a fortnight before by students in Beiping, Shanghai and all over.

Awash in a human wave, I was taken over and forced to run west at the crowd's pace. In moments I was unwittingly infected with its mood. My breathing became heavier. I could hear the veins thumping in my temples. Anyone beside me looking round would have seen the same fervour in my face.

"Down with the thievery of imperialism!"

Countless voices joined in an angry, roaring climax. The buildings on either side seemed to shake, and from the trams and buses came an almost pitiful chaos of flustered cries.

Sheaves of leaflets were hurled at any vehicle, blowing hither and thither to submerge the glinting tramlines and the unique woodblock road, their black and white trodden underfoot by the advancing, chanting crowd.

All at once the human wave hit a reef and recoiled. I heard heavy thudding noises and standing on tiptoe saw red-faced foreign concession police brandishing truncheons and pulling and hitting at people.

The May Thirtieth Incident! I thought straight back to the textbook description. Here was I living a scene from it in person.

"No retreat! No retreat!" The wave swept back on, threatening

狂大的海啸。立刻之间,我的前后左右挤满了人体;向这边看看,一个个激昂的脸,向那边看看,一个个激昂的脸。白色的纸片在空中纷纷飘扬。我捉住一张来看,上面用特别大的铅字印着"打倒强盗样的帝国主义"。

我明白了。半个月来,北平、上海以及各地的学生都在干这种工作,现在是上海市民来那本分内的一手。

冲在人群的波浪里,我身不由主,只能应合着大众的步调朝西跑。不知道怎么,一会儿我就传染了大众的情绪。我的呼吸沉重起来。我听见太阳穴的血管突突作响。如果旁边的人回头来看我,一定也看见个激昂的脸。

"打倒强盗样的帝国主义!"

无数人的声音合并成一个浪潮的怒吼。两旁的建筑物都像震动了,电车和汽车慌张地叫喊,显得混乱和可怜。

一叠叠的传单向无论什么车辆扔过去。飘散开来,掩没了亮得发青的电车轨道,掩没了唯一的用木块铺成的马路。人群就踏着那些白纸黑字,前进,呼号。

突然间,人群的波浪冲着了礁石,反激地往后退了。我听见重实的拍拍拍的声音。点起脚来看,是好些个脸红红的外国巡捕挥动着木棍,在向人身上乱抽乱打。

"五卅"事件!我立刻想到教科书中所讲的这个题目,现在我亲身经历当时的一幕了!

"不要退啊!不要退啊!"浪头回冲过去,直欲推翻那挡在前面的礁石。

to engulf the reef in its path.

The wanton thud of the truncheons took up again. People went down, their prostrate forms kicked savagely by the heavy boots and the fresh red of trickling blood staining the sheets of white paper. Cries of suffering and anger fell like arrows, goading the people to the brink of madness.

I cannot convey the revulsion I felt. No one who had seen with his own eyes that living manifestation of imperialism could ever call it an empty word. We did not bring it down. We could only lie on the ground and bleed.

Eventually, however, the crowd retreated to the corridors of the Continental Stores and to Shandong Road. After a couple of minutes of peculiar calm, a voice suddenly burst out: "Gather at the entrance to Xianshi's!"

"Come on, arm in arm!" The voice seemed to be that of a young woman, particularly resonant in the solemn air after the outburst.

And the procession moved off once again, arm in arm.

At this point I began to think of my work and regretfully declining the arm extended by a blue-clad friend made a detour along Jiujiang Road to my destination.

Back at the publisher's, having reported to the head of department, I could not but tell some of the other trainees what I had just seen. It was so new, so exciting that I would have burst if I had kept it to myself. I could not rest until I had it off my chest. I recounted the fervour of the crowd and the climactic outburst of chanting; I recounted the wanton violence of truncheon and boot and the shock of the fresh blood trickling on to the road; and I re-

拍！拍！拍！拍！木棍又是一阵放肆。有一些人倒了下去。巨大的皮鞋就在横倒的人身上狠命地乱踢。鲜红的血淌出来了，染上白色的纸片。又凄惨又愤怒的叫声像一枝枝的箭，刺得人几乎发狂。

我描摹不出我当时的愤恨。谁说帝国主义只是口头的一个名词，眼前这一幕就是它活生生的表现！我们不把它打倒，只好横倒在地上淌血！

但是人群终于退进了大陆商场的过道以及山东路。经过两三分钟的异样的沉默，忽然霹雳似的声音响了起来："先施公司门前去集合啊！"

"我们手挽着手走去啊！"似乎是青年女子的声音，在霹雳过后的严肃空气中，特别显得清朗。

于是手挽着手的行列重又流动起来。

这当儿我开始想到我的任务。很抱歉地谢绝了一位穿青布衣服的朋友伸过来的一只手，从九江路绕着圈子到了我所要去的地方。

回到书局里，向部长交了差，不由得把刚才看见的告诉几个同学。这对于我太新鲜了，太刺激了，藏在肚子里会发胀，必须吐露一下才觉得痛快。我叙述了激昂的人群，浪潮样霹雳样的呼号；我叙述了木棍和皮鞋怎样地放肆，鲜红的血淌在马路上怎样地惊心动魄；我也叙述了

英汉对照
English-Chinese
中国文学宝库
Gems of Chinese Literature
现代文学系列
Modern Literature

counted my feelings, my oblivion of myself as of a drop in that human tide.

Some bit their lips as they listened.

It was three in the afternoon when I was called to see the gentleman with the black beard in his office. Uncle Zhang was already there, his face a picture of awkwardness. I realized that it was something to do with me, and my heart gave an involuntary jump.

Uncle Zhang coughed twice drily and explained: "They don't want you here any longer. You're to leave today. You were well off here. Why did you have to go and join in a street demonstration?"

There was a buzzing inside my head, and the walls began to turn. I pulled myself together and defended myself with the facts: "Certainly I was caught up in a crowd, but never went with the intention of joining in."

"So that was it." Uncle Zhang turned a humble smile on the gentleman with the black beard. "Surely it's pardonable," he pleaded, "since he didn't expressly join in? We should be beholden to your sense of fairness if you could see your way to countermanding the order."

"Expressly or not, that is quite beside the point," he said, meeting no-one's eyes, then took a black-printed paper from a file and continued his monologue: "Here are the terms of his apprenticeship. Article seven states clearly: 'The employer may terminate the agreement at any time it feels the trainee to be unsatisfactory, whereupon he shall be withdrawn by his sponsor.' I am acting upon this article." Taking a fountain pen, he scratched two words in red on the paper and handed it to Uncle Zhang. "It is

我当时的心情,我差不多忘了自己,人群如果是海潮,我就是其中的一滴。

几个同学听得都咬住了嘴唇皮。

下午三点钟光景,忽然被那位黑胡须先生传到他屋子里去。张伯伯先在那里了,一副尴尬的脸色。我知道一定是关于我的什么事情,不觉心跳起来。

张伯伯咳了两声干嗽,给我说明:"这里用不着你了,教你今天就出去。你好好地在这里,为什么要去参加大马路的游行呢!"

我听见头脑里嗡的一声,墙壁随即转动起来。我定一定神,根据实际情形为自己分辩:"被挤在人群中间是有的;特地去参加,可没有这回事!"

"原来如此。"张伯伯转过脸去,露出卑下的笑容向那黑胡须先生恳情说:"他既不是存心去参加,似乎情有可原。感激你的大德,请你收回了成命吧!"

"存心去不存心去都没有关系,总之,他在这里不适宜就是了。"黑胡须先生对谁都不看一眼。他从文件橱里取出一张印有黑字的纸张来,又独白似地说:"这是他的'习业契约',第七条条文写得明白:'书局认为不适宜时,得随时废约,由管护人领回。'现在我的根据就是这一条。"他拿起钢笔,刹刹地在纸面写上两个红字,就递给张伯伯,"批明作废了,你带了去。"接着

英汉对照
English-Chinese
中国文学宝库
Gems of Chinese Literature
现代文学系列
Modern Literature

officially terminated. Take it. Here is his guarantee," he went on, "and his sixty dollars surety. Count it." And with this he struck a match and proceeded to smoke a cigarette.

Easy, wasn't it?

I stayed with Uncle Zhang last night but could not get to sleep at all, more wretched than I can say, though without shedding a tear. Today he wrote me a letter to prove it had not been my fault. I have to take the two'clock train home, but I scarcely dare face them for thinking of Mother's frowns and Father's sighs.

1936
Translated by Simon Johnstone

说:"这是他的保单。这是他的保证金,六十块钱,你点一点。"说罢,他划着火柴自去抽他的纸烟。

这不是太容易了吗?

昨夜晚我睡在张伯伯那里,一夜没有睡熟,说不出地难过,可是没淌眼泪。今天张伯伯给我写了信,证明我没有错处。我得乘两点钟的火车回去。但是,想到妈妈的眉心,想到爸爸的叹气声,我怎么敢回去见他们呢!

1936 年

A Declaration

The school principal received a telegram. As his habit was, he looked first at the end where he saw "Education Bureau" and the date. Next, his eyes flashed to the beginning of the telegram and travelled slowly over the mimeographed blue characters. Ah, it was nothing serious. He breathed more freely.

The telegram merely instructed him to find out and report back immediately who had drafted the declaration issued recently by some teachers in his school.

"I saw the declaration in the papers but I don't know who wrote it," thought the principal. "I must be the only one kept in the dark. More than fifty teachers from different schools signed the declaration. All twenty or so of my staff, except for the civics teacher, put down their names. Yet no one mentioned anything to me. They behaved as if nothing had happened even when it was published in the papers. I remarked, 'So you've made a declaration.' Mr. Zhang, sitting opposite me, answered with his eyes on the wall, 'Yes, we've made a declaration. We are so fed up with this mess that we had to say something to make ourselves feel better.' The others went on reading their text-books and making notes as if they had heard nothing. Two hurried away pretending to have remembered something. In a word, they didn't want to discuss it with me. I'm not a fool, I can see clearly. Why should I insist on

一篇宣言

校长先生接到了一个电报。依习惯先看末尾，写着"教厅叩"三字，是教育厅来的。眼光像闪电一般射到电文的开头，又像蚂蚁那么爬，爬过那些蓝色复写的文字。原来并不是什么严重的事情，这才定了心。

电文的意思不过是你们那里有一班教职员最近发布一篇宣言，那篇宣言是谁的手笔，望调查清楚，立即电复。

"宣言确曾在报上看见过，谁的手笔可不知道，"校长先生。"他们干这件事情仿佛只瞒着我一个人，各校教职员签名的有五六十个，我校的二十几个同事，除掉一个公民教员，都在里头了。直到报上把那篇宣言登了出来，他们还是若无其事，不对我提起一声。我说，'今天你们发表了一篇宣言？'张先生正在我的对面，他眼睛看着墙壁，说，'不错，我们发表了一篇宣言。这样乌烟瘴气，喉咙口忍不住了，说了这一番话，才觉得爽快一点。'其余几个人好像没听见我的话，顾自看他们的教本，批他们的笔记，还有一个装作忽然想起了什么事情的样子，匆匆走开了。总之，他们不愿意同我谈到那篇宣言，我不是瞎子，我看得明白，我为什么定要同

英汉对照
English-Chinese
中国文学宝库
Gems of Chinese Literature
现代文学系列
Modern Literature

179

A Declaration

talking about it?"

But the telegram in his hands said the Education Bureau was waiting for a reply. He must have a talk with his staff. He could find out by other means, of course, but that would take longer, and making inquiries among the teachers of other schools would be more awkward than among his own. There were more than twenty of them. Whom should he ask? Not those tiresome fellows who had pretended not to hear him. Perhaps Mr. Zhang would do. Although he kept his eyes on the wall he had at least answered him. All the principal wanted from him was the name of the man who had drafted the declaration. He would report this to the Education Bureau. Then his task would be done.

So Mr. Zhang the drawing master was summoned to the principal's office and asked to sit down. "I want to know who drafted your declaration. Can you tell me?" This was a simple enough question.

"It was Mr. Wang Yongyi," Mr. Zhang answered without hesitation.

"Mr. Wang? You don't say!" His task was not so very simple, it seemed. The principal felt as if an invisible noose was falling over his head.

"Though he drafted it, the content was decided by us all," explained Mr. Zhang, running his fingers through his long hair. We had a meeting to discuss it. Different people raised different points. After talking them over we put our ideas together. Somebody suggested, 'Let Mr. Wang Yongyi do the writing. He is the language teacher. He writes well.' Mr. Wang did not refuse and

他们多谈呢?"

　　但是,教育厅的电报执在手里,那边在等着电复,现在是不得不再同他们谈一谈了。私下打听也未尝不可,可所费的时间多。去问别的学校参加签名的教职员,又当然不及问自己的同事来得直捷痛快。自己的同事有二十几个,问谁呢?那几个假作没听见的有点讨厌,不去问他们。还是张先生,他虽然跟睛看着墙壁,对于人家的询问总算给了个理睬。只要他说一声,那篇宣言是谁写的,把那人的姓名回复教育厅,一件公务就办了了。

　　于是美术教员张先生被请到校长办公室。校长先生让他坐下,就提出简单的问话:"你们的宣言由谁起的草?我要知道这个,请你告诉我。"

　　"王咏沂王先生起的草,"张先生毫不迟疑地说。

　　"王先生起的草?我可没有料到!"校长先生立刻感到这件公务并不怎样轻松,仿佛有一条拖泥带水的长鞭子抽过来,缠着他的身体,一时未必容易把它解脱。

　　"虽然由王先生起草,意思却是共同决定的,"张先生说着,用手指梳理他的留得很长的头发。"那天大家聚在一起商量,一个说,这一层应得提一提,另一个说,那一层也得说一说。大家斟酌过后,凑齐了一串的意思。记不清是谁提议道,'就请王咏沂先生把这一串意思写下来吧,他是国文教师,笔下来得。'王先生当仁不让,回来就起草了那篇宣言。"

英汉对照
English-Chinese
中国文学宝库
Gems of Chinese Literature
现代文学系列
Modern Literature

brought his draft to our next meeting."

Tap, tap, tap! Drumming on the desk, the principal gazed fixedly at a couplet written by Zhang Binlin in the style of ancient inscriptions. "It doesn't look too good," he murmured, then checked himself. Regret showed on his face. After half a minute's consideration, his gaze fell on Mr. Zhang. "The Education Bureau has sent a telegram asking me to find out who made the draft," he said softly.

"Find out who made the draft? What does that mean?"

"Who knows? But I can assure you that they are not going to ask him to be their secretary general because they like the style of the declaration! Mr. Wang ought not to have done it. There are language teachers in the other schools too. Why should an old man like him look for trouble?"

"But there was nothing wrong in making the draft."

The principal looked at the drawing master who had been a student himself not long ago and sighed. "You are too naive, Mr. Zhang! You would think differently if you had been a teacher longer. You say there is nothing wrong? This investigation proves there is something wrong — how serious, we don't know. Even if it is only a little thing, how annoying to have this happen in our school!"

"Is that so?" Bewildered as well as indignant, the drawing master was lost for words.

"Well, I have to report the truth. But I will warn Mr. Wang," said the principal to himself. He rang for the usher and told him to invite Mr. Wang over.

校长先生一个手指敲着桌面,搭,搭,搭,搭,眼睛直望着章炳麟写的一副篆字对子,自言自语说,"事情只怕有点不妙。"说了这句随即缩住,脸上现出后悔的神色。但是经过了半分钟光景的踌躇,眼光终于移到张先生脸上,轻轻地说,"教育厅刚才来了电报,叫我调查起草人呢。"

"调查起草人,这是什么意思?"

"谁知道什么意思?总之不会因为那篇宣言写得太好,要请起草人去当总秘书,这是一定的。王先生当时不担任起草也罢了,旁的学校也有国文教师,何必他老先生出手?"

"担任起草并没有错儿呀。"

校长先生对这个离开学生生活不久的美术家看了一眼,叹息说,"张先生,你的想头太天真了。你多担任几年教师,想头就会跟此刻不同。你说没有错儿,依我想,他们在调查,保证有错儿,只不知是重是轻。即使很轻,偏偏落在我们学校里,你想,岂不是麻烦的事情?"

"这样吗?"美术教师感觉怅惘,又有点愤愤,一时说不出什么。

"既然是王先生起的草,我不能不据实回复,不过总得告诉他一声,"校长先生重又自言自语。随即按电铃招来一个校工,叫他去请王先生。

英汉对照
English-Chinese
中国文学宝库
Gems of Chinese Literature
现代文学系列
Modern Literature

A Declaration

Mr. Wang arrived and sat down, tugging at his beard as usual. His threadbare, shiny cuffs were stained with red ink. He flushed and showed a trace of agitation when he heard what the principal had to say, but he replied calmly, "Yes, I made the draft. You can report it to the Education Bureau. There is nothing outrageous in a declaration which merely expressed our wish to maintain our territorial integrity and sovereignty. Every Chinese, every right-minded Chinese, must cherish the same thoughts day and night."

"A few days ago, the professors from more than twenty universities in Beijing issued a simple straightforwawd declaration, quite similar to ours," put in Mr. Zhang. "That is to say, we all feel the same."

"It may not be appropriate for middle-school teachers to say what the professors say. You ought...." Thinking better of it, the principal changed the subject. "Since you drew up the draft, Mr. Wang, I cannot but report the truth. It is good to find you so understanding. But by way of extenuation we might add that you simply recorded the consensus of opinion." This was said in a tone of concern, while the principal peered sympathetically through his large glasses at the somewhat uneasy face of Mr. Wang, as if he were a small boy who had misbehaved.

"All right," said Mr. Wang, and withdrew with Mr. Zhang from the principal's office.

That same evening, after telegraphing his reply the principal received another telegram instructing him to send express to the bureau the composition books of the two forms Mr. Wang taught. "Just as I feared!" He shuddered, as if a noose were tightening

王先生来了。坐定下来，依习惯摘着胡须根，油亮的袖底几乎涂满了红墨水迹。听完了校长先生的叙述，他有点激动，两颊发红，可是沉静地说，"这确是我起的草，请校长回复教育厅就是了。我想，这里头并没有什么大逆不道的话。要维护领土的完整，要保持主权的独立，无非这一点意思。只要是中国人，只要是有心肝的中国人，醒里梦里谁不想着这一点意思？"

张先生接上说，"前几天北平二十多个大学教授发表一篇简单明了的宣言，意思也是这样。用一句老话，可以说人同此心。"

"大学教授可以说的话，在中学教员嘴里也许就不配说了，所以最好还是……"校长先生觉得这样说下去未免多事，就换个头绪说，"那篇宣言既然是王先生起的草，对于教育厅方面，我不能不据实回复。你王先生也谅解这一层，自然再好没有。不过为减轻责任起见，不妨说明意思是共同的，只是由一个人执笔罢了。"校长先生的声调显得非常关切，怜悯的眼光透过大圆眼镜落在王先生不很自在的脸上，好像面对着一个淘气而不见得可厌的孩子。

"这样也好，"王先生接着说，就同张先生退出了校长办公室。

校长先生把复电打出以后，当天晚上，接到教育厅的电报，叫把王咏沂所教两班学生的作文本子快邮寄去。"果然不出所料，"这样的一念闪过校长先生的心头，缠在身上的无形的鞭

round his neck. This was not an ordinary check-up of the work. It presaged calamity. If this calamity, like a shower of meteors, fell not on one individual but on the whole school, the result would not bear contemplating! The night was chilly and he turned icy cold as if he had changed suddenly into thin clothes.

Mr. Wang collected the composition books from his pupils. The principal suggested that they work all night on them.

"Do you mean we should go through all these exercise books? I don't think it's necessary," said Mr. Wang who was quite sure of himself. "I've confidence in my corrections — they're carefully done."

"It's not that, Mr. Wang. Just think how serious it would be, especially for you, if there were anything wrong with these compositions!"

"Anything wrong?" Mr. Wang laughed. "I assure you I am most careful and our boys have always been taught to behave themselves. How could 'anything wrong' crawl like worms into these exercise books?"

"Discretion is always necessary. We must be discreet in everything." The principal felt not a little embarrassed, but he was determined to carry out his plan. "As the principal, I ask you to have some consideration for our school and look over these exercise books with me," he insisted.

There was no escape for Mr. Wang. The two men sat up all night, not reaching the end of their laborious task till the early sparrows were cheeping on the eaves at the break of day. By then characters were reeling before their eyes like flies swarming round

子仿佛更收紧了许多。这不比平常的抽查成绩,显然是祸事临头的预兆。如果祸事像一群陨石,不只打着一个人,却落在多数人头上,那真不堪设想。天气本来已经寒冷,这当儿尤其觉得凛冽,好像换穿了单衣似的。

两班学生的作文本子由王先生收了来,校长先生就留住王先生,请他陪同做一夜的夜工。

王先生泰然说,"校长的意思是把这些本子复看一遍吗?我想不用了。对于批改的工作,我自己有数,不至于马虎的。"

"不是这么说。王先生,你想,如果这些本子里有什么不妥当的话,事情不是很糟吗,尤其对于你?"

"不妥当的话?"王先生笑了,"我自问是个最妥当的人,我们的学生也被管教得妥当不过,不妥当的话怎么会像蛀虫一样钻进这些本子里去呢?"

"什么事情总得谨慎,谨慎是不嫌多余的。"校长先生有点儿窘,但是越想越觉得他的主张非贯彻不可,于是说,"我以校长的名义,请你为学校着想,帮同我复看一遍吧。"

这就没有什么说的了。王先生和校长先生直看了一夜的作文本子,天刚发亮,早起的麻雀在檐头唧唧叫着的时候,他们才把这辛苦的工作做完。眼睛虽然离开了本子,还只见歪歪斜

a garbage can or crows wheeling in the evening sky. Mr. Wang had read each composition first, then passed it on for the principal to check. Carefully, the principal chewed over every phrase and sentence for a hidden meaning, not going on to the next expression until he was certain that this one was genuinely correct and loyal. The result of a whole night's work was the discovery that in writing an essay entitled *The Countryside in Autumn* seven boys had referred to peasants harvesting rice with "sickles." This struck the principal as improper, and he changed all seven sickles into knives.

"Nothing else wrong, is there?" said the principal, yawning and turning out the light.

Mr. Wang, tired out and thoroughly annoyed, reflected that one minute would have sufficed to change seven "sickles," instead of sitting up, shivering all night. "Not after you've read them, sir," he replied indifferently.

Rousing his secretary out of his warm bed, the principal told him to wrap up the composition books and send someone with them at once to the post office. They were to be dispatched express as soon as the post office opened.

News of the two telegrams soon spread among the teachers, who felt sickened by it, as if smeared with slime and unable to wash themselves clean. This was the chief topic of conversation in the staff room.

"They want to look at the compositions he corrected just because he made the draft. Any fool can see there's something wrong with the declaration."

斜的字迹,像垃圾箱上面的苍蝇,像傍晚天空的乌鸦,飞舞着,回旋着。王先生担任的是初读,读过一本,递给校长先生去复读。校长先生读得尤其当心,一个词儿,一句句子,都得细细咀嚼,辨出它含在骨子里的滋味。那滋味是妥当的,王道的,才放过了,再辨另外的词儿和句子。可是辨了一夜的结果,只发见在《秋天的郊野》那个题目之下,有七个学生提起农人割稻,用了"镰刀"两个字。校长先生认为不很妥当,把七个"镰"字都涂去了。

"大概没有什么毛病了吧?"校长先生打着呵欠说,同时捻灭了悬空的电灯。

王先生非常疲倦,又生气,早知道仅仅涂去七个"镰"字,一分钟工夫就够了,何必磨整个的寒夜?他似理不理地说,"校长亲自看过,大概没有什么毛病了。"

校长先生把书记员从热被窝里叫起来,叫他把两班学生的作文本子分包封固,立刻派人去等候邮局开门,快邮寄出。

教育厅来了两个电报的消息在全校教职员间传播着,各人心头仿佛沾着了湿泥,很讨厌,可是粘粘地剔不去。教员预备室里的谈话就集中在这上头。

"起草了一篇宣言,就要看他批改的作文本子,傻子也揣得透,那篇宣言有问题了。"

英汉对照
English-Chinese
中国文学宝库
Gems of Chinese Literature
现代文学系列
Modern Literature

"What's wrong with it? It says no more than you can find in the papers. Why shouldn't we say what educational circles elsewhere and the Beijing students are saying?"

"Have you seen yesterday's newspaper? The Shanghai students have published a similar statement."

"That's just the point. How can the teachers take the part of the students? The Beijing students are being arrested and beaten. Now that we have made a declaration we should expect to be investigated."

"You mean that teachers should take the opposite stand from the students?"

"Precisely! That's how it is today. If we don't take the opposite stand, how can we teach? If we want to keep our jobs we must join the opposition.... I am not pulling your leg. This is the truth, whether you like it or not."

"Then we ought not to have made any declaration?"

"That's another thing. We have a dual personality, being Chinese as well as teachers. As Chinese we must speak, be there listeners or not. But a teacher, like a soldier, must obey orders. No freedom of speech for us! Has anyone ever seen a declaration issued by a platoon of soldiers in such-and-such a company?"

"All we did was sign our names. We didn't say we were teachers. That meant we were signing as Chinese."

"What if others classify us as teachers?"

"Then we're in for disciplinary action!"

Here the conversation stopped. The ticking of the clock was suddenly heard. Indefinable doubts and misgivings filled their minds.

"有什么问题呢?里头说的只是顶起码的话,报上在说,别地方的教育界在说,北平的学生也在说,难道我们就不能说?"

"不看见昨天的报吗?上海的学生也在那里发表意思,和我们的宣言差不了多少。"

"问题大概就在这里。学生闹的事情,教职员怎么可以附和在一起呢?北平的学生该打该抓,我们发表宣言,就该受侦察了。"

"这样说起来,教职员要和学生对立才是呢。"

"哈哈,这原是现在的真理!如果不和学生对立,也就做不成教职员。我们能够在这里吃一碗饭,多少总得站在和学生对立的阵线上——并不是拆自己的衙门,真理是这样,不说也还是这样。"

"那末,我们根本就不应该发表宣言?"

"这个是得分开来说。我们有双重的人格,一个中国人,又是一个教职员。在中国人的立场上,人家听不听且不问,这一番话非说不可。至于教职员,好比编配在队伍里的兵士,惟有绝对地服从,不能够自由说一句话。谁会看见几连第几排的兵士发表过什么宣言?"

"我们各自签上名,并没有写什么学校的教职员,正是站在中国人的立场上。"

"人家把我们移到了教职员的立场上去呢?"

"那只有受处分的份儿了。"

谈话中止了,墙上时计的的搭声突然显得响亮起来。种种微妙的思想像蚯蚓一样在各人心里钻动,钻动,画成种种模糊的总之不见可爱的图画。

"What if Mr. Wang is the only one penalized?" asked the drawing master Mr. Zhang eagerly, looking at the faces around him.

"We'll stand up for him. He has done nothing wrong."

"He only put down what everyone agreed on. All of us should be responsible if we were in the wrong."

"Why should we say we were wrong?"

"Let's get everyone who signed to go in a body to the commissioner of education and tell him that all we did was to voice our love for our country. Are we not allowed to love our country?..."

Just then the principal's shadow, obliquely framed by the doorway, fell on to the floor. The ticking of the clock was heard once more.

Two days later the third telegram arrived from the Education Bureau. The principal opened it with trembling fingers. A long sigh of relief escaped him, the noose round his neck seemed to loosen.

The telegram read: Nothing improper was found in Wang Yongyi's composition books. Dismiss him immediately. No reprimand.

The principal showed Mr. Wang the telegram to save himself the trouble of talking. With a sinking heart Mr. Wang saw in his mind's eye his homeless compatriots in the northeast, refugees suffering hunger and cold in the Yellow and Yangtse River valleys, the unemployed in the big cities ... and among these scenes of desolation he glimpsed himself. Coming out of this daze, he quietly took his luggage and left the school without once turning his head. He took a rickshaw to the station which was crammed with passengers waiting for various trains. They were saying that no

"如果处分落在王先生一个人身上呢?"美术教员张先生环视着各人的脸,热切地问。

"我们替他辩白,他没有错儿。"

"况且是大家的公意,他不过动手写了下来罢了,即使有错儿,也该大家有份。"

"为什么要自己承认有错儿呢?"

"我们可以联合所有签名的人一同去见厅长,对他说,我们无非爱国的意思,难道现在已经到了不准爱国的时候吗?……"

这当儿,校长先生的身影镶嵌到映在地板上的斜方门框里,时计的搭声重又显得响亮起来。

过了两天,教育厅的第三个电报又来了。校长先生慌张地拆开来看。看完之后,缠在身上的无形的鞭子似乎抽回去了,他长长地吐了一口舒畅的气。

电报的内容是这样:查阅王咏沂批改的作文本子,还没有什么不妥当,除立即解除教职外,不再给他旁的处分。

校长先生省得口说麻烦,就把这电报送给王先生看。王先生只觉身子往下一沉,模模糊糊之中,他看见东北无家可归的同胞,他看见黄河流域长江流域饥寒交迫的灾民,他看见大都市中成群结队的失业大众,而他自己的形象就隐隐约约在这些活动图画里面出现,这一幅里有,那一幅里也有。等到清醒过来的时候,他悄悄地带了行李,头也不回地走出校门,坐上一辆人力车,直奔火车站。火车站上挤满了好几趟

英汉对照
English-Chinese
中国文学宝库
Gems of Chinese Literature
现代文学系列
Modern Literature

trains were likely to come because the Shanghai students were on strike. Yet still they waited. From time to time they went to the edge of the platform, braving the cutting wind, to look at the motionless signal. Mr. Wang joined these passengers and, tugging at his beard, waited disconsolately with them.

When news of Mr. Wang's departure reached the staff room, the disgust in each mind was tempered by the dubious speculation: "Suppose I'd been the one to draft that declaration!"

Translated by Yu Fanqin

车的旅客,大家在那里说,上海学生闹事,只怕火车不会开来了。虽然这么说,大家还是等着,时时走到月台沿边去,冒着刮面的冷风,望那平指的扬旗。王先生加入这批旅客中间,手指摘着胡须根,也就怅怅的等着。

学校的教员预备室里传到王先生走了的消息的时候,大家有一种反胃似的感觉,同时朦朦胧胧浮起这么一个想头:"如果那篇宣言由我起的草呢?"

A Minor Flutter

Mr. Wu sprang to his feet to turn off the wireless, and the room seemed unusually quiet, the only sound being the faint clatter of mahjong tiles from the back courtyard.

"A-er!" Mr. Wu switched off his study light and hurried impatiently out. "Light your lamp, quick. I'm going out immediately."

"Oh. Right."

Mrs. Wu overhearing this in the back courtyard called archly, "Who's standing treat this time? Come home early after drinking. These days the weather's bad and there's a heavy dew. If you're late you may catch cold."

"Who's going to drink?" muttered Mr. Wu as he strode to the gate where A-er was lighting the rickshaw lamp. Mr. Wu climbed over his shoulder to take his seat.

"Where to, sir?" A-er pocketed his match-box, then picked up the shafts.

"Nowhere special. Just take me for a run."

The rubber tires rolled over the bumpy, stony road. The evening wind ruffled Mr. Wu's hair and his hands went up of their own accord to smooth it. He realized then that he had forgotten his felt hat.

"Stop here." Mr. Wu held out a note in his right hand. "Change this for five dollars' worth of coppers."

一个小浪花

　　吴先生忽地站起来,把收音机的开关旋转,室内就显得异常静寂,只从后进的屋子送来轻微的骨牌声。

　　"阿二,"吴先生把电灯开关也关上,不耐烦地跑出书室,"快去点灯,我立刻要出去。"

　　"噢,是啦。"

　　吴夫人在后进听见了,娇声娇气地问:"谁又请你吃酒?吃了酒早点回来。这几天天气不好,露水重,回来晚了恐防伤风。"

　　"谁吃什么酒?"吴先生咕噜了一声,急忙赶到门前。阿二正在那里点着灯,吴先生就跨过阿二的肩膀坐上包车。

　　"先生,到那里?"阿二把自来火盒儿塞进衣袋,随即把车柄提起。

　　"不到那里,你拉着跑就是了。"

　　胶皮轮在碎石路上一高一低地转动。晚风吹乱吴先生的头发,使他不由自主地抬起手来梳掠,这才省悟忘戴了呢帽子。

　　"这里停一停,"吴先生伸出右手,手里拿着一张钞票。"兑五块钱铜板。"

英汉对照
English-Chinese
中国文学宝库
Gems of Chinese Literature
现代文学系列
Modern Literature

A-er parked the rickshaw, took the note and changed the money in a tobacconist's. The rate was 3,400 coppers per dollar, so for five dollars he got exactly seventeen packets. Having carried these out in both hands to put them on the foot-board, A-er set off again at a run.

"Change this for another five dollars' worth of coppers." In Mr. Wu's hand was another note. Glancing at the enamel noticeboard he muttered, "This shop gives only 3,390, ten coppers less." Still he didn't retract the hand holding the note.

A-er glanced in some mystification at his master, then once more fetched a pile of coppers to heap on the foot-board.

He changed money like this at each tobacconist's they passed. By the time they had covered several main roads Mr. Wu's lower limbs were virtually hemmed in by coppers; coppers on the foot-board reaching up to his knees; coppers below the seat making it stick up; coppers on both sides of his buttocks cutting painfully into his pelvis; coppers on his thighs which seemed heavier at each step.

"That'll do," gasped Mr. Wu. "Go back."

Without a word, gulping in a breath, A-er started running back. Sweat was zigzagging down his face.

By the time they reached home Mrs. Wu's mahjong party had broken up and the guests had left. Mrs. Wu and the old lady were peeling lotus seeds.

A-er followed Mr. Wu inside with the first armful of coppers which he put at the foot of the wooden wall.

"So you weren't out drinking?" asked Mrs. Wu. "What have

阿二放下车柄,接了钞票,向烟纸店兑铜板。洋价三千四,五块钱兑换整整的十七包。两手捧着,放上包车的脚踏,阿二重又拔脚奔跑。

"再兑五块钱铜板,"吴先生手里又是一张钞票。他瞅见那块搪瓷牌,不禁咕噜说:"这一家只有三千三百九,要吃亏五个铜板呢。"可是他并不把拿着钞票的手缩回来。

阿二有点摸不清头脑,向主人家看了一眼,又去捧来一堆铜板压在脚踏上。

就像这样,遇见烟纸店就兑钱,兑了钱再跑。跑过几条大街,吴先生的下半截身躯差不多给铜板围困住了:脚踏上是铜板,齐到膝盖,坐垫下是铜板,把坐垫顶了起来,屁股两旁是铜板,嵌得坐骨部分很不舒服,大腿上也是铜板,只觉得行一步加重一步。

"好了,"吴先生喘吁吁地说,"回去吧。"

阿二口也不开,咽了口气就跑回头路。他脸上挂着曲折的小河流。

到家里的时候,吴夫人的马将局快已经散场,客人去了,吴夫人陪着老太太在那里剥莲心。

阿二跟着吴先生把第一捧的铜板送进来,放在板壁脚下。吴夫人就问:"你没有去吃酒吗?兑了这些铜板做什么?"

you changed those coppers for?"

"There's a lot more than this. This one trip I've changed a hundred and five dollars into coppers. I'd have kept on, only the rickshaw wouldn't hold any more."

"Are you crazy?" His wife was bewildered.

A-er mopped his perspiring face with one sleeve, standing stock-still for the moment, his eyes on his master. He too was wondering, "Are you crazy?"

"Crazy?" Mr. Wu clenched his fists and pounded his thighs. "See here, tomorrow there's bound to be a big drop in the price, maybe to three thousand, maybe two thousand, who knows? By changing a hundred and five dollars today, I'll have cut my losses by at least ten to twenty dollars." He told A-er, "Bring in the rest of the coppers outside."

When A-er had gone Mr. Wu went closer to where his wife and mother were sitting.

"It's coming tomorrow, what we've been dreading for so long," he whispered.

"Are you sure?" Catching on at once, they asked virtually in unison.

"Of course I'm sure. I just heard the announcement on the radio — it's set for tomorrow."

"Why, you...." Mrs. Wu sprang up, hesitated, then went off at a tangent. "Why didn't you tell me earlier instead of going out for coppers? Think ten or twenty dollars such a fine scoop? We're going to lose more than ten times that amount. More than twenty or thirty times!"

"何止这些？我出去一趟,兑了一百零五块钱的铜板呢。实在车子里放不下了,不然还得多兑。"

"发什么痴?"吴夫人有点惊讶。

阿二用衣袖擦着脸上的汗,暂时站定不动,一双眼睛看定主人家,肚子里也含着一句"你发什么痴?"

"发痴?"吴先生两手执着拳头捶两条大腿。"你看,明天洋价准保大跌,或是三千,或是二千,都说不定。今天我兑一百零五块钱,至少可以便宜一二十块钱。"说到这里,他盼咐阿二说:"外面的铜板再去拿进来呀。"

待阿二走了,吴先生凑近吴夫人和老太太的座头,轻轻地说:"我们好久好久担心着的那件事情,明天要来了!"

"真的吗?"吴夫人和老太太立刻会意,差不多齐声喊出来。

"怎么不真？我听见无线电的报告,说那件事情来了,就在明天!"

"你这个……"吴夫人霍地站起来,顿了一顿,转换话头说:"你怎么不早点对我说？倒去兑铜板！你以为一二十块钱便宜得要命了,不想想吃亏的地方何止十个一二十块钱,何止二十个三十个一二十块钱!"

英汉对照
English-Chinese
中国文学宝库
Gems of Chinese Literature
现代文学系列
Modern Literature

"Cutting your losses by ten or twenty dollars is always to the good." The old lady had no way of assessing the situation. As usual she was just taking her son's side.

"What time is it now?" Mrs. Wu looked at her watch. "Seven thirty-eight. The night market won't have closed yet. I'm going shopping."

"What are you going to buy?" asked the old lady.

"A few bracelets. They may be too countrified to wear, but gold doesn't depreciate."

"That's true. Metal's not like paper." The old lady expressed complete approval.

Mr. Wu scratched his head as he pointed out gloomily, "The banks won't open till nine tomorrow morning."

"Never you mind. A-er! Don't bring those coppers in. Put them in the gate-house. I want to go out right away."

"Oh. Right." A-er put down the second armful of coppers, then turned and ran out.

Mrs. Wu hastily washed her hands. Not stopping to change her clothes, she picked up her little purse and hurried to the gate. The coppers under the seat had not yet been removed, much to her annoyance. "Botheration! Quick! Get a move on!"

A-er hastily made two trips to clear out all the coppers under the seat. Then, like a hound ready to retrieve game, he strained forward between the shafts.

Mrs. Wu having seated herself ordered briefly, "To Tianbao on Ziyang Street!"

The few shop-assistants in Tianbao were yawning. Electric lights

"便宜一二十块钱总是好的,"老太太下不来判断,只是依照老习惯回护她的儿子。

"现在什么时候了?"吴夫人看手表,"七点三十八分。夜市还没有收。我要出去买东西。"

"你去买什么?"老太太问。

"我去兑几副镯子。虽然乡气腾腾不要戴,摆在那里究竟是硬货。"

"不错,究竟是硬货,"老太太表示极端信服。

吴先生搔搔头皮,颓丧地说:"银行要明天上午九点才开门呢。"

"你不用管。阿二,你的铜板不要搬进来了,就放在门房里。我立刻要出去。"

"噢,是啦。"阿二放下第二捧的铜板,转身向外跑。

吴夫人匆匆洗了手,衣服也不换,拿起小皮包赶到门前。坐垫底下的铜板还没有拿出来,这使她生气了,"讨厌!快点!快点!"

阿二急急忙忙来回两趟,才把坐垫底下的铜板出清,他自己就像预备去攫取鸟兽的猎狗一样,伏在两条车柄中间。

吴夫人坐上包车,简捷地说:"到紫阳街天宝。"

天宝里的几个伙计正在那里打呵欠。电灯

shone on silver trinkets in glass cabinets, and the shop seemed as forlorn as an empty square in the moonlight. Reanimated by Mrs. Wu's arrival, the attendants stretched themselves. On hearing that she wanted to buy bracelets, the short fat fellow serving her smiled and ushered her into a reception room at the back. His colleagues, also rather bucked, looked enviously after his short fat back.

"I suppose you want the latest fashion, madam?"

"Please bring me some to choose from." Mrs. Wu sat down on a teak armchair. "I want solid gold."

Fatty brought in a teak tray, and as he unwrapped a white paper package said, "This is a Western design, the latest style." He unwrapped another, announcing, "This one has only this little decoration, but it looks comfortable." When he had unwrapped half a dozen packages, the teak tray was filled with gold, glittering objects.

It was not the design, however, which interested Mrs. Wu, who simply selected three of the largest. "Please weigh these," she said.

He came back having done this to announce, "Together the three weigh 9.67 ounces."

"Today's price is a hundred and fifteen dollars." Mrs. Wu had looked up at the figure chalked on the copper plate in a golden frame.

"That's right, madam, a hundred and fifteen dollars." Fatty screwed up his eyes. "It's already gone down in price. A few days ago it rose to a hundred and eighteen."

"Work out what the cost will be."

光照着玻璃橱里的那些银家伙,店堂里好像月光下的空场那样凄清。待吴夫人走进来,几个伙计才领一领神,伸一伸腰和胳膊。既而听说要兑镯子,接生意的矮胖子脸上露出了笑意,把吴夫人让到店堂背后的客室里去。另外几个伙计也有点兴奋,大家用欣羡的眼光送那矮胖子的背影。

"大概要摩登式样吧?"

"请你拿出来让我挑,"吴夫人在一把红木交椅上坐下。"要实心的。"

矮胖子捧出一只红木盘,取一个白纸包解开来说:"这是西洋图案,顶摩登的。"接着又取一个白纸包解开来说:"这一副只有这么一点小花样,戴起来也满写意。"他一连解了六七个纸包,红木盘里就排满了黄澄澄的家伙。

可是吴夫人并不留心什么花样,只挑比较大的三副,说:"请你称一称吧。"

"三副共计九两六钱七,"矮胖子称了之后回来报告。

"今天是一百十五块,"吴夫人抬头看金边镜框里乌金纸上写着的粉字。

"不错,一百十五块,"矮胖子眯齐着眼睛说。"今天已经便宜了,前几天涨到一百十八块呢。"

"算一算够多少钱。"

He took an abacus and flicked the beads with his short, pudgy fingers, then wagging his head said, "1,112 dollars 5 cents. Plus three dollars each for the making, comes to another nine. That makes a total of 1,121 dollars 5 cents." He flicked two more beads on the abacus. "We won't count the odd dollar five cents, just charge you 1,120 dollars." This said, his eyes strayed to Mrs. Wu's small blue purse.

She opened it and took out a wad of notes, which she threw on the table like a ball of waste-paper. "I'll first give a deposit of a hundred dollars, and pay the rest tomorrow when I come to collect them."

Fatty moistened two fingers in his mouth, assenting, "Very good, madam." Then with the skill born of practice he counted the notes. "A hundred dollars, no mistake. May I ask your honourable name?"

"Wu. I'll come for them tomorrow, according to today's...." She broke off here.

"Of course, of course, according to today's price. Even if gold rises to a hundred and twenty tomorrow, after taking your deposit we can't charge you a cent extra."

"Yes, that's the rule." Keeping up her pose of sophistication, Mrs. Wu took the receipt and left the shop to mount the rickshaw. Struck by a sudden idea she said to herself, "A rickshawful of coppers — what use is that!"

"Home now?" A-er turned to ask as he picked up the shafts.

"Go to Yeshengxing. I want to buy some chicken marinated in soy sauce."

矮胖子取来了算盘,短短的几个粗手指一阵滴历搭刺,他颠头簸脑说:"一千一百十二块零五分。加上打工,三块一副,三三得九。两共一千一百二十一块零五分。"他又拨动算盘上的两颗子,说:"一块零五分不要算了,整数是一千一百二十块钱。"他说着,眼光就溜到吴夫人那个蓝色小皮包上。

吴夫人解开小皮包,取出一叠钞票,像扔一团字纸那样扔在桌上,说:"先付一百块定洋,明天带钱来取东西。"

矮胖子伸两个指头在嘴里蘸了点唾液,连声说"好的,好的,"就用熟练的手法数钞票。"一百块,不错。请教贵姓?"

"吴,口天。——明天来取,照今天的……"说到这里,就缩住了。

"当然,当然,照今天的行情。既然收了您的定洋,明天即使涨到一百二十块,也不能多算您一毛钱。"

"照规矩这样的,"吴夫人不脱老口的身分。一会儿接了收据,走出天宝,跨上包车。忽然想到了什么,她自言自语说:"一车子的铜板,真是死东西!"

"回家去吗?"阿二提起车柄回转头问。

"到叶盛兴,我要买酱鸡。"

英汉对照
English-Chinese
中国文学宝库
Gems of Chinese Literature
现代文学系列
Modern Literature

The next morning when the local paper was delivered, Mr. Wu grabbed it to look at the front page. Mrs. Wu craned forward, her head level with his ear. The old lady waited wide-eyed for them to read out the news.

"Six emergency laws. From today on the notes issued by the three central banks are to be the legal tender. Legal tender, not cash, must be used in all business transactions. All silver dollars must be exchanged for legal tender...."

"What does that mean?" asked the old lady mystified.

"You can't use silver dollars, but must change any you have into banknotes," Mr. Wu answered loudly.

"Who's willing to do that?" This really made no sense to the old lady.

"The paper says anyone who hoards silver dollars will be punished according to the law."

"You mean I must change those three hundred dollars in my chest for banknotes?" the old lady fumed.

"Of course," replied Mrs. Wu casually. A cheering thought had just struck her.

"If you don't, you won't be able to use them," added Mr. Wu.

"I'd rather not use them then," said the old lady stubbornly. "Snow-white dollars are always worth their weight in silver and bound to come in useful. If they're not safe in my chest, I can dig a hole under the floor and bury them. Who's got second sight to know I have dollars there?"

"I doubt whether that would be safe," said Mr. Wu thoughtfully.

第二天早上,当地的报纸送来了,吴先生抢在手里看头一版。吴夫人把脑袋挤到吴先生的耳朵边。老太太张大眼睛等他们读出什么来。

"六项紧急法令。从今天起,把中央中交三家银行的钞票定为法币。一切收付都用法币,不得行使现金。谁有银洋,就得去兑换法币。"

"怎么说?"老太太缠不清了。

"就是不用现洋,有现洋快去换钞票,"吴先生高声回答。

"谁肯这样做呢?"老太太实在想不透。

"报纸上说的,故意收藏现洋,就得按照法律治罪。"

"那末我箱子里的三百块现洋也得拿出去换钞票了?"老太太愤愤地说。

"当然罗,"吴夫人悠然说。她正想到什么快意的事情。

"不去换也用不出去呀,"吴先生接上一句。

"我宁可用不出去,"老太太固执地说,"雪白的现洋,究竟是真价实货,放在那里总有用处的。箱子里不稳当,我会在地板底下挖一个坑,把现洋藏在里头。谁又有神仙的眼睛,知道我地板底下藏着现洋?"

"地板底下恐怕也不稳当,"吴先生想了一

"Didn't you tell me, mother, that in the time of the Long Hairs[①] people hid silver in vats buried in the ground? But after the Long Hairs left and they dug up the vats, there was nothing in them but dirty water."

"Bah, I don't believe such talk!" Mrs. Wu eyed her husband contemptuously and moved her head away.

"It happened all right. But those folk were unlucky, or their silver wouldn't have changed into dirty water. In our case, gracious Buddha...." The old lady stopped as A-er ran eagerly in.

"You did the smart thing, sir, changing those notes into coppers yesterday," he blurted out loudly. "There are no exchange rates up in the tobacconists' today. When people ask for coppers they say they haven't any!"

"Hear that?" Mr. Wu couldn't help looking at his wife with a complacent smile.

But she ignored him, turning her head away.

"All the prices have gone up! Heavens! Just flour has risen two coppers!"

"Hear that?" Mrs. Wu pouted at her husband. "And you thought you were making a killing by changing a hundred and five dollars."

"Everyone's saying you can't use silver dollars, only notes. Using silver dollars is illegal! Amah Zhang in the Li family across the way has thirty dollars saved up. When she heard that, she beat her

---

① The Taiping insurgents of the 19th century who wore their hair loose round their shoulders instead of in Manchu-style queues.

想说。"妈妈,你不是说过的么?从前长毛时候,人家把银子装进罐子,埋在泥土里。后来长毛平了,他们在原地方掘开来,只见满罐子的脏水。"

"嗤,我不相信有这样的事情!"吴夫人用鄙夷不屑的眼光瞥着吴先生,同时她的脑袋离开了吴先生的耳朵边。

"事情是有的。不过那人家正在倒运,银子才会变脏水。像我们,阿弥陀佛……"老太太说到这里就咽住了,因为阿二正在兴冲冲跑进来。

"先生昨天兑铜板正兑得着,"阿二总是那么大声大气。"今天烟纸店都不挂牌子,人家去兑铜板,他们回说没有铜板!"

"如何?"吴先生不免得意,看着吴夫人微笑。

吴夫人把头偏转一点,给他个不睬。

"东西都涨价了!娘的,光面一涨涨了两个铜板!"

"如何?"吴夫人这才向吴先生努一努嘴,"你以为兑了一百零五块钱便宜得要命了!"

"大家在那里说,洋钱不用了,只准用钞票,用洋钱就犯法!对门李家的张妈积下三十只

英汉对照
English-Chinese
中国文学宝库
Gems of Chinese Literature
现代文学系列
Modern Literature

breast and burst out sobbing. Nobody can get her to stop. She's still sobbing away!"

"It's a scandal!" The old lady's heart bled for Amah Zhang.

"I'll tell you a joke," A-er chortled. "I've no silver dollars and no banknotes either. So whatever's used, I shan't lose any sleep. I've the strength to feed myself. If silver dollars can't be used, fine; the same goes for banknotes too. That way I can't lose out over counterfeit dollars or notes. Does that make sense to you, sir?"

Mr. Wu grunted noncommittally, then asked, "Has my study been cleaned out?" Before A-er could answer, his eyes had fixed on the newspaper again.

Translated by Wenxue

羊,听见了这个信息,拍着胸脯大哭。大家劝她劝不醒,直哭到此刻还不曾停哩。"

"作孽,"老太太对于那个张妈大表同情。

"我说笑话,"阿二一副嘻嘻哈哈的神气,"我身边洋钱也没有,钞票也没有,用什么哩,不用什么哩,都打搅不来我的夜梦。我只要气力换得来饭吃。不用洋钱,好,不用钞票,也好,省得吃坏洋钱和假钞票。先生,我的话中听吗?"

"唔,"吴先生随随便便应了一声。接着问:"书房里收拾了没有?"不等阿二回答,他的眼光又射到报纸上去了。

A Year of Good Harvest

In front of Wan Sheng Rice Shop was a wharf, and moored at all angles to this wharf were the open boats in which the villagers had come to sell their rice. These boats, loaded with new rice, were riding low in the water. The space between them was filled with cabbage leaves and refuse, round which swirled greasy bubbles of white scum.

From the wharf climbed narrow steps, up which no more than three men could walk abreast. The rice shop stood at the top of these steps. The morning sun, slanting down through gaps in the tiles of the roof, shed broad beams of light on the tattered felt hats bobbing up to the counter.

The owners of the felt hats had risen at dawn to row here. And once at the wharf, not waiting to catch their breath, they rushed up to this counter to see what fate had to offer.

"Polished rice, five dollars. Paddy, three," was the manager's laconic answer to their question.

"What!" The peasants in the old felt hats could hardly believe their ears. Their hopes were dashed to the ground. They were dumbfounded.

"In June you paid thirteen dollars, didn't you?"

"We paid as much as fifteen, let alone thirteen."

"How could the price drop so sharply?"

多收了三五斗

万盛米行的河埠头,横七竖八停泊着乡村里出来的敞口船。船里装载的是新米,把船身压得很低。齐船舷的菜叶和垃圾给白腻的泡沫包围着,一漾一漾地,填没了这船和那船之间的空隙。

河埠上去是仅容两三个人并排走的街道。万盛米行就在街道的那一边。朝晨的太阳光从破了的明瓦天棚斜射下来,光柱子落在柜台外面晃动着的几顶旧毡帽上。

那些戴旧毡帽的大清早摇船出来,到了埠头,气也不透一口,便来到柜台前面占卜他们的命运。

"糙米五块,谷三块,"米行里的先生有气没力地回答他们。

"什么!"旧毡帽朋友几乎不相信自己的耳朵。美满的希望突然一沉,一会儿大家都呆了。

"在六月里,你们不是卖十三块么?"

"十五块也卖过,不要说十三块。"

"那里有跌得这样厉害的!"

英汉对照
English-Chinese
中国文学宝库
Gems of Chinese Literature
现代文学系列
Modern Literature

"What else do you expect in times like these? Rice is flooding the market. A few more days and the price will fall even lower."

Coming here, the men had plied their oars as if rowing in the dragon-boat race, but now all the energy drained out of them. This year Heaven had been kind, rain had fallen in due season, there had been no plague of pests and each *mu* had yielded a few pecks more than usual. This time, they had thought they could have a breathing space. To end up even worse off than the previous year was the last thing they had expected.

"Let's not sell. Row it home and keep it!" cried one simple soul indignantly.

The manager uttered a sarcastic laugh. "Do you think folk are going to starve because you won't sell? The whole country's full of foreign rice and flour. Before the first lot's finished, foreign steamboats are shipping in a second."

Foreign rice, foreign flour and foreign steamboats were too remote to worry them. But not to sell the rice in their boats was unthinkable. That was simply angry talk. They had to sell. The landlord would be coming for his rent, and old debts must be cleared — they had run into debt to pay day-labourers and buy fertilizer and food.

"Why don't we try Fanmu?" It occurred to one of them that they might find a better price there.

But the manager snorted with laughter again and tweaked his sparse beard as he said: "Even if you go to the city, you'll find our rice guild has reached a common agreement. The price everywhere these days is five dollars for polished rice, three for paddy."

"现在是什么时候,你们不知道么?各处的米像潮水一般涌来,过几天还要跌呢!"

刚才出力摇船犹如赛龙船似的一股劲儿,现在在每个人的身体里松懈下来了。今年天照应,雨水调匀,小虫子也不来作梗,一亩田多收这么三五斗,谁都以为该得透一透气了。那里知道临到最后的占卜,却得到比往年更坏的课兆!

"还是不要粜的好,我们摇回去放在家里吧!"从简单的心里喷出了这样的愤激的话。

"嗤,"先生冷笑着,"你们不粜,人家就饿死了么?各处地方多的是洋米,洋面,头几批还没吃完,外洋大输船又有几批运来了。"

洋米,洋面,外洋大输船,那是遥远的事情,仿佛可以不管。而不粜那已经送到河埠头来的米,却只能作为一句愤激的话说说罢了。怎么能够不粜呢?田主方面的租是要缴的,为了雇帮工,买肥料,吃饱肚皮,借下的债是要还的。

"我们摇到范墓去粜吧,"在范墓,或许有比较好的命运等候着他们,有人这么想。

但是,先生又来了一个"嗤",捻着稀微的短髭说道:"不要说范墓,就是摇到城里去也一样。我们同行公议,这两天的价钱是糙米五块,谷三块。"

英汉对照
English-Chinese
中国文学宝库
Gems of Chinese Literature
现代文学系列
Modern Literature

"It's no good going to Fanmu," put in one of the peasants. "You have to pass two toll-houses, and there's no knowing how much they'd charge by way of tax. Who's got so much money to spare?"

"Won't you raise that price a little, sir?" another pleaded.

"That's easy to ask. We've sunk capital into this business, I'd have you know. To raise the price would mean giving you something for nothing. Do you take me for a fool?"

"But this price is too low, honestly it is. Who ever dreamed of such a thing? Last year we sold at seven dollars fifty. This summer rice went up to thirteen, no, fifteen, sir, as you said yourself just now. We were sure this year we'd get at least more than seven dollars fifty. Only five dollars — no!"

"Give us last year's price, sir! Seven fifty."

"Have a heart, sir. Be content with a smaller profit."

Another merchant, losing patience, hurled the stub of his cigarette into the street. "So you think the price too low!" He glared round at them. "You came of your own free will. You weren't asked to come. What's all this fuss about? We have silver dollars. If you don't sell, others will. Look, more boats have just stopped at the wharf."

Three or four more old felt hats were mounting the stone steps, the ruddy faces beneath them bright with hope. The sunlight slanted on the shoulders of their tattered cloth jackets as they joined the group.

"Wait till you hear this year's price!"

"It's even worse than last year — a paltry five dollars!" Utter

"到范墓去粜没有好处,"同伴间也提出了驳议。"这里到范墓要过两个局子,知道他们捐我们多少钱!就说依他们捐,那里来的现洋钱?"

"先生,能不能抬高一点?"差不多是哀求的声气。

"抬高一点,说说倒是很容易的一句话。我们这米行是拿本钱来开的,你们要知道。抬高一点,就是说替你们白当差,这样的傻事谁肯干?"

"这个价钱实在太低了,我们做梦也没想到。去年的粜价是七块半,今年的米价又卖到十三块,不,你先生说的,十五块也卖过;我们想,今年总该比七块半多一点吧。那里知道只有五块!"

"先生,就是去年的老价钱,七块半吧。"

"先生,种田人可怜,你们行行好心,少赚一点吧。"

另一位先生听得厌烦,把嘴里的香烟屁股扔到街心,睁大了眼睛说:"你们嫌价钱低,不要粜好了。是你们自己来的,并没有请你们来。只管多罗嗦做什么!我们有的是洋钱,不买你们的,有别人的好买。你们看,船埠头又有两只船停在那里了。"

三四顶旧毡帽从石级下升上来,旧毡帽下面是表现着希望的酱赤的脸。他们随即加入先到的一群。斜伸下来的光柱子落在他们的破布袄的肩背上。

"听听看,今年什么价钱。"

英汉对照
English-Chinese
中国文学宝库
Gems of Chinese Literature
现代文学系列
Modern Literature

despair was on the speaker's face.

"What!" Hope vanished like a pricked bubble.

But though hope vanished, they had no choice but to sell the rice in their boats. And fate compelled them to sell to Wan Sheng Rice Shop. For the rice shop had silver dollars, and silver dollars were precisely what the empty pockets of those tattered cloth jackets lacked.

As they haggled over the grading of the rice and whether the measure was full enough or not, the rice boats were slowly emptied of their loads. They rode higher in the water, and the cabbage leaves and refuse between them disappeared. The peasants in the old felt hats carried the rice they had grown into Wan Sheng's godown in exchange for varying numbers of notes.

"Give me silver dollars, sir!" White rice should at least be exchanged for white silver dollars. If not, the bargain seemed an even worse one.

"Ignorant clods!" A hand holding a fountain-pen rested on the abacus, while scornful eyes looked at them from over spectacles. "A dollar note is as good as a silver dollar. You're not being cheated of a single cent. We don't have silver dollars here, only notes."

"Let me have notes of the Bank of China then." Judging by the design, the notes in this speaker's hand were from some other bank.

"Pah! These *are* from the Central Bank of China." The accountant levelled the forefinger of his left hand. "If you refuse them, we can take you to court."

"比去年都不如,只有五块钱!"伴着一副懊丧到无可奈何的神色。

"什么!"希望犹如肥皂泡,一会儿又迸裂了三四个。

希望的肥皂泡虽然迸裂了,载在敞口船里的米可总得粜出;而且命里注定,只有卖给这一家万盛米行。米行里有的是洋钱,而破布袄的空口袋里正需要洋钱。

在米质好和坏的辩论之中,在斛子浅和满的争持之下,结果船埠头的敞口船真个敞口朝天了;船身浮起了好些,填没了这船那船之间的空隙的菜叶和垃圾就看不见了。旧毡帽朋友把自己种出来的米送进了万盛米行的廒间,换到手的是或多或少的一叠钞票。

"先生,给现洋钱,袁世凯,不行么?"白白的米换不到白白的现洋钱,好像又被他们打了个折扣,怪不舒服。

"乡下曲辫子!"夹着一支水笔的手按在算盘珠上,鄙夷不屑的眼光从眼镜上边射出来,"一块钱钞票就作一块钱用,谁好少作你们一个铜板。我们这里没有现洋钱,只有钞票。"

"那末,换中国银行的吧。"从花纹上辨认,知道手里的钞票不是中国银行的。

"吓!"声音很严厉,左手的食指强硬地指着,"这是中央银行的,你们不要,可是要想吃官司?"

英汉对照
English-Chinese
中国文学宝库
Gems of Chinese Literature
现代文学系列
Modern Literature

Why should refusing bank-notes be a crime? None of them understood that. After checking the figures on the notes and exchanging half-convinced, half-sceptical glances, they tucked the money into the empty pockets of their shabby jackets or the empty wallets at their belts.

Cursing under their breath, they left Wan Sheng Rice Shop as another group mounted the steps from the wharf. More bubbles of hope were pricked, destroying all the joy the peasants had taken since early autumn in their heavy ears of paddy. They carried their precious white rice into Wan Sheng's godown in exchange not for white silver dollars but paper notes.

The streets began to hum.

The owners of the old felt hats had come to the market today intending to buy many different imported products. They had run out of soap and must take back another ten bars or so, as well as a few packages of matches. Paraffin bought from the pedlars who came to the villages cost ten coppers for a small ladle, if several households combined to buy a tin they would get much better value. Moreover it was said that the foreign prints displayed in the shop windows were only eighty-five cents a foot, and for months now the womenfolk had been dreaming of buying some. That was why they had insisted on coming today when the rice was to be sold, having worked out exactly how many feet they needed for themselves, how many for Big Treasure and Small Treasure. Some of the women's plans included one of those oval foreign mirrors, a snowy white square towel or a pretty knitted cap for baby. Surely this year, when Heaven had been kind and each *mu* had yielded an extra

不要这钞票就得吃官司,这个道理弄不明白。但是谁也不想弄明白;大家看了看钞票上的人像,又彼此交换了将信将疑的一眼,便把钞票塞进破布袄的空口袋或者缠着裤腰的空褡裢。

一批人咕噜着离开了万盛米行,另一批人又从船埠头跨上来。同样地,在柜台前迸裂了希望的肥皂泡,赶走了入秋以来望着沉重的稻穗所感到的快乐。同样地,把万分舍不得的白白的米送进万盛的廒间,换到了并非白白的现洋钱的钞票。

街道上见得热闹起来了。

旧毡帽朋友今天上镇来,原来有很多的计划的。洋肥皂用完了,须得买十块八块回去。洋火也要带几匣。洋油向挑着担子到村里去的小贩买,十个铜板只有这么一小瓢,太吃亏了;如果几家人家合买一听分来用,就便宜得多。陈列在橱窗里的花花绿绿的洋布听说只要八分半一尺,女人早已眼红了好久,今天粜米就嚷着要一同出来,自己几尺,阿大几尺,阿二几尺,都有了预算。有些女人的预算里还有一面蛋圆的洋镜,一方雪白的毛巾,或者一顶结得很好看的绒线的小团帽。难得今年天照应,一亩田多收

英汉对照
English-Chinese
中国文学宝库
Gems of Chinese Literature
现代文学系列
Modern Literature

three or four pecks, they were entitled to loosen the purse-strings usually held so tightly. For there ought to be something left over even after paying the rent, their debts and the guild. With this in mind, a few of them had even toyed with the idea of buying a thermos flask. Now that was an extraordinary thing! Without a fire, the hot water you'd poured in stayed just as hot hours later when you poured it out. The difference between heaven and earth could hardly be greater than between a thermos flask and the straw-lined box in which they kept the teapot warm.

Cursing beneath their breath, they left Wan Sheng Rice Shop like gamblers who have lost — lost yet again! The extent of their losses was still not clear to them. At all events, of the wad of notes in their pockets not half a note or ten cents was truly their own. In fact, they would have to raise a good many more notes somewhere to discharge their obligations — they had no idea how they were going to satisfy their creditors.

It was clear anyway that they had lost, and rowing straight home would not save the situation. If they strolled round the town and made a few purchases that would merely put them a little further in the red. Besides, there were some things they simply had to buy. So the streets began to hum.

In threes and fours, casting short shadows behind them, they walked the narrow streets. The men muttered over the price they had just been given and damned all black-hearted rice merchants. The women, a basket on one arm a baby on the other, let their eyes dart from shop to shop on both sides of the street. As for the children, they were fascinated by the celluloid dolls, tigers and

这么三五斗,让一向捏得紧紧的手稍微放松一点,谁说不应该?缴租,还债,解会钱,大概能够对付过去吧;对付过去之外,大概还有多余吧。在这样的心境之下,有些人甚至想买一个热水瓶。这东西实在怪,不用生火,热水冲下去,等会儿倒出来照旧是烫的;比起稻柴做成的茶壶窠来,真是一个在天上,一个在地下。

他们咕噜着离开万盛米行的时候,犹如走出一个一向于己不利的赌场——这回又输了!输多少呢?他们不知道。总之,袋里的一叠钞票没有半张或者一角是自己的了。还要添补上不知在那里的多少张钞票给人家,人家才会满意,这要等人家说了才知道。

输是输定了,马上开船回去未必就会好多少;镇上走一转,买点东西回去,也不过在输账上加上一笔,况且有些东西实在等着要用。于是街道上见得热闹起来了。

他们三个一群,五个一簇,拖着短短的身影,在狭窄的街道上走。嘴里还是咕噜着,复算刚才得到的代价,咒骂那黑良心的米行。女人臂弯里钩着篮子,或者一只手牵着小孩,眼光只是向两旁的店家直溜,小孩给赛璐珞的洋囝囝,

英汉对照
English-Chinese
中国文学宝库
Gems of Chinese Literature
现代文学系列
Modern Literature

dogs from abroad, as well as the red and green tin drums and tin trumpets — also made abroad. It was almost impossible to drag them away.

"Look, sonny, at this fine foreign drum, this foreign trumpet! Want one?" Tempting voices were followed by a rub-a-dub-dub, a toot-toot-toot!

Dong-dong-dong! "Highest quality face-basins of foreign enamel! At forty cents apiece they're going dirt cheap. Buy a basin, friends!"

"Walk up, friends! Here's a splendid variety of foreign prints selling at cut prices. Eighty-five cents a foot! Let me measure a few feet for you!"

The assistants in the chief shops were going all out, shouting to the villagers at the top of their voices, pulling at their cotton sleeves. For this was the only day in the year when the peasants' pockets were lined. This was a chance not to be missed.

After some deliberation spent in cutting down their budgets, the villagers handed one note and then another to the shop assistants. Soap, matches and the like were necessities, but they bought a little less than originally planned. The price of a tin of foreign paraffin was so shocking that they refrained from buying; they would have to go on purchasing a ladleful at a time from the pedlar. As for cloth, those who had decided to make two suits bought cloth for one; those who had planned new jackets for mother and son, bought enough for the son only. The oval foreign mirror, after being lovingly handled, was replaced on the counter. The knitted cap proved a perfect fit for baby; but his father's sharp veto made

老虎,狗,以及红红绿绿的洋铁铜鼓,洋铁喇叭勾引住了,赖在那里不肯走开。

"小弟弟,好玩呢,洋铜鼓,洋喇叭,买一个去,"故意作一种引诱的声调。接着是——冬,冬,冬,——叭,叭,叭。

当,当,当,——"洋瓷面盆刮刮叫,四角一只真公道,乡亲,带一只去吧。"

"喂,乡亲,这里有各色花洋布,特别大减价,八分五一尺,足尺加三,要不要剪些回去?"

万源祥大利老福兴几家的店伙特别卖力,不惜工本叫着"乡亲",同时拉拉扯扯地牵住"乡亲"的布袄;他们知道惟有今天,"乡亲"的口袋是充实的,这是不容放过的好机会。

在节约预算的踌躇之后,"乡亲"把刚到手的钞票一张两张地交到店伙手里。洋火,洋肥皂之类必需用,不能不买,只好少买一点。整听的洋油价钱太"咬手",不买吧,还是十个铜板一小瓢向小贩零沽。衣料呢,预备剪两件的就剪了一件,预备娘儿子俩一同剪的就单剪了儿子的。蛋圆的洋镜拿到了手里又放进了橱窗。绒线的帽子套在小孩头上试戴,刚刚合式,给爷老子一句"不要买吧",便又脱了下来。想买热水

mother put it hastily down again. Those who had wanted a thermos flask dared not even ask the price. It might be as much as a dollar or a dollar fifty. If one threw caution to the winds and bought one, white-haired granddad and granny would be bound to scold: "Hard times like these — yet all you can think of is comfort! Throwing away a dollar fifty on a falderal like that! No wonder you've never amounted to anything. We've managed all these years without a thermos." No, life would not be worth living. Some mothers couldn't resist the longing in their children's eyes and bought the cheapest and smallest celluloid doll: you could move its arms and legs, make it sit down, stand up or raise its arms. Naturally, the children without one were green with envy, while even the grown-ups were much impressed.

Finally, having bought a little wine and some pork from the butcher's, the villagers went back to their own boats moored by the Wan Sheng wharf. From the stern they brought out dishes of pickled vegetables and beancurd; then the men sat down in the bow to drink while the women started cooking in the stern. Presently smoke was rising from most of the boats, and tears were flowing from the peasants' eyes. The children alone, tumbling and rolling in the empty holds or playing with grimy treasures rescued from the water, were happier than words can tell.

Wine loosened the peasants' tongues. Neighbours or strangers, the same fate had befallen them all, and they drank together on the river. Raising his wine bowl one would voice his views, while another, putting down his chopsticks, would chime in with approbation or an oath according to the sentiments expressed. They needed

瓶的简直不敢问一声价。说不定要一块块半吧。如果不管三七二十一买回去,别的不说,几个白头发的老太公老太婆就要一阵阵地骂:"这样的年时,你们贪安逸,花了一块块半买这些东西来用,永世不得翻身是应该的!你们看,我们这么一把年纪,谁用过这些东西来!"这罗嗦也就够受了。有几个女人拗不过孩子的欲望,便给他们买了最便宜的小洋团团。小洋团团的腿臂可以转动,要他坐就坐,要他站就站,要他举手就举手;这不但使拿不到手的别的孩子眼睛里几乎冒火,就是大人看了也觉得怪有兴趣。

"乡亲"还沽了一点酒,向熟肉店里买了一点肉,回到停泊在万盛米行船埠头的自家的船上,又从船梢头拿出咸菜和豆腐汤之类的碗碟来,便坐在船头开始喝酒。女人在船梢头煮饭。一会儿,这条船也冒烟,那条船也冒烟,个个人淌着眼泪。小孩在敞口朝天的空舱里跌交打滚,又捞起浮在河面的脏东西来玩,惟有他们有说不出的快乐。

酒到了肚里,话就多起来。相识的,不相识的,落在同一的命运里,又在同一的河面上喝酒,你端起酒碗来说几句,我放下筷子来接几声,中听的,喊声"对",不中听,骂一顿:大家觉得正需要这样的发泄。

英汉对照
English-Chinese
中国文学宝库
Gems of Chinese Literature
现代文学系列
Modern Literature

this outlet for their feelings.

"Five dollars a bushel, devil take it!"

"Last year a flood, a poor crop — we lost out. This time a good year, a big crop — but we lose out again."

"We are worse off this year than last. Last year we still got seven dollars fifty."

"We've had to sell the rice we need ourselves. Heaven! The men who grow the grain can't eat it!"

"Why did you have to sell it, you old devil? I'd have kept some for the wife and sonny. I wouldn't pay the rent, but let them have the law of me and lock me up."

"We can't pay the rent whether we want to or not. To pay the rent we'd have to run up fresh debts. If we borrow more money at forty or fifty per cent interest, what's to become of us? Next year we'd be crushed by debt."

"There's no living to be made on the land any more."

"Give up the land, I say, and take the road. Tramps have a better time of it than we do."

"Famine refugees needn't pay their debts or guild money. A good idea. I'm for the road."

"Who'll be the leaders? Refugees always have a few leaders whom all the others — men and women, old and young — must obey."

"Seems to me it wouldn't be a bad idea to go to Shanghai to find work. Young Wang of our village went, didn't he? He works in a Shanghai factory and gets fifteen dollars a month. Fifteen dollars — that's worth three bushels of rice today."

"五块钱一担,真是碰见了鬼!"

"去年是水灾,收成不好,亏本。今年算是好年时,收成好,还是亏本!"

"今年亏本比去年都厉害;去年还粜七块半呢。"

"又得把自己吃的米粜出去了。唉,种田人吃不到自己种出来的米!"

"为什么要粜出去呢,你这死鬼!我一定要留在家里,给老婆吃,给儿子吃。我不缴租,宁可跑去吃官司,让他们关起来!"

"也只好不缴租呀。缴租立刻借新债。借了四分钱五分钱的债去缴租,贪图些什么,难道贪图明年背着更重的债!"

"田真个种不得了!"

"退了租逃荒去吧。我看逃荒的倒是满写意的。"

"逃荒去,债也赖了,会钱也不用解了,好打算,我们一块儿去!"

"谁出来当头脑?他们逃荒的有几个头脑,男男女女,老老小小,都听头脑的话。"

"我看,到上海去做工也不坏。我们村里的小王,不是么?在上海什么厂里做工,听说一个月工钱有十五块。十五块,照今天的价钱,就是三担米呢!"

英汉对照
English-Chinese
中国文学宝库
Gems of Chinese Literature
现代文学系列
Modern Literature

"You're behind the times, you fool! In Shanghai the Japs are fighting. Most of the factories have closed down. Young Wang's a beggar now, didn't you know?"

Every road was closed. They were silent for a moment. Their bronzed faces flushed with sun and wine were ugly, as if dark blood were oozing through their skin.

"Who are we sweating for every year anyway?" asked one man hoarsely after a swig of wine.

"It's staring you in the face. We're sweating for them!" Someone pointed to the tarnished gilt signboard of Wan Sheng Rice Shop. "We nearly kill ourselves growing the rice and running into debt at wicked rates of interest. And without moving a muscle they say: 'Five dollars a bushel!' They might as well tear out our hearts and have done with it."

"If only we could fix the price ourselves! We'd be fair. I wouldn't ask more than eight dollars a bushel."

"Are you crazy? Didn't you hear? The rice merchants sink capital into the business — they can't let us have something for nothing."

"Well, we sink capital into the land. Why should we give them something for nothing? Why should we give the landlord something for nothing?"

"In the godown just now I was thinking: You're sitting pretty today with all this rice stored here. But if a time comes when we've nothing to eat, we'll be back to help ourselves." The speaker kept his voice down, his bloodshot eyes flickering towards the shore.

"If men are starving, it's no crime to take a little rice from those

"你翻什么隔年旧历本!上海东洋人打仗,好多的厂关了门,小王在那里做叫化子了,你还不知道?"

路路断绝。一时大家沉默了。酱赤的脸受着太阳光又加上一酒力,个个难看不过,好像就会有殷红的血从皮肤里迸出来似的。

"我们年年种田,到底替谁种的?"一个人呷了一口酒,幽幽地提出疑问。

就有另一个人指着万盛的半新不旧的金字招牌说:"近在眼前,就是替他们种的。我们吃辛吃苦,赔重利钱借债,种了出来,他们嘴唇皮一动,说'五块钱一担!'就把我们的油水一古脑儿吞了去!"

"要是让我们自己定价钱,那就好了。凭良心说,八块钱一担,我也不想多要。"

"你这囚犯,在那里做什么梦!你不听见么?他们米行是拿本钱来开的,不肯替我们白当差!"

"我刚才在廒间里这么想:现在让你们沾便宜,米放在这里;往后没得吃,就来吃你们的!"故意把声音压得很低,网着红丝的眼睛向岸上斜溜。

"真个没得吃的时候,什么地方有米,拿点来吃是不犯王法的!"理直气壮的声口。

英汉对照
English-Chinese
中国文学宝库
Gems of Chinese Literature
现代文学系列
Modern Literature

who have plenty." This was said in righteous tones.

"This spring, didn't they break into the Fengqiao rice shops?"

"The militia opened fire and two men were killed."

"There may be shooting here this year, for all we know."

Nothing came, naturally, of this wild talk. When the wine was drunk and the food eaten, they rowed back to their respective villages. The wharf was left silent and deserted, lapped by dark, dirty green water.

The next day another batch of boats rowed up to moor here and the same scene was re-enacted in the town. This scene was being enacted in towns all over the country. In fact, it was only too common.

"When grain is cheap the peasants suffer." This old saying made the headlines in the papers in town.

The landlords, finding it hard to collect their rent, held meetings and dispatched telegrams. The gist of these was: This year there was a bumper harvest. A glut in grain has caused a drop in prices and the peasants are destitute. Public assistance should be given.

The financiers, anxious to do business, drafted a plan for relief: 1. Funds should be raised by the large banks and money-changers for the purchase of rice from all parts of the country, and appropriate places appointed for its storage. The rice was to be sold the next spring when there was a shortage of food. This would keep the rice price stable. 2. The rice should be mortgaged as security for loans to prevent the rice merchants from buying up the whole crop and hoarding it. 3. The financiers should be responsible for col-

"今年春天,丰桥地方不是闹过抢米么?"

"保卫团开了枪,打死两个人。"

"今天在这里的,说不定也会吃枪,谁知道!"

散乱的谈话当然没有什么议决案。酒喝干了,饭吃过了,大家开船回自己的乡村。船埠头便冷清清地荡漾着暗绿色的脏水。

第二天又有一批敞口船来到这里停泊。镇上便表演着同样的故事。这种故事也正在各处市镇上表演着,真是平常而又平常的。

"谷贱伤农"的古语成为都市间报上的时行标题。

地主感觉收租棘手,便开会,发通电,大意说:今年收成特丰,粮食过剩,粮价低落,农民不堪其苦,应请共筹救济的方案。

金融界本来在那里要做买卖,便提出了救济的方案:(一)由各大银行钱庄筹集资本,向各地收买粮米,指定适当地点屯积,到来年青黄不接的当儿陆续售出,使米价保持平衡;(二)提倡粮米抵押,使米商不至群相采购,造成无期的屯

lecting the fund to buy grain to be stored. The funds should be paid back after the sale of grain with interest calculated according to the profit made or losses incurred.

The industrialists said nothing. The drop in the price of rice was to their advantage since it freed them from the necessity of giving their workers a "rice subsidy."

The social scientists published their views in different journals. They marshalled statistics and theories to prove that it was ridiculous to talk of a glut in grain, and not necessarily true that "when grain is cheap the peasants suffer." Even if grain were not cheap, the peasants would suffer anyway under the double oppression of imperialism and feudalism.

Since all this happened in the towns the villagers remained totally ignorant of it. Some of them sold rice they needed for themselves, or their gaunt, half-starved buffalo. Some borrowed money at forty to fifty per cent interest to pay the rent. Some stubbornly refused to pay and were arrested. In bitterness of spirit some paid a few cents today, a few more tomorrow, depriving themselves of food. Some took to gambling, hoping for a run of luck enabling them to win nine or ten dollars. Some begged friends to put in a good word for them to the landlord, so that they might stop renting his land, for they would be better off without. Some left home to seek their fortune, buying a fourth-class ticket on the train to Shanghai.

Translated by Gladys Yang

积;(三)由金融界负责募款,购屯粮米,到出售后结算,依盈亏的比例分别发还。

工业界是不声不响。米价低落,工人的"米贴"之类可以免除,在他们是有利的。

社会科学家在各种杂志上发表论文,从统计,从学理,指出粮食过剩之说简直是笑话;"谷贱伤农"也未必然,谷即使不贱,在帝国主义和封建势力双重压迫之下,农也得伤。

这些都是都市里的事情,在"乡亲"是一点也不知道。他们有的粜了自己吃的米,卖了可怜的耕牛,或者借了四分钱五分钱的债缴租;有的挺身而出,被关在拘押所里,两角三角地,忍痛缴纳自己的饭钱;有的沉溺在赌博里,希望骨牌骰子有灵,一场赢它十块八块;有的求人去说好话,向田主退租,准备做一个干干净净的穷光蛋;有的溜之大吉,悄悄地爬上开往上海的四等车。

英汉对照
English-Chinese
中国文学宝库
Gems of Chinese Literature
现代文学系列
Modern Literature

Lotus Root and Water Shield

As I sit drinking with friends and chewing thin slices of snowy lotus root I am suddenly reminded of home. At home, on any early autumn morning, many countryfolk would pass my door: the men with bronzed arms and protruding calf muscles, their bodies tall and upright, evoking a sense of well-being; the women, usually with white turbans dotted with dark flowers, go barefoot and wear short coarse linen skirts, and while they are not as tall as the men, they still have their own brand of healthy beauty. Each carries a shoulderpole with bundles full of long, fresh and tender sections of lotus root the colour of white jade. In the ponds where the lotus roots grow, by the winding small rivers outside town, they are washed again and again until they become this pure white. It is as if the countryfolk consider lotus roots to be precious delicacies or an important element in an early morning scene in a painting, and if the roots were all smeared with mud it would destroy people's appreciation; this is a sin the countryfolk are reluctant to bear, so first they scrub them until they are sparkling white and then they bring them into town. When they want to rest a while they lay down their bamboo pole, sit on top of it and casually choose an extra-tender lotus root "spear" or a rather older "blunt knife" and chew large mouthfuls of it to quench their thirst. Passersby come to a halt: young ladies dressed in red select a length; old granddads buy a couple of pieces. And thus it is that their delicate,

藕与莼菜

　　同朋友喝酒,嚼着薄片的雪藕,忽然怀念起故乡来了。若在故乡,每当新秋的早晨,门前经过许多乡人:男的紫赤的胳膊和小腿肌肉突起,躯干高大且挺直,使人起健康的感觉;女的往往裹着白地青花的头巾,虽然赤脚,却穿短短的夏布裙,躯干固然不及男的那样高,但是别有一种健康的美的风致;他们各挑着一副担子,盛着鲜嫩的玉色的长节的藕。在产藕的池塘里,在城外曲曲弯弯的小河边,他们把这些藕一再洗濯,所以这样洁白。仿佛他们以为这是供人品味的珍品,这是清晨的画境里的重要题材,倘若涂满污泥,就把人家欣赏的浑凝之感打破了;这是一件罪过的事,他们不愿意担在身上,故而先把它们洗濯得这样洁白,才挑进城里来。他们要稍稍休息的时候,就把竹扁担横在地上,自己坐在上面,随便拣择担里嫩的"藕枪"或是较老的"藕朴"大口地嚼着解渴。过路的人就站住了,红衣衫的小姑娘拣一节,白头发的老公公买两支。

英汉对照
English-Chinese
中国文学宝库
Gems of Chinese Literature
现代文学系列
Modern Literature

Lotus Root and Water Shield

sweetly refreshing flavour reaches every household. This is a daily occurrence right into late autumn when the leaves start to fall.

Here in Shanghai, lotus roots are virtually precious delicacies. They are probably brought in from my old home. Not many, however, and most are snatched up by tea-houses catering to the rich; the rest go to comparatively large fruit shops and are ranked alongside Californian apples and fragrant Luzon mangoes, awaiting the highest bid. It does happen that bundles of them are carried in and sold on the streets, but if they are not as thin as the limbs of a beggar they pucker up your mouth like an unripe persimmon so that it is impossible to enjoy them. That is why, with that sole exception, we have not eaten lotus root once this year.

And even then we did not buy them — neighbours gave them to us. They had not bought them either — a relative brought them in from home. It was probably quite some time since the lotus roots had left their home, for they were no longer jade-coloured but covered in rusty blotches. It was not easy to peel them because the knife kept slipping. Even after they were sliced and we began chewing them there was only a hint of sweetness and none of that fresh, tender sensation. Instead it seemed as if we had a mouthful of dregs, which made us reluctant to eat another slice. Only the children were happy — they finished off all the slices and surprisingly did not demand anything else for half an hour.

Thinking of lotus root makes me think in turn of water shield. At home in springtime we ate water shield practically every day. Water shield does not have much taste of its own — it is all in the cooking broth. And yet with its tender green colour and rich, almost poetic

清淡的甘美的滋味于是普遍于家家户户了。这样情形差不多是平常的日课,直到叶落秋深的时候。

在这里上海,藕这东西几乎是珍品了。大概也是从我们故乡运来的。但是数量不多,自有那些伺候豪华公子硕腹巨贾的帮闲茶房们把大部分抢去了;其余的就要供在较大的水果铺里,位置在金山苹果吕宋香芒之间,专待善价而沽。至于挑着担子在街上叫卖的,也并不是没有,但不是瘦得像乞丐的臂和腿,就是涩得像未熟的柿子,实在无从欣羡。因此,除了仅有的一回,我们今年竟不曾吃过藕。

这仅有的一回不是买来吃的,是邻舍送给我们吃的。他们也不是自己买的,是从故乡来的亲戚带来的。这藕离开它的家乡大约有好些时候了,所以不复呈玉样的颜色,却满被着许多锈斑。削去皮的时候,刀锋过处,很不爽利。切成片送进嘴里嚼着,有些儿甘味,但是没有那种鲜嫩的感觉,而且似乎含了满口的渣,第二片就不想吃了。只有孩子很高兴,他把这许多片嚼完,居然有半点钟工夫不再作别的要求。

想起了藕就联想到莼菜。在故乡的春天,几乎天天吃莼菜。莼菜本身没有味道,味道全在于好的汤。但是嫩绿的颜色与丰富的诗意,

英汉对照
English-Chinese
中国文学宝库
Gems of Chinese Literature
现代文学系列
Modern Literature

quality, that no-taste taste can be really quite intoxicating. In the small canals alongside every road there are always a couple of sailless boats resting by the stone banks, their holds filled to the brim with water shield culled from Lake Tai. When it is that easy to come by it is no wonder that we could have a bowl of it every day.

It is not like that here in Shanghai — it is hard to find unless you go to a restaurant. Of course we do not go to restaurants, or if we do go to return friends' hospitality once or twice, it is always just at the time when water shield is not available, so we have not had it once this year. Recently Boxiang's Hangzhou relatives came and gave him some jars of West Lake water shield. He gave me a jar and it was as if I had tasted it for the first time again.

When I, who had never loved my old home, think of all this, I feel that my home is truly lovable after all. Why it should evoke such a strong emotion I do not understand. On reflection, however, the reason is really very simple: it is because there are things to be loved at home, and those things are only to be found at home, so that you become entangled and cannot cut free. For example, my intimate family is there and so are my close friends, so how can I not feel love? How can I not cherish its memory? And yet is it simply for the sake of loving one's old home? No, it is just that some people there tie us to it. If there were no such ties what else would there be to love and cherish there? In my case I have become linked again now to my old home through lotus root and water shield and thus remember it with fondness.

Wherever we find love, that is where we find home.

Translated by Alison Bailey

无味之味真足令人心醉。在每条街旁的小河里，石埠头总歇着一两条没篷的船，满舱盛着莼菜，是从太湖里捞来的。取得这样方便，当然能日餐一碗了。

而在这里上海又不然；非上馆子就难以吃到这东西。我们当然不上馆子，偶然有一两回去叨扰朋友的酒席，恰又不是莼菜上市的时候，所以今年竟不曾吃过。直到最近，伯祥的杭州亲戚来了，送他瓶装的西湖莼菜，他送给我一瓶，我才算也尝了新。

向来不恋故乡的我，想到这里，觉得故乡可爱极了。我自己也不明白，为什么会起这么深浓的情绪？再一思索，实在很浅显：因为在故乡有所恋，而所恋又只在故乡有，就萦系着不能割舍了。譬如亲密的家人在那里，知心的朋友在那里，怎得不恋恋？怎得不怀念？但是仅仅为了爱故乡么？不是的，不过在故乡的几个人把我们牵系着罢了。若无所牵系，更何所恋念？像我现在，偶然被藕与莼菜所牵系，所以就怀念起故乡来了。

所恋在哪里，哪里就是我们的故乡了。

英汉对照
English-Chinese
中国文学宝库
Gems of Chinese Literature
现代文学系列
Modern Literature

Before Leaving

A soft, fine rain was falling as I got off the streetcar. An eddying wind brought the rain swirling over me. The light of the streetlamps was very dim and the black shadow of the train station jutted up from a dark grey emptiness. A row of trees lined the street there, their sighing branches tossing and dancing like hair. Suddenly I thought: undoubtedly this is to make it harder for me to bear, deliberately putting on an autumn face ahead of time! I felt myself become submerged in wretchedness and the wine I had just drunk sat uneasily on my stomach.

This is what I conjecture: to leave on a fine sunny day beats leaving on a chilly, damp and desolate one; to leave early in the morning beats leaving at nightfall. Although no two leave-takings can be compared and although this leave-taking has not yet taken place, I still believe in the main that my proposition holds true. Yet since the steamer for Fuzhou departs at twelve, there is no alternative but to part at nightfall. And, as autumn encroaches in this way, when there is a gust of wind and a flurry of rain such as this and I know what has been arranged for that evening six days hence, does it not seem even more likely that it will be a chilly damp and desolate leave-taking?

Nothing must be moved: a jumble of volumes, incomplete

将 离

跨下电车,便是一阵细且柔的密雨。旋转的风把雨吹着,尽向我身上卷上来。电灯光特别昏暗,火车站的黑影兀立在深灰色的空中。那边一行街树,枝条像头发似的飘散舞动,萧萧作响。我突然想起:难道特地要叫我难堪,故意先期做起秋容来么!便觉得全身陷在悽怆之中,刚才喝下去的一斤酒在胃里也不大安分起来了。

这是我的揣想:天日晴朗的离别胜于风凄雨惨的离别,朝晨午昼的离别胜于傍晚黄昏的离别。虽然一回离别不能二者并试以作比较,虽然这一回的离别还没有来到,我总相信我的揣想是大致不谬的。然而到福州去的轮船照例是十二点光景开的,黄昏的离别是注定的了。像这样入秋渐深,像这样时候吹一阵风洒一阵雨,又安知六天之后的那一夜,不更是风凄雨惨的离别呢?

一点东西也不要动:散乱的书册,零星的原

英汉对照
English-Chinese
中国文学宝库
Gems of Chinese Literature
现代文学系列
Modern Literature

Before Leaving

drafts, containers for ink, inkstones piled up haphazardly ... all in their original positions. Not the slightest alteration will be allowed: get up at six, eat breakfast, write a bit, off punctually to the office, home in the evening, chat a while, play with the kids ... it's all life as usual. There is certainly no sense of departure, nothing to give a feeling of urgency. It is as if this event were not soon approaching.

I remember last year when Pingbo went abroad. We were both in the hotel, knowing full well there was less than an hour left before the sharp knife of parting would sever us. And so with every word and gesture I felt as if there were unseen ties pulling me, binding my whole body tight; my chest felt so constricted I could hardly bear it. I did my utmost to shake it off, deliberately adopting a nonchalant air leaning back in my chair, raising my cup to drink a mouthful of tea and chatting away about this and that. But it was useless, I felt it was only a polite pretence, that I was just being pulled, bound and constricted ever more tightly. And so I thought: the atmosphere of parting has already solidified around us, we must not think any more of shattering it, for it must break us apart.

This time I will not allow that atmosphere to solidify, hoping thus to avoid all the snares of being pulled, bound and constricted. I have this wish that when the time comes to leave it will be right in the middle of a deep sleep when the power to think has vanished and therefore there will be nothing of which to think. And yet, on awakening to find oneself a lonely traveller on a lone ship in the midst of the ocean, it will be impossible to avoid feeling a profound melancholy; but the hardest part will already have sped by and the

稿纸，积着墨汁的水盂，歪斜地摆着的砚台……一切保持原来的位置。一点变更也不让有：早上六点起身，吃了早饭，写了一些字，准时到办事的地方去，到晚回家，随便谈话，与小孩胡闹……一切都是平淡的生活。全然没有离别的气氛，还有什么东西会迫紧来？好像没有快要到来的这回事了。

记得上年平伯去国，我们一同在一家旅馆里，明知不到一小时，离别的利刃就要把我们分割开来了。于是一启口一举手都觉得有无形的线把我牵着，又似乎把我浑身捆紧；胸口也闷闷的不大好受。我竭力想摆脱，故意做出没有什么的样子，靠在椅背上，举起杯子喝口茶，又东一句西一句地谈着。然而没有用，只觉得十分勉强，只觉得被牵被捆被压得越紧罢了。我于是想：离别的气氛既已凝集，再也别想冲决它，它是非把我们拆开来不可的。

现在我只是不让这气氛凝集，希望免受被牵被捆压的种种纠缠。我又这么痴想，到离去的一刻，最好恰正在沉酣的睡眠里，既泯能想，自无所想。虽然觉醒之后，已经是大海孤轮中的独客，不免引起深深的惆怅；但是最难堪的一关已经闯过，情形便自不同了。

英汉对照
English-Chinese
中国文学宝库
Gems of Chinese Literature
现代文学系列
Modern Literature

situation will not be the same.

And yet that atmosphere does solidify and accumulate after all. I walk into my home and see the newly washed and mended bedding, shirts, trousers and gowns all piled up on the table. There is no need to ask — these are my travelling companions. "With so much to do and everything already arranged, why couldn't these have been packed earlier?" I think with slight annoyance. And yet since it is already established that they must be taken away they can be made ready at any time and how can I be heartless enough to be reproachful? In fact, I should not be reproachful but grateful.

And yet I am coming up against that atmosphere. I am smelling its odour which is exactly the same as the one I sensed last year in the hotel, only that was not as thick as this. I know that it will gradually thicken like the evening mist over West Lake; in the end it will possess a great force which will bear down on me so that I cannot leave here freely.

I talk as usual, write, eat, lie in the rattan chair, but it is all a bit different, a bit unnatural.

I had a dream in the night. I dreamed I was on a platform at the railway station. The train arrives in a flash, I quickly lift in my luggage, get on board and the train swiftly departs. I feel as if I have left something on the platform, and as I check I realize it is not things that I have left there but people. The strangest thing is that I did not say a single goodbye, nor did I give them my hand;

然而这气氛终于会凝集拢来。走进家里，看见才洗而缝好的被袱，衫褥长袍之类也一叠叠地堆在桌子上。这不用问，是我旅程中的同伴了。"偏要这么多事，事已定了，为什么不早点儿收拾好！"我略微颇烦地想。但是必须带走既属事实，随时预备尤见从容，我何忍说出责备的话呢——实在也不该责备，只该感激。

然而我触着这气氛了，而且嗅着它的味道了，与上年在旅馆里感到的正是同一的种类，不过还没有这样浓密而已。我知道它将要渐渐地浓密，犹如西湖上晚来的烟雾；直到最后，它具有一种强大的力量，便会把我一挤；我于是不自主地离开这里了。

我依然谈话，写字，吃东西，躺在藤椅上；但是都有点儿异样，有点儿不自然。

夜来有梦，梦在车站月台旁。霎时火车已到，我急忙把行李提上去，身子也就登上，火车便疾驰而去了。似乎还有些东西遗留在月台那边，正在检点，就想到遗留的并不是东西，是几个人。很奇怪，我竟不曾向他们说一声"别了"，竟不曾伸出手来给他们；不仅如此，登上火车的

英汉对照
English-Chinese
中国文学宝库
Gems of Chinese Literature
现代文学系列
Modern Literature

not only that, when I got on the train I forgot them completely. I am filled with regret — how could I not have said anything or even shaken hands? It is like saying that shaking hands — the more the better — makes a parting complete. "Let me go back and make up for it! Let me go back and make up for it!" But the train ignores me and races on full steam ahead.

My departure in this dream when I completely forget the people on the platform is quite different from my hopeful fancy of leaving in the midst of blissful sleep. The experience of this dream tells me that such a departure would only arouse regrets and is by no means necessarily any better. So why do I have such fancies? And yet, after all, how can parting be easy when one is awake, with just a word and a shaking of hands?

"You should write lots of letters with plenty of detail; even though there's a gap of three to five days between each steamer, it is always a great delight and comfort to a lonely traveller to pull out a thick wad of letters from a package."

"I may not be able to write much or in great detail. I haven't been in that line for quite some time; I'm bombarded with all kinds of things — big, little, thick, thin — and it's enough dealing with them one at a time, so who knows how much time and energy I'll have left to sit down and take up a pen!"

If the taste of leaving is bitter, here it is mixed with an acrid flavour.

Translated by Alison Bailey

时候简直把他们忘了。于是深深地悔恨,怎么能不说一声,握一握手呢!假若说了,握了,究竟是个完满的离别,多少是好。"让我回头去补了吧!让我回头去补了吧!"但是火车不睬我,它喘着气只是向前奔。

这梦里的登程,全忘了月台上的几个人,与我痴心盼望的酣睡时离去,情形正相仿佛。现在梦里的经验告诉我,这只有勾引些悔恨,并不见得比较好些。那么,我又何必作这种痴想呢?然而清醒地说一声握一握的离别,究竟何尝是好受的!

"信要写得勤,要写得详;虽然一班轮船动辄要隔三五天,而厚厚的一叠信笺从封套里抽出来,总是独客的欣悦与安慰。"

"未必能够写得怎样勤怎样详吧。久已不干这勾当了;大的小的粗的细的种种事情箭一般地射到身上来,逐一对付已经够受了,知道还有多少坐定下来执笔的功夫与精神!"

离别的滋味假若是酸的,这里又搀入一些苦辛的味道了。

英汉对照
English-Chinese
中国文学宝库
Gems of Chinese Literature
现代文学系列
Modern Literature

Traveller's Words

The best time to depart after all is at noon on a fine, bright day.

"Everything's fine. Go back on shore, it's almost time to leave." I say this with seeming courage but, in fact, given the situation, I cannot speak otherwise. And yet it is not entirely false. Pears and bananas have already been bought for me. There is nothing more to be said. The hustle and bustle of the ship's crew and the fragrant steaminess of the cabin can no longer provide distraction. We are silently crowded together and suddenly the invisible web around my desolate heart tightens still more — surely it would be better to part a little sooner?

What I cannot explain to myself is that I felt compelled to escort them to the ship's rail and, indeed, to go with them down the gangplank and on to the quayside. Was I not just about to set off on a journey? In the end I took on the role of host. A host sees off his guests before turning back to enter his home and see his own people. And yet, this time — what of this turning back?

It was certainly not cowardice that made me look casually elsewhere as I promised to obey the admonition, "Write soon." Nor did I feel anything except that suddenly my heart was like a void (to be honest, it is indescribable). At last I knew that I should go back on board, so I climbed the gangway, combing through my dishevelled hair with my fingers as I went.

客　语

　　侥幸万分的竟然是晴明的正午的离别。

　　"一切都安适了,上岸回去吧,快要到开行的时刻了。"似乎很勇敢地说了出来,其实呢,处此境地,就不得不说这样的话。但也不是全不出于本心。梨与香蕉已经买来给我了,话是没有什么可说了,夫役的扰攘,小舱的郁蒸,又不是什么足以赏心的,默默地挤在一起,徒然把无形的凄心的网织得更密罢了,何如早点儿就别了呢?

　　不可自解的是却要送到船栏边,而且不止于此,还要走下扶梯送到岸上。自己不是快要起程的旅客么?竟然充起主人来。主人送了客,回头踱进自己的屋子,看见自己的人。可是现在——现在的回头呢?

　　并不是懦怯,自然而然看着别的地方,答应"快写信来"那些嘱咐。于是被送的转身举步了。也不觉得什么,只仿佛心里突然一空似的(老实说,摹写不出了)。随后想起应该上船,便跨上扶梯;同时用十个指头梳满头散乱的头发。

英汉对照
English-Chinese
中国文学宝库
Gems of Chinese Literature
现代文学系列
Modern Literature

Leaning against the ship's rail, I watched those on shore move off a short distance before turning to wave in this direction. Without awaiting instruction my right hand flew up and waved domineeringly above my head. It came to me then that this was a very beautiful situation with a flavour worth savouring. When I looked again towards those on shore I found no trace of them — perhaps they had turned a corner to board a streetcar.

Any phenomenon not yet experienced makes a layman out of the uninitiated and so when it is finally experienced, it is hard to avoid laughing at oneself. At first I had believed that on leaving the mouth of the Wusong there would be a vast expanse of sea and sky with mountainous waves beating against the ship and dispersing like torn silk and tossed pearls, and so I leaned against the ship's rail and waited. Imagine my surprise that, on leaving the estuary, there should still be endless sandy beaches and a continuous line of green mountains, the sea remaining as calm as before and the ship as steady and yet, while my field of vision might not have widened greatly, it did seem somehow much emptier. However, it was no more interesting than taking a small steamer on inland waters. And so, disappointed, I returned to my cabin and climbed into my upper berth, reading perforce to pass the time. The gentleman in the lower berth had long been emitting the occasional, abrupt snore.

I had not read many pages before I felt a reverie come upon me. "Reverie" is the correct term, for I was certainly not asleep — I was still aware of the noise of the engine and the ship's movement, but it was simply an awareness without a trace of thought or

倚着船栏，看岸上的人去得不远，而且正回身向这里招手。自己的右手不待命令，也就飞扬趷扈地舞动于头顶之上。忽地觉得这刹那间这个境界很美，颇堪体会。待再望岸上人，却已没有踪迹，大概拐了弯赶电车去了。

没有经验的想象往往是外行的，待到证实，不免自己好笑。起初以为一出吴淞口便是苍茫无际的海天，山头似的波浪打到船上来，散为裂帛与抛珠，所以只是靠着船栏等着。谁知出了口还是似尽又来的沙滩，还是一抹连绵的青山，水依然这么平，船依然这么稳。若说眼界，未必开阔了多少，却觉空虚了好些；若说趣味，也不过与乘中小汽轮一样。于是失望地回到舱里，爬上上层自己的铺位，只好看书消遣。下层那位先生早已有时而猝发的鼾声了。

实在没有看多少页书，不知怎么也朦胧起来了。只有用这朦胧二字最确切，因为并不是睡着，汽机的声音和船身的微荡，我都能够觉知，但仅仅是觉知，再没有一点思想一毫情绪。

英汉对照
English-Chinese
中国文学宝库
Gems of Chinese Literature
现代文学系列
Modern Literature

emotion. This reverie was like an acute drunken spell — I passed the night and it was morning again, but I did not awake other than to get up out of necessity on occasion to eat biscuits, beef and bananas and the like, just letting it take its course — remaining in my reverie.

Is this not how life must be in a cradle? I have no recollection of my infancy, but surely it must have been rather like this, just an awareness with no thought or emotion? Naturally even the pain of parting is given temporary leave of absence.

I have never been this close to nature before and feel a great enhancement in my interest. Beyond my study window, and with only a field between, the Min River flows lazily on. The mountains on the other bank extend out and pile upwards, sometimes newly adorned in bright green and sometimes covered in a light veil of mist. Sometimes clouds appear as if from nowhere to link the mountains with the house and then they seem even more to abound with strange vistas. The field outside my window is the territory of several dozen sheep and ten cows. The shepherd apparently does not encourage a *laissez faire* attitude, for as soon as his troops have eaten he starts prodding them with a bamboo stick and orders them back. I often hear what sounds like people cutting the grass and then think how free those cows are, still wandering at will in the field. It is their milk that I drink every day — thick, white and fragrant — there is no bounty like it.

My bedroom window looks out on to the foot of a mountain with bare black rocks, stunted pines and a ravine through which spring

这朦胧仿佛剧烈的醉,过了今夜,又是明朝,只是不醒,除了必要坐起来几回,如吃些饼干牛肉香蕉之类,也就任其自然——连续地朦胧着。

　　这不是摇篮里的生活么?婴儿时的经验固然无从回忆,但是这样只有觉知而没有思想没有情绪,该有点儿相像吧。自然,所谓离思也暂时给假了。

　　向来不曾亲近江山的,到此却觉得趣味丰富极了。书室的窗外,只隔一片草场,闲闲地流着闽江。彼岸的山绵延重叠,有时露出青翠的新妆,有时披上轻薄的雾帔,有时不知从什么地方来了好些云,却与山通起家来,于是更见得那些山郁郁然有奇观了。窗外这草场差不多是几十头羊与十条牛的领土。看守羊群的人似乎不主张放任主义的,他的部民才吃了一顿,立即用竹竿驱策着,叫它们回去。时时听得仿佛有几个人在那里割草的声音,便想到这十头牛特别自由,还是在场中游散。天天喝的就是它们的奶,又白又浓又香,真是无上的恩惠。

　　卧室的窗对着山麓,望去有裸露的黑石,有矮矮的松林,有泉水冲过的涧道。间或有一两

英汉对照
English-Chinese
中国文学宝库
Gems of Chinese Literature
现代文学系列
Modern Literature

water rushes. Occasionally when one or two people go to the mountaintop to gather firewood I watch their tiny shapes moving around up there and catch the faint and indistinct rustling sound of dry grass. It is like the realm of a hermit from ancient times, read about in some poem or seen in a painting. There is certainly something fresh and appealing about being a hermit from ancient times for a while.

The moon is still up there in the mountains and the gorges, vast and dark, seem even gloomier. A wind gets up, its constant sharp whistling accompanied by the soughing of the pines. Suddenly I remember a scene from my childhood: I went hiking with classmates on Tianping Mountain and we stayed overnight at Gaoyiyuan on ricestraw mattresses lying haphazardly on the ground. I awoke in the middle of the night. There was no light whatsoever, just a sound like a rushing flood, a sound which seemed to encompass all else; I felt chilled and wrapped my cover more firmly around me. I was unable to sleep and until dawn broke all I could do was try and identify that deafening yet overpoweringly silent and profoundly significant sensation. In thirty years that is the only time I have ever made a "mountain sojourn." And now I hear that sound again, yet while it is not as awesome as on that night, I will be hearing more of it as the winds increase. Whether or not I can always maintain that child-like sense of awe I do not know....

There are crickets here, lots of crickets and, after all, any place without crickets is an accursed anomaly. I lie on the bed and listen: what a marvellous ensemble they make! Sometimes manifold and garrulous, sometimes in complete unison, yet always it feels

个人在山顶上樵采,形体藐小极了,看他们在那里运动着,便约略听得微茫的干草瑟瑟的声响。这仿佛是古代的幽人的境界,在什么诗篇什么画幅里边遇见过的。暂时充当古代的幽人,当然有些新鲜的滋味。

月亮还在山的那边,仰望山谷,苍苍的,暗暗的,更见得深郁。一阵风起,总是锐利的一声呼啸一般,接着便是一派松涛。忽然忆起童年的情景来:那一回与同学们远足天平山,就在高义园借宿,稻草衬着褥子,横横竖竖地躺在地上,半夜里醒来了,一点儿光都没有,只听得洪流奔放似的声音,这声音差不多把一切包裹起来了;身体颇觉寒冷,因而把被头裹得更紧些。从此再也不想睡,直到天明,只是细辨那喧而弥静静而弥旨的滋味。三十年来,所谓山居就只有这么一回。而现在又听到这声音了,虽然没有那夜那么宏大,但是往后的风信正多,且将常常更甚地听到呢。只不知童年的那种欣赏的心情能够永永持续否……

这里有秋虫,有很多的秋虫,没有秋虫的地方究竟是该诅咒的例外。躺在床上听听,真是奇妙的合奏,有时很繁碎,有时很凝集,而总觉

英汉对照
English-Chinese
中国文学宝库
Gems of Chinese Literature
现代文学系列
Modern Literature

just right and thoroughly pleasing to the ear. In their midst is a kind unknown to me whose call is resonant and long, like string music, arousing the fancy that one is watching a musician playing leisurely.

The sound of the pines and the insects gradually diminishes, diminishes and at last disappears....

Cangqian Mountain is practically just a garden, a road, a clump of flowers, a house and a driver, each of which has a poetic quality to them. Especially captivating is that time when the evening sunlight fades, a bell sounds from the temple and girls with flowered paper umbrellas walk under the green shade.

Accompanying Shaoyu and his wife on a walk in the mountains I recognized the very similar litchi and longan trees and the banyan tree with its long, wispy, floating aerial roots. Looking towards the mountain where we lived, we saw sunset clouds the colour of rouge in the west. We sat on a low brick wall by the road to rest. Gradually it became darker all around and the distant mountains looked like nothing more than a few faint brust-strokes staining grey paper. Countrywomen hurried home, turning naturally to look at us as they passed. They made me think of people from ancient times when I saw their unsophisticated appearance and strange ornaments (the most eye-catching being three very long silver hair-pins, like three small swords, two placed horizontally and the other vertically, to hold the hair fast. I thought that if two of them walked abreast the horizontal pins would cut the other person's head). Furthermore it seemed to me that any element of modernity or any

得恰合刚好,足以娱耳。中间有一种不知名的虫,它们的声音响亮而曼长,像是弦乐,而且引起人家一种想象,仿佛以一位乐人在那里徐按慢抽地演奏。

松声与虫声渐渐地轻微又轻微,终于消失了……

仓前山差不多一座花园,一条路,一丛花,一所房屋,一个车夫,都有诗意。尤其可爱的是晚阳淡淡的时候,礼拜堂里送出一声钟响,绿荫下走过几个张着花纸伞的女郎。

跟着绍虞夫妇前山后山地走,认识了两相仿佛的荔枝树与龙眼树,也认识了长鬓飘飘的生着气根的榕树,眺望了我们所住的那座山,又看了胭脂似的西边的暮云,于是坐在路旁的砖砌的矮栏上休息。渐渐地四围昏暗了,远处的山只像几笔极淡的墨痕染渍在灰色的纸上。乡间的女人匆匆地归去,走过我们身边,很自然地向我们看一看。那种浑异的意态,那种奇蔚的装束(最足注目的是三支很长的银发钗,像三把小剑,两横一竖地把发髻拢住,我想,两个人并肩走时,横插的剑锋会划着旁人的头皮),都使我想到古代的人。同时又想,什么现代精神,什

kind of dispute would become as hazy as the distant mountains here, as if deep within a dream.

There was no moon on the night of the Mid-autumn Moon Festivel, but that was alright because I had not hoped to see a mid-autumn moon anyway. It was like any ordinary moonless night and I was shut up in my study doing some homework under the broad, beautiful sweep of lamplight before going to bed.

The next evening the sky was full of clouds and the surface of the river was dark. A west wind shook the window lattices until they rattled. Suddenly I felt as if everything were wrong. And yet it cannot be "everything" — one has to make a stand somewhere and this time I made mine by leaning listlessly against the window. Yet what point is there in being listless?

It seemed as if Shaoyu had guessed something because he walked over to urge me to take a stroll by the river. Waves slapped and dashed against the rocks on the beach. A broad-sweeping yet very light sound like the wind spread over the surface of the river — the tide was retreating again. I quoted a couple of lines from one of my old poems:

> *The tide's sound has not yet changed,*
> *But already the traveller's mood is different.*

Seven years ago I saw Molin off to Nantong. Leaving town, staying overnight in a hotel by the river and waiting for a boat served to

么种种的纠纷,都渺茫得像此刻的远山一样,仿佛沉在梦幻里了。

中秋夜没有月,这倒很好,我本来不希望看什么中秋月。与平常没有月亮的晚上一样,关在书室里,就美孚灯光下做了一点功课,就去睡了。

第二天的傍晚,满天是云,江面黯然。西风震动窗棂,"吉格"作响。突然觉得寂寥起来,似乎无论怎样都不好。但是又不能什么都不,总要在这样那样里占其一,这时候我占的是倚窗怅望。然而怅望又有什么意思呢?

绍虞似乎有点儿揣度得出,他走来邀我到江边去散步。水波被滩石所挡,激触有声。还有广遍而轻轻的风一般的音响平铺在江面上,潮水又退出去了。便随口念旧时的诗句:

潮声应未改,客绪已频更。

七年以前,我送墨林去南通。出得城来,在江滨的客店里歇宿候船,却成了独客。荒凉的

make me a lonely traveller. The desolate waterfront was more than enough to make one sad, especially on a night of parting, and I truly felt as if nothing were quite right. A thought came to my mind and I made up a poem to help pass the time. The lines above are from that poem. Ah, once again it is the sound of the tide and the traveller's mood!

This "traveller's mood" is exactly like thick winter clouds which even the wind cannot disperse. They just amass and grow still thicker — and what good is there in this medicinal stroll? It was almost dark when we returned to the room but we did not light the lamps for a while, sitting instead in the dim dusk. I said, "Jiequan in Beijing used to say there was something special about sitting for a while as dusk deepens and a faint glow comes from the stove." Shaoyu made an assenting sound but said nothing more. How strange it was that both our voices should sound so very isolated, as if we were in a vast, open and eternally soundless void which reverted to silence as our few sounds, making barely a ripple, died away.

There is undoubted pain in thinking of that "something special" of which Jiequan spoke. His "something special" certainly was "special" and I can appreciate what he meant.

After the lamps were lit letters eagerly awaited and not easily obtained arrived unexpectedly. A paddle-boat had come here yesterday. The first letter made my heart constrict again. The second was from Pingbo. He mentioned some random jottings I had written several days previously, "After all, there is no alternative to this waiting and one cannot but lament, and yet if one does lament,

江滨晚景已够叫人怅怅,又况是离别开始的一晚,真觉得百无一可了。聊学雅人口占一诗,藉以排遣。现在这两句就是这一首诗里的。唉,又是潮声,又是客绪!

所谓客绪,正像冬天的浓云一般,风吹不散,只是越凝集越厚,散步的药又有什么用处。回到屋里,天差不多黑了,我们暂时不点火,就在昏暗中坐下。我说:"介泉在北京常说,在暮色苍茫之际,炉火微明,默然小坐,别有滋味。"绍虞接应了一声就不响了。很奇怪,何以我和他的声音都特别寂寞,仿佛在一个广大的永寂的虚空中,仅仅荡漾着这一些声音,音波散了,便又回复它的永寂。

想来介泉所说的滋味,一定带着酸的。他说"别有",诚然是"别有",我能够体会他的意思了。

点灯以后,居然送来了切盼而难得的邮件,昨天有一艘轮船到这里了。看了第一封,又把心挤得紧一点。第二封是平伯的,他提起我前几天作的一篇杂记,说:"……此等事终于无可

one feels as though one is sinking into weakness. In the end there is nothing to be done and that's the truth...."

I feel as if this is weakness and so I should not be lamenting.

And yet I think what is there to lament about? Missing my old home? All that is fit to be missed at home are things like lotus root and water shield, and are they worth lamenting over? Missing the apartment in the city that is like a pigeon-roost? I am no pigeon, so why should I lament if I flew away? Frankly, in brief, it is simply the desire to live together with those I love most dearly that has suddenly made me dissatisfied, that is all. Where is life's interest if one cannot live with those one loves best? It is because I am dissatisfied that I lament and, in truth, what weakness is there in that? Indeed, why should I not lament?

A lamenting heart is like fuel to a lit fire — thick smoke comes belching out before flames appear. Pingbo's letter is like a piece of firewood which kindles on being put close and then starts to blaze....

October 1, 1923
Translated by Alison Bailey

奈何,不呻吟固不可,作呻吟又觉陷于怯弱。总之,无一而可,这是实话。……"

似乎觉得这确是怯弱,不要呻吟吧。

但是还要去想,呻吟为了什么?恋恋于故乡?故乡之足以恋恋的,差不多只有藕与莼菜这些东西了,又何至于呻吟?恋恋于鹁鸽箱似的都市里的寓居么?既非鹁鸽,又何至于因为飞开了而呻吟?老实地说,简括地说,只因一种愿与最爱与同居的人同居的心情,忽然不得满足罢了。除了与最爱与同居的人同居,人间的趣味在哪里?因为不得满足而呻吟,正是至诚的话,有什么怯弱不怯弱?那么,又何必不要呻吟呢?

呻吟的心本来如已着了火的燃料,浓烟郁结,正待发焰。平伯的信恰如一根火柴,就近一引,于是炽盛地燃烧起来了……

英汉对照
English-Chinese
中国文学宝库
Gems of Chinese Literature
现代文学系列
Modern Literature

Selling Gingkos

The lanes gradually became shrouded with the sunset hue of dusk and a row of streetlights came on. Groups of men and women in twos and threes, all apparently very serious, stood at the corners of each lane talking about something. A few kids, their shoes not properly slipped on, chased each other, their soles flapping against the cement.

At this point a man carrying a shoulder-pole came into the lane. He looked left and right, paused and then went forward a few steps. This is his way of assessing potential customers — customers have to be assessed for after all, he is not carrying that shoulder-pole for fun, is he? When he reached the entrance to the fourth lane he put down his pole. We looked his load over. On the back end there was a wooden bucket, covered so that you could not see the contents. The front end was interesting though — it was fitted with a tiny stove, like the kind we use for making tea, and on top there was a small cauldron. Tiny petals of flame licked ineffectually at the cauldron's sides. It made for a strange sight in this dusk-filled lane.

He took off the cauldron lid and flipped the contents with an oyster-shell while singing out rather unmelodiously, "Fresh hot gingkos! Come and get 'em!" His voice was very high and had an urgent ring to it. His chant had no mean impact — children came

卖白果

总弄里边不知不觉笼上昏黄的暮色,一列电灯亮起来了。三三两两的男子和妇女站在各弄的口头,似乎很正经的样子,不知在谈些什么。几个孩子,穿鞋没拔上跟,他们互相追赶,鞋底擦着水门汀地,作"替替"的音响。

这时候,一个挑担的慢慢地走进弄来,他向左右观看,顿一顿再向前走两三步。他探认主顾的习惯就是如此;主顾确是必须探认的,不然,挑着担子出来难道是闲耍么?走到第四弄的口头,他把担子歇下来了。我们试看看他的担子。后头有一个木桶,盖着盖子,看不见盛的是什么东西。前头却很有趣,装着个小小的炉子,同我们烹茶用的差不多,上面承着一只小镬子;瓣状的火焰从镬子旁边舔出来,烧得不很旺。在这暮色已浓的弄口,便构成个异样的情景。

他开了镬子的盖子,用一爿蚌壳在镬子里拨动,同时不很协调地唱起来了:"新鲜热白果,要买就来数。"发音很高,又含有急促的意味。这一唱影响可不小,左弄右弄里的小孩子陆续

英汉对照
English-Chinese
中国文学宝库
Gems of Chinese Literature
现代文学系列
Modern Literature

Selling Gingkos

racing out of the lanes to the right and left, already entranced by the small nuts in the cauldron. Behind them came adults, calling out, "Slow down a bit!" To the children, however, it was just a distant murmur.

Traditionally, when you hear gingkos being sold the heat of summer has already given way to a new coolness; and while you cannot go as far as to discard your fan yet, it has nonetheless become a little *passé*. That is why this particular seller's cry seems to bring a wave of coolness in its wake. This year, however, there has been an Indian summer and even when you do nothing at home after work, you still feel it is very close and sweaty. Just as we sit opposite each other, sighing as if there will be no end to it, suddenly in comes that cry with its heralding of coolness arousing in me brief illusions of happiness and making me truly grateful.

That cry makes me recall the gingko-sellers in my old home. While naturally more than one person does this trade, their cries all sound the same, melodious and light, just as the symbol of coming coolness should be and with far more character than the cries of gingko-sellers here in Shanghai. Their cry is almost like a nursery rhyme. I once learned it from an adult when I was young and used to copy them singing:

> *Warm up your hands with hot gingkos.*
> *Tasty, oh tasty and stick-in-your-mouth.*
> *One copper cash'll buy you three nuts.*
> *Three copper cash'll buy you three nuts.*
> *If you want to buy, come and count them out.*

奔出来了,他们已经神往于镬子里的小颗粒,大人在后面喊着慢点儿跑的声音,对于他们只是微茫的喃喃了。

据平昔的经验,听到叫卖白果的声音时,新凉已经接替了酷暑;扇子虽不至于就此遭到捐弃,总不是十二分时髦的了;因此,这叫卖声里似乎带着一阵凉意。今年入秋转热,回家来什么也不做,还是气闷,还是出汗。正在默默相对,仿佛要叹息着说莫可奈何之际,忽然送来这么带着凉意的一声两声,引起我片刻的幻想的快感,我真要感谢了。

这声音又使我回想到故乡的卖白果的。做这营生的当然不只是一个,但叫卖的声调却大致相似,悠扬而轻清,恰配作新凉的象征;比较这里上海的卖白果的叫卖声有味得多了。他们的唱句差不多成为儿歌,我小时候曾经受教于大人,也摹仿着他们的声调唱:

> 烫手热白果,
> 香又香来糯又糯;
> 一个铜钱买三颗,
> 三个铜钱买十颗。
> 要买就来数,
> 不买就挑过。

Selling Gingkos

If you don't want to buy, then get on out!

The words are coarse and vulgar, but when you hear them sung out in a quiet lane at night, neither too slow nor too fast, neither too bold nor too soft, they can have a truly relaxing effect, stilling your thoughts and immersing you in a world of pleasure and beauty. Indeed, if you discount art, and talk simply from the point of view of the sound, then all the songs sung by workers, the cries of small stall-holders and the opera tunes sung by maids, scholars, heroines and long-beards have considerable ability to move you. There is no need to distinguish the words or their meaning, instead just sing out their cadence, rhythm, rounds, twists and turns with relish; nor is there any need to be as diligent as a textual critic or expert, studying the origins of a certain vulgar song or whether a particular tune is a new version of an old measure and therefore terribly precious. No, it is enough just to find a pleasurable sound and to hear it again. In this way you can gain considerable delight and enjoyment. And if the singing is also artistically fine that is even more to the good and needs no justification.

The main reason why the cries of the Shanghai gingko-sellers do not match up to those of my old home is because their tone is not very good. Another factor is that this neighbourhood is not sufficiently quiet enough to act as a proper foil. The medley of noises in the neighbourhood, the sound of the cars on the streets beyond and the machines in the factories, all mingle together to prevent silence. Even if an extremely talented musician were to come here and play with the most consummate skill of his life, he would still

这真是粗俗的通常话,可是在静寂的夜间的深巷中,这样不徐不疾,不刚劲也不太柔软地唱出来,简直可以使人息心静虑,沉入享受美感的境界。本来,除开文艺,单从声音方面讲,凡是工人所唱一切的歌,小贩呼唤的一切叫卖声,以及戏台上红面孔白面孔青衫长胡子所唱的戏曲,中间都颇有足以移情的。我们不必辨认他们唱的是些什么话,含着什么意思,单就那调声的抑扬徐疾送渡转折等等去吟味;也不必如考据家内行家那样用心,推究某种俚歌源于什么,某种腔调是从前某老板的新声,特别可贵;只取足以悦我们的耳的,就多听它一会;这样,也就可以获得不少赏美的乐趣。如果歌唱的也就是极好的文艺,那当然更好,原是不待说明的。

这里上海的卖白果的叫卖声所以不及我故乡的,声调不怎么好自然是主因,而里中欠静寂,没有给它衬托,也有关系。全里的零零碎碎的杂声,里外马路上的汽车声,工厂里的机器声,搅和在一起,就无所谓静寂了。即使是神妙的音乐家,在这境界中演奏他生平的绝艺,也要

lose out — how much more so would the insignificant cry of a gingko-seller?

And yet it arouses in me brief illusions of happiness for which it is deserving of both thanks and praise.

August 22, 1924
Translated by Alison Bailey

打个很大的折扣,何况是不足道的卖白果的叫卖声呢。

  但是它能引起我片刻的幻想的快感,总是可以感谢而且值得称道的。

英汉对照
English-Chinese
中国文学宝库
Gems of Chinese Literature
现代文学系列
Modern Literature

Late-Night Food

The main gate of the compound, though it shut at nine, had in it a wicket gate through which one person could enter or leave, and this was open all night, being seen by the landlord as a convenience for the residents, who could thus come in or go out at any time they liked. Vigilance was maintained by a doorman who slept on the spot. Perhaps it was not such a bad idea. It was certainly convenient to be able to come and go as one wished, but the vigilance not infrequently lapsed and villains made off with residents' belongings, though one could not conclude irrefutably that this was due to the conveniently open wicket.

I think if anyone was necessarily grateful for the open wicket, beyond a doubt it was the pedlars vending food. When I awoke in the middle of the night, which was not often, I would hear them crying their wares: "Spiced tea eggs!" "Hot ham rice cakes!" "Spiced dried beancurd!" "Sweet cassia flower and lotus seed porridge!" and various others shouted by Cantonese, of which, try as I would, I could make out nothing at all but a string of unfamiliar sounds. The crowd noise had died down by this time, and despite the last persisting remnants of mahjong tiles, laughter and babies crying to show that not everyone in the compound had gone to bed, it was nothing like the daytime world. The hoarse cries, borne tremulously and mournfully through this domain, pointed up its

深夜的食品

里的总门虽然在九点钟光景关上了,总门上的小门,仅容一个人出入的,却终夜开着。房主以为这是便利住户的办法,随便什么时候要进要出都可以;门口就有看门人睡在那里,所以疏失是不至于有的。这想法也许不错,随时可以进出确实便利;然而里里边却出了好几回疏失,贼骨头带着住户的东西走了。这是否由于小门开着的便利,固然不能确凿断定。

我想有一些人必然感激这小门的开着,是不容怀疑的,那就是挑售食品的小贩们。我中夜醒来(这是难得的事),总见他们的叫卖声:"五香茶叶蛋!""火腿热粽子!""五香豆腐干!""桂花白糖莲心粥!"还有些是广东人呼喊的,用心细辨也辨不清,只听见一连串生疏的声音而已。这时候众喧已息,固然有些骨牌声、笑语声、儿啼声在那里支持残局,表示这里里的人还没有全部入睡,但究竟不比白天的世界了。这些叫卖声大都是沙哑的;在这样的境界里传送过来,颤颤地,寂寂地,更显出这境界的凄凉与

英汉对照
English-Chinese
中国文学宝库
Gems of Chinese Literature
现代文学系列
Modern Literature

chill and emptiness. The voices, too, suggested their owners' appearances, withered forms with protruding noses and cheekbones, listless eyes and anaemic skin carrying baskets and poles, raising their feet as if lifting stones, their spines bent like bows. In short, the sound of their voices brought to mind the cast list of *The Black Book of Wronged Souls*.

The vendors were not without their customers, but who was it bought these things to eat late at night? The categoric answer was, not us. We had always gone to bed early as a family, never after eleven at the latest, and of course we rose early too. We had become infected with rustic habits since moving to the country for three years and had come increasingly to embody the folk of yore, dining with the sun still on the rooftops and going to our rest at the going down of the same, our lights lit only for the briefest space of time. Our recent move back to the refinement of Shanghai should in theory have brought progress and expunged some of our rustic ways, but these had by and large reverted to type. Local refinement touched our rusticity not at all. We still dined and retired early. Sometimes friends would visit when we were about to go to bed. "Have you had any dinner?" we would ask, only to get some clever reply such as, "We've just finished tea, thanks. There are two or three hours to dinner yet." I was ashamed but at the same time thought it natural that these long-time Shanghai residents should be much more refined in their ways than we were. People like us were not going to put off going to bed just to buy spiced tea eggs and the like to eat, much less crawl out of bed at the sound of the first vendor and go outdoors to buy them. So whatever the

空虚。从这些声音又可以想见发声者的形貌，枯瘦的身躯，耸起的鼻子与颧颊，失神的眼睛，全没有血色的皮肤；他们提着蓝子或者挑着担子，举起一步似乎提起一块石头，背脊是弯得像弓了。总之，听了这声音就会联想到《黑籍冤魂》里的登场人物。

有卖东西的，总有吃东西的。谁在深夜里还买这些东西吃呢？这可以断然回答，决不是我们。我家向来是早睡的，至迟也不过十一点钟（当然也是早起的）。自从搬到乡下去住了三年，沾染了鄙野的习俗，益发实做其太古之民了。太阳还照在屋顶，我们就吃晚饭；太阳没了，我们就"日入而息"，灯自然要点一点的，然而只有一会儿工夫。近来搬到这文明的地方上海来住，论理总该有点进步，把鄙野的习染洗刷去一部分，但是我们的习染几乎化为本性了；地方虽然文明，与我们的鄙野全不相干，我们还是早吃晚饭早睡觉。有时候朋友来访，我们差不多要睡了，就问他们："晚饭吃过了吧？"谁知他们回答得很妙："才吃过晚点，晚饭还差两三个钟头呢。"这使我惭愧了，同时才想起他们是久居上海的，习染自然比我们文明得多。像我们这样的情形，决不会特地耽搁了睡觉，等着买五香茶叶蛋等等东西吃的；更不会一听到叫卖声就从床上爬起来，开门出去买。所以半夜的里

英汉对照
English-Chinese
中国文学宝库
Gems of Chinese Literature
现代文学系列
Modern Literature

tremulous, mournful cries that haunted the compound at midnight, we were not the prime customers.

Who then were? Some, I suppose, must have been the unflagging night-long male and female devotees of the card table who, their stomachs functioning unabated through sleeplessness, had by now digested most of their evening meal and would of course be gulping saliva, helpless before the advertised temptations of the sweet and savoury delicacies. A temporary win, perhaps smaller than usual, would see them shelling out on a little something to keep up the spirits, while a chance windfall that normally had a gambler paying off the rickshaw man engaged to wait for him at the den door in dollars rather than dimes would scarcely leave him less liberal than was his wont when it came to things like spiced tea eggs for his own consumption, and the loser, exculpating himself on the grounds that his luck might change, that a better-lined stomach might greatly sharpen his wits and thus turn the tables and that food might be the currency with which the others were footing the bill, would on reflection airily call, "Three tea eggs!" or "One bowl of lotus seed porridge!"

Another class of customers was of course made up of those who belonged to the same drug culture as the vendors themselves, who only emerged to ply their trade when they had satisfied their crude — crude opium — hunger or gorged themselves on some pill or other, thus to a certain extent restoring their spirits. Ranged on the same couch, deft with the same pipe, they conducted an evenly matched barter when, as was natural, the banishment of nocturnal fatigue contributed to the whetting of their appetites. Most opium

里虽然常常颤颤地寂寂地喊着什么什么东西，而我们决非他们的主顾。

那么他们的主顾是谁呢？我想那些神明不衰，通宵打牌的男男女女总该是其中的一部分。他们尚未睡眠，胃的工作并不改弱，到半夜里，已经把吃下去的晚餐消化得差不多了；怎禁得那些又香又甜又鲜美的名称一声声地引诱，自然要一口一口地咽唾沫了。手头赢了一点的呢，譬如少赢了一些，就很慷慨地买来吃个称心如意（黄包车夫在赌场门口候着一个赌客，这赌客正巧是赢了钱的，往往在下车的时候很不经意地给车夫过量的钱，洋钱当作毛钱用；何况五香茶叶蛋等等东西是自己吃下去的，当然格外地慷慨了）。输了的呢，他想藉此告一小段落，说不定运气就会转变过来；把肚皮吃得充实些，头脑也会灵敏得多，结果"返本出赢钱"，吃的东西还是别人会的钞。他这么想的时候，就毫不在乎地喊道，"茶叶蛋，来三个！""莲心粥，来一碗！"

其次，与叫卖者同属黑籍的人们当然也是主顾。叫卖者正吞饱了土（烟土）皮，吃足了什么丸，精神似乎有点回复，才出来干他们的营生；那些一榻横陈，一枪自持的，当然也正是宿倦已消，情味弥佳的当儿，他们彼此做个交易，正是适合恰当，两相配合。抽大烟的人大都喜

英汉对照
English-Chinese
中国文学宝库
Gems of Chinese Literature
现代文学系列
Modern Literature

Late-Night Food

smokers like their food scalding hot, often with a predilection for the cloyingly sweet, and almost all the wares on offer were kept at the requisite temperature over braziers of glowing charcoal chips, the sellers of hot ham rice cakes catering neatly to demand by also carrying rice cakes stuffed with sweet larded beanpaste or sugared jujubes, whose consumption boosted the appetite for a late night around the lamp drawing heavily and deeply on a few more pipes.

Others, such as revellers returning home from theatres or houses of entertainment, night staff from newspaper offices and the like and those with a bad case of the refinement habit, citizens who never went to bed before two or three in the morning, unaffected by the lateness of the hour would also stop the street pedlars for a bite to eat, either from boredom or hunger, so they too were customers of the night vendors.

I doubt strongly whether the same was true of night workers such as cobblers who were their own masters and invariably stitched soles until two or three in the morning, menials in beancurd mills who rose in the grey hours to do the grinding or late-night rickshaw men duty-bound to stay awake all night: these worked doubly hard through the night to shoulder the heavy burden of their own and their families' livelihood and were unlikely ever to be able to spare enough money for a tea egg or a ham rice cake. Rapt and drooling as they might be at the sound of the fragrant, sweet, delicious names, they would never go so far as actually to stop one of the vendors.

The lack of their customers did not affect the vendors, however. I knew from the neighbours' talk and from what I heard when I

欢吃烫热的东西,有的欢喜吃甜腻的东西。那些待沽的东西几乎全是烫热的,都搁在一个小炉子上,炉子里红红地烧着炭屑;而卖火腿热粽子的,也带着猪油豆沙粽、白糖枣子粽;这可谓恰投所好了;买来吃下去,烫的感觉,甜的滋味,把深夜拥灯的情味益发提起来了,于是又重重地深深地抽上几管烟。

其他像戏馆里游戏场里散归的游人,做夜间工作的像报馆职员之类,还有文明的习染已深,非到两三点钟不睡的居民,他们虽然不觉得深夜之悠悠,或者为着消消闲,或者为着点点饥,也就喊住过路的小贩买一些东西吃。所以他们也是那些深夜叫卖者的主顾。

我想夜间的劳工们未必是主顾吧。老板伙计一身兼任的鞋匠,扎鞋底往往要到两三点钟;豆腐店里的伙计,黄昏时候就要起身磨豆腐了;拉夜班的黄包车夫,是义务所在,终夜不得睡觉的,他们负着自己和全家的生命的重担,就是加倍努力地做一夜的工作,也未必能挣得到够买一个茶叶蛋一只火腿粽的闲钱来;他们虽然听着那些又香又甜又鲜美的名称而神往,而垂涎,但是哪里敢真个把叫卖者喊住呢!

他们不敢喊住,对于叫卖者却没有什么影响,据同里的人谈起,以及我偶尔醒来的时候听

chanced to wake that tea eggs and the like made their appearance every evening, sufficient proof that they were all sold, and the business showed no sign of abating for want of participation on the part of rustics such as us and workpeople.

March 26, 1924
Translated by Simon Johnstone

见的,知道茶叶蛋等等是每晚必来的;这足以证明那些东西自会卖完,这一宗营生决不因为我们这样鄙野的人以及劳工们的不去作成它而会见得衰颓的。

英汉对照
English-Chinese
中国文学宝库
Gems of Chinese Literature
现代文学系列
Modern Literature

Three Kinds of Boat

I hadn't been back to Suzhou to visit the graveyard for three years running, but this autumn I found the time. It is simply a matter of paying the caretakers so that they know that the family graves are not yet safe to sell on the sly. To get to my family plot you have to take a boat, the way people in Suzhou have always visited the graves, and in fine weather it makes for a really very pleasant escape from the city confines for anything up to a whole carefree day breathing the fresh air that abounds on the river. I took one of the boats I knew well, peeled almost bare of paint, its windows awry and its deck split, a picture of dilapidation. Indeed the boatman told me when I inquired that it had not been out of the water for repairs for some years, having had to make do with stopping in the bankside shallows throughout the summer drought, when the dearth of business meant a corresponding dearth of money for shore repairs. It had in fact always been the lot of the boats in previous years to stay tied up from dawn till dusk except during the spring visits to the graves. Recently small steamers had begun to serve every town and hamlet, or one could take one of the Shaoxing men's Dangdang boats, no slower than the steamers and cheaper into the bargain. The Suzhou city boats would doubtless have been chopped up for firewood willy-nilly had it not been for these graveyard visits, which were generally on the decline anyway, becoming

三种船

　　一连三年没有回苏州去上坟了。今年秋天有点儿空闲,就去上一趟坟。上坟的意思无非是送一点钱给看坟的坟客,让他们知道某家的坟还没有到可以盗卖的地步罢了。上我家的坟得坐船去。苏州人上坟向来大都坐船,天气好,逃出城圈子,在清气充塞的河面上畅快地呼吸一天半天,确是非常舒服的事。这一趟我去,雇的是一条熟识的船。涂着的漆差不多剥光了,窗框歪斜,平板破裂,一副残废的样子。问起船家,果然,这条船几年没有上岸修理了。今年夏季大旱,船只好胶住在浅浅的河浜里,哪里还有什么生意,又哪里来钱上岸修理。就是往年,除了春季上坟,船也只有停在码头上迎晓风送夕阳的份儿。近年来到各乡各镇去,都有了小轮船,不然,可以坐绍兴人的"嘡嘡船",也不比小轮船慢,而且价钱都很便宜。如果没有上坟这件事,苏州城里的船恐怕只能劈做柴烧了。而上坟的事大概是要衰落下去的,就像我,已经改变为三年上一趟坟了。

英汉对照
English-Chinese
中国文学宝库
Gems of Chinese Literature
现代文学系列
Modern Literature

Three Kinds of Boat

limited, as in my case, to one every three years.

The Suzhou city boats were called "fast boats," not that in reality they were faster than any elsewhere. They were not made for crossing large expanses of water and consequently had a shallow draught and broad, flat bottoms. Apart from the bows, which were open to the elements, they were divided into a forward cabin, a middle cabin and a stern section with an awning. The forward cabin was built high enough to allow one to stand up straight without cracking one's head and was furnished down either side with two or three delicate armchairs and an equally delicate tea table. Its front eaves were hung with red and green horn-paned lanterns, hung in their turn with red and green tassels. The deck beneath one's feet was formed of Guangzhou-varnished planks, usually six, supported on longitudinal and transverse timbers and removable to reveal the boatman's storeroom beneath. The middle cabin was also floored with planks but these almost touched the boat's bottom, so that access from the forward cabin required a step down of about a foot. There were two rows of small, square windows along either side, the top row of which could be suspended and the bottom row taken out so as to afford whoever leant out a view over the side. At one time the windows had been fitted out with bright tile work, sometimes a mosaic surrounding a tiny square of glass. The glass gradually grew to predominate until there was nothing else. Dividing the middle cabin from the forward cabin and the stern awning were six screen doors decorated with painting and calligraphy, each running in separate grooves above and below and needing only to be pushed to the left or right to open or close. Their adornments, mostly in

苏州城里的船叫做"快船",与别地的船比起来,实在是并不快的。因为不预备经过什么长江大湖,所以吃水很浅,船底阔而平。除了船头是露天以外,分做头舱中舱和艄篷三部分。头舱可以搭高,让人站直不至于碰头顶,两旁边各有两把或者三把小巧的靠背交椅,又有小巧的茶几。前檐挂着红绿的明角灯,明角灯又挂着红绿的流苏。踏脚的是广漆的平板,一般是六块,由横的直的木条承着。揭开平板,下面是船家的储藏库。中舱也铺着若干块平板,可是差不多贴着船底,所以从头舱到中舱得跨下一尺多。中舱两旁边是两排小方窗,上面的一排可以吊起来,第二排可以卸去,以便靠着船舷眺望。以前窗子都配上明瓦,或者在拼凑的明瓦间镶这么一小方玻璃,后来玻璃来得多了,就完全用玻璃。中舱与头舱艄篷分界处都有六扇书画小屏门,上方下方装在不同的几条槽里,要开要关,只须左右推移。书画大多是金漆的,无

英汉对照
English-Chinese
中国文学宝库
Gems of Chinese Literature
现代文学系列
Modern Literature

gold lacquer, were confined to such things as "At night by river in cold rain to Wu" and "Crows called at moonset in the frosty sky," accompanied by plum blossom, orchids, bamboo and chrysanthemums. The rear and starboard of this cabin were provided with long benches where passengers might rest; the addition of two extra at the rear gave those on an overnight trip somewhere to spread their bedding. On the port side just under the windows four small, square stools surrounded a small, square table, which could accommodate a dinner party of up to ten if a round top was put on it. The benches, like the deck in the forward cabin, afforded seating, supplemented by stools arranged in the corners. The stern awning was the boatman's self-contained world and had, like the forward cabin, a space under the deck. Here were pots and pans, cupboards and a stove, as well as sundries such as bedding and clothes chests. A removable hatch in the deck allowed the boatman to squat below chopping meat and boiling vegetables. Here was also where the oarsmen stood, two plying the starboard oar and two the port, one on the shaft and one on the cable of each. Any of the boatman's children that could not yet walk lay in cribs in the upturned poop; those that could were allowed to crawl there restrained by a rope secured around their waists and tied to the awning pillars lest they tumbled off into the river. Four parallel poles protruded at an angle from the side of the stern, once no doubt weapons of defence but turned to decorative use. Guangzhou varnish was used on all parts above the waterline — windows, doors, decks and pillars — thus avoiding the off-putting odour of tung oil common on other boats. Things so varnished were easily

非"寒雨连江夜入吴","月落乌啼霜满天"以及梅兰竹菊之类。中舱靠后靠右搁着长板,供客憩坐。如果过夜,只要靠后多拼一两条长板,就可以摊被褥。靠左当窗放一张小方桌,方桌旁边四张小方凳。如果在小方桌上放上圆桌面,十来个人就可以聚餐。靠后靠右的长板以及头舱的平板都是座头,小方凳摆在角落里凑数。末了儿说到艄篷,那是船家整个的天地。艄篷同头舱一样,平板以下还有地位,放着锅灶碗橱以及铺盖衣箱种种东西。揭开一块平板,船家就蹲在那里切肉煮菜。此外是摇橹人站着摇橹的地方。橹左右各一把,每把由两个人服事,一个当橹柄,一个当橹绳。船家如果有小孩,走不来的躺在困桶里,放在翘起的后艄,能够走的就让他在那里爬,拦腰一条绳拴着,系在篷柱上,以防跌到河里去。后艄的一旁露出四条棍子,一顺地斜并着,原来大概是护船的武器,后来转变成装饰品了。全船除着水的部分以外,窗门板柱都用广漆,所以没有其他船上常有的那种难受的桐油气味。广漆的东西容易擦干净,船

cleaned, and no small amount of water got on the sides of a boat. Provided the boatman was not lazy, the boat could be spick and span at all times.

So tiresome did married daughters on visits to parents or matrons calling on young ladies find it in days gone by to use a sedan chair that they changed to the comfort of travelling by fast boat, where it was no trouble to lie down and possible to take tea or smoke a water pipe or even opium. The only drawback was the filth of the city waterways, to which household rubbish, dyer's effluent and the cleaning of rice, vegetables and clothes and the swilling of chamberpots that took place on their banks imparted colours and odours which there are no adequate words to describe, not to mention the odd bloated cadaver of a cat or dog and the summer proliferation of red-, white- or yellow-lined watermelon rinds, surely one of the less enviable traits of Venice, of which Suzhou with its many canals had been called the oriental counterpart. Yet these ladies and their like did not mind, caring not a whit for anything beyond the comfort of their little world. Familiarity indeed had made all this second nature and so spared them even the effort of raising a hand to hold their noses. How much more delightful, then, must it have been to take a fast boat along the broader, fresher out-of-town waterways to a neighbouring community when a fine spring or autumn day occasioned an outing to the hills or — that important item in a religious society — a visit to the graves. The food served by boatmen, "boat food" as it was designated, was unrivalled in any eating house, and no one meal could exhaust the elaborations of the real thing, from its dishes proper to its varied snacks. Even

旁边有的是水,只要船家不懒惰,船就随时可以明亮爽目。

　　从前,姑奶奶回娘家哩,老太太看望小姐哩,坐轿子嫌吃力,就唤一条快船坐了去。在船里坐得舒服,躺躺也不妨,又可以吃茶,吸水烟,甚至抽大烟。只是城里的河道非常脏,有人家倾弃的垃圾,有染坊里放出来的颜色水,淘米净菜洗衣服涮马桶又都在河旁边干,使河水的颜色和气味变得没有适当的字眼可以形容。有时候还浮着肚皮胀得饱饱的死猫或者死狗的尸体,到了夏天,红里子白里子黄里子的西瓜皮更是洋洋大观。苏州城里河道多,有人就说是东方的威尼斯。威尼斯像这个样子,又何足羡慕呢?这些,在姑奶奶老太太等人是不管的,只要小天地里舒服,以外尽不妨马虎,而且习惯成自然,那就连抬起手来按住鼻子的力气也不用花。城外的河道宽阔清爽得多,到附近的各乡各镇去,或逢春秋好日子游山玩景,以及干那宗法社会里的重要事项——上坟,唤一条快船去当然最为开心。船家做的菜是菜馆比不上的,特称"船菜"。正式的船菜花样繁多,菜以外还有种种点心,一顿吃不完。非正式地做几样也还是

英汉对照
English-Chinese
中国文学宝库
Gems of Chinese Literature
现代文学系列
Modern Literature

specialities outside its usual range had a refinement due to the simple training of the boatmen, nothing to which they applied their skill ever escaping the style of boat food, the mystery of whose excellence lay in individual preparation with small pots and pans, so that everything was different, with no mixing of sauces or adulteration of ingredients, and everything tasted as it should, leaving the mouth still watering after all had been consumed. Had a boatman fried his prawns or boiled his chicken in the capacious utensils of a large restaurant kitchen, there would no doubt have been falls from grace. Be that as it may, given the excellence of the boat food, the added relaxation of the journey with its opportunities for sightseeing, light banter and night-long indulgence generally created a demand in excess of supply. "Slump" was not in the vocabulary of the idle Suzhou tripper of those days, nor was any such notion in his head, and the fast boats were in the right place at the right time to play the part of fortune's favourite.

Their cooking apart, the boatmen showed a wonderful facility for insult. But purely defensive insult incapable of attack was rated no rarity. It was a second-rate performer, too, who stopped short after a couple of words without progressing to endless, creeper-like convolutions, and even then mere conventional grammar stripped of rhetorical variation did not constitute brilliance. Only one without scruple on these three counts could give a proper account of himself in navigatory invective. The boatman who foresaw possible collision with a load of firewood up from the country or from reckless oarwork ahead of him on a narrow canal would leap witheringly to the attack. "You blind or what, splashing and bashing around

精,船家训练有素,出手总不脱船菜的风格。拆穿了说,船菜所以好就在于只准备一席,小镬小锅,做一样是一样,汤水不混和,材料不马虎,自然每样有它的真味,叫人吃完了还觉得馋涎欲滴。倘若船家进了菜馆里的大厨房,大镬炒虾,大锅煮鸡,那也一定会有坍台的时候的。话得说回来,船菜既然好,坐在船里又安舒,可以眺望,可以谈笑,玩它个夜以继日,于是快船常有求过于供的情形。那时候,游手好闲的苏州人还没有识得"不景气"的字眼,脑子里也没有类似"不景气"的想头,快船就充当了适应时地的幸运儿。

除了做船菜,船家还有一种了不得的本领,就是相骂。相骂如果只会防御,不会进攻,那不算希奇。三言两语就完,不会像藤蔓似的纠缠不休,也只能算次等角色。纯是常规的语法,不会应用修辞学上的种种变化,那就即使纠缠不休也没有什么精彩。船家与人家相骂起来,对于这三层都能毫无遗憾,当行出色。船在狭窄的河道里行驶,前面有一条乡下人的柴船或者什么船冒冒失失地摇过来,看去也许会碰撞一下,船家就用相骂的口吻进攻了,"你瞎了眼睛

英汉对照
English-Chinese
中国文学宝库
Gems of Chinese Literature
现代文学系列
Modern Literature

Three Kinds of Boat

right, left and centre? Who're you trying to catch up with, death?" This was ever the way. A riposte boosted the exchange to a level of inextricability where hands simply fell away from oar and pole and insults were traded back and forth as anger — it was always the other guy's fault — became uncontainable. It seldom came to blows however, since to them invective stopped short of coiling up the male queue and wrenching the female bosom. And one had, on these occasions, to appreciate their rhetorical accomplishment. No example comes readily to mind, but one would feel, listening to turns of phrase one would never have thought utterable, that they were nonetheless the only way of subsuming resentment, spite, arrogance, scorn and much else besides. I doubt seriously whether any compiler of a learned work on geographical anthropology has considered the genius for invective fostered among boatmen by the urban waterways of Suzhou.

They had practised the art of rowing along these waterways to such perfection that they generally took excellent care to avert collisions as boat scraped past boat. Out of town they used towlines in a headwind and hoisted a scrap of sail if the wind was behind them, but did not have resources of propulsion possessed by other craft. In a really strong wind they would turn you away, telling you with great circumspection that today was quite impossible. My visit to the graveyard, for instance, involved a crossing of Stone Lake, which, *pace* Mr. Wu Qiu'an's poetic descriptions of its "waves 'neath a windy sky" and "mounts that dipped and soared for me," is a lake of no great breadth flanked by a small, square-topped hill on which witches congregate to burn incense on the eighteenth of

吗？这样横冲直撞是不是去赶死？"诸如此类。对方如果有了反响，那就进展到纠缠不休的阶段，索性把摇橹撑篙的手停住了，反复再四地大骂，总之错失全在对方，所以自己的愤怒是不可遏制的。然而很少骂到动武，他们认为男人盘辫子女人扭胸脯不属于相骂的范围。这当儿，你得欣赏他们的修辞的才能。要举例子，一时可记不起来，但是在听他们那些话语的时候，你一定会想，从没有想到话语可以这么说的，然而惟有这么说，才可以包含怨恨、刻毒、傲慢、鄙薄种种成分。编辑人生地理教科书的学者只怕没有想到吧，苏州城里的河道养成了船家相骂的本领。

他们的摇船技术是在城里的河道训练成功的，所以长处在于能小心谨慎，船与船擦身而过，彼此绝不碰撞。到了城外去，遇到逆风固然也会拉纤，遇到顺风固然也会张一扇小巧的布篷，可是比起别种船上的驾驶人来，那就不成话了。他们敢于拉纤或者张篷的时候，风一定不很大，如果真个遇到大风，他们就小心谨慎地回复你，今天去不成。譬如我去上坟必须经过石湖，虽然吴瞿安先生曾做诗说石湖"天风浪浪"什么什么以及"群山为我皆低昂"，实在是个并不怎么阔大的湖面，旁边只有一座很小的上方山，每年阴历八月十八，许多女巫都要上山去烧

英汉对照
English-Chinese
中国文学宝库
Gems of Chinese Literature
现代文学系列
Modern Literature

Three Kinds of Boat

every eighth month. The crew, on being told that I wished to cross it, scanned the heavens for traces of wind, and as we entered the lake their features tensed and laughter ceased as faint gurglings from the bows elicited casual warnings to each other of "Waves, waves!" One year my family was visiting the graveyard when the wind rose after ten o'clock and the boatman, though not liking to talk of turning back, refused to cross Stone Lake, so that our poor legs had a scenic journey of twenty *li* if we were to get there and back.

Then there were the Dangdang boats, plied by men from Shaoxing. The peculiar name derived from a gong mounted on board and struck first as a signal when they set out and again to attract passengers they passed through towns on the way: "Dang-dang-dang-dang!" There were none in Suzhou when I was small, and I cannot say when they first appeared. I never ran across them until I went to Luzhi to teach. They had moored outside town, it was said, and had been in a fight with the original river boats, which had been driven to mount a resistance when they saw their custom being eroded. But the Dangdang boats were run by hard men who took on resistance when they saw it, and it can only have taken a few tussles before the river boatmen realized they were outclassed and rereated into scornful contemplation of the newcomers making free with their erstwhile waters. Whether recourse was ever had to litigation or registration I could not say, but in short the Shaoxing men set up routes of their own by the power of their wrists: that was fact. "Shaoxing men are sparrowpats," we used to say, meaning that you would find the one where you found the other: the distribution was equal.

香的。船家一听说要过石湖就抬起头来看天，看有没有起风的意思。到进了石湖的时候，脸色不免紧张起来，说笑都停止了。听得船头略微有汩汩的声音，就轻轻地互相警戒，"浪头！浪头！"有一年我家去上坟，风在十点过后大起来，船家不好说回转去，就坚持着不过石湖。这一回难为了我们的腿，来回跑了二十里光景才上成了坟。

现在来说绍兴人的"啗啗船"。那种船上备着一面小铜锣，开船的时候就啗啗啗啗敲起来，算是信号，中途经过市镇，又啗啗啗啗敲起来，招呼乘客，因此得了这奇怪的名称。我小时候，苏州地方没有那种船。什么时候开头有的，我也说不上来。直到我到甪直去当教师，才与那种船有了缘。船停泊在城外，据传闻，是与原有的航船有过一番斗争的。航船见它来抢生意，不免设法阻止。但是"啗啗船"的船夫只知道硬干，你要阻止他们，他们就与你打。大概交过了几回手吧，航船夫知道自己不是那些绍兴人的敌手，也就只好用鄙夷的眼光看他们在水面上来去自由了。中间有没有立案呀登记呀这些手续，我可不清楚，总之那些绍兴人用腕力开辟了航线是事实。我们有一句话，"麻雀豆腐绍兴

Sheer comparison between the Dangdang boats and the river boats was proof of how efficiently the Shaoxing men struggled for survival. The equal distribution was no accident. For this see below. I will describe the working of the Dangdang boats.

They were a subspecies of Black Awning boat, having square bows, an uplifted stern, a vaulted awning and only width enough for two men to sit side by side, which made them seem very long. Their sides were painted green above and red below, so that when they were lightly loaded a line of red appeared above water level, contrasting violently with the green. The awnings were quite black. The steering oar, red or green, was not used, being fixed reversed to the stern and bearing, usually in white, the names of the places through which the boat passed. All the fabric was crude and cobbled together with the sole aim of preventing the boat being swamped, with crossbeams and upright planks haphazardly placed like patches on torn clothes. Other boats one boarded from the bows and thence entered the cabin. Not so the Dangdang boats, where one normally stepped on to the gunwale and insinuated oneself into the cabin between pushed back sections of awning. It was as straightforward as that. No one liked to negotiate the cabin door, so the men simply blocked it by piling freight there. Stepping on to the gunwale, though, required caution. The Dangdang boats were scarcely larger than West Lake rowboats, with which anyone who has been to Hangzhou will be familiar, and shared their stability. You had to watch for your chance, get your centre of gravity over the foot on the side then lightly bring the other foot down to meet the deck of the cabin. Once inside you had to sit.

人",意思是说有麻雀豆腐的地方也就有绍兴人,绍兴人与麻雀豆腐一样普遍于各地。试把"啯啯船"与航船比较,就可以证明绍兴人是生存斗争里的好角色,他们与麻雀豆腐一样普遍于各地,自有所以然的原因。这看了后文就知道,且让我把"啯啯船"的体制叙述一番。

"啯啯船"属于"乌篷船"的系统,文头,翘尾巴,穹形篷,横里只够两个人并排坐,所以船身特别见得长。船旁涂着绿釉,底部却涂红釉,轻载的时候,一道红色露出水面,与绿色作强烈的对照。篷纯黑色。舵或红或绿,不用,就倒插在船艄,上面歪歪斜斜标明所经乡镇的名称,大多用白色。全船的材料很粗陋,制作也将就,只要河水不至于灌进船里就成,横一条木条,竖一块木板,像破衣服上的补缀一样,那是不在乎的。我们上旁的船,总是从船头走进舱里去。上"啯啯船"可不然,我们常常踩着船边,从推开的两截穹形篷中间把身子挨进舱里去,这样见得爽快。大家既然不欢喜钻舱门,船夫有人家托运的货品就堆在那里,索性把舱门堵塞了。可是踩船边很要当心。西湖划子的活动不稳定,到过杭州的人一定有数,"啯啯船"比西湖划子大不了多少,它的活动不稳定也与西湖划子不相上下。你得迎着势,让重心落在踩着船边的那只脚上,然后另一只脚轻轻伸下去,点着舱里铺着的平板。进了舱你就得坐下来。两旁船边搁

英汉对照
English-Chinese
中国文学宝库
Gems of Chinese Literature
现代文学系列
Modern Literature

Three Kinds of Boat

The seats were two narrow, thin planks along either side, no more than a foot clear of the deck, so that you sat with your knees raised up in intimate contact with those of anyone opposite you. You could rest your upper body against the awning, but any attempt to sit up straight made you aware how cramped the space was by making you hit your head against the roof. First arrivals usually sat in the space where the awning had been pushed back, for although in this major thoroughfare one was forever having to lean out of other people's way, these were the superior seats, affording fresh air and a view of the passing scene, as well as the chance to alleviate the fatigue of prolonged sitting by taking turns to put one's arms on the gunwale, though this advantage was lost when rain or particularly cold weather made it necessary to pull the awning and equality was restored. Everyone was engulfed in the stagnant darkness.

The Dangdang boats hardly ever had a crew of over forty, and these were powerful men, unstinting of their strength and rowing amain from the start. Five stood on either side of the raised stern, each on one oar, its handle in one hand and its cable in the other. The oars were lighter and thinner than those on other boats. The men's bodies thrust forward as they pushed the handles of the oars away from them, almost in the attitude of one about to rumble into the water, then as they hauled back fell into a squatting position as if they were about to sit down. The hull flew forward to the mighty strokes of the oars, and the pace was of course increased when an extra oarsman sat in the bows, leaning forward to his task. The only sound was the delicate tune of water slapping its way aft, and of the men singing snatches of Shaoxing opera or trading salacious

着又狭又薄的长板就是坐位,这高出铺着的平板不过一尺光景,所以你坐下来就得耸起你的两个膝盖,如果对面也有人,那就实做"促膝"了。背心可以靠在船篷上,躯干最好不要挺直,挺直了头触着篷顶,你不名免要起局促之感。先到的人大多坐在推开的两截穹形篷的空档里,这里虽然是出入要道,时时有偏过身子让人家的麻烦,却是个优越的位置,透气,看得见沿途的景物,又可以轮流把两臂搁在船边,舒散久坐的困倦。然而遇到风雨或者极冷的天气,船篷必须拉拢来,那位置也就无所谓优越,大家一律平等,埋没在含有恶浊气味的阴暗里。

"啕啕船"的船夫差不多没有四十以上的人,身体都强健,不懂得爱惜力气,一开船就拼命划。五个人分两边站在高高翘起的船艄上,每人管一把橹,一手当橹柄,一手当橹绳。那橹很长,比旁的船上的橹来得轻薄。当推出橹柄去的时候,他们的上身也冲了出去,似乎要跌到河里去的模样。接着把橹柄挽回来,他们的身子就往后顿,仿佛要坐下来似的。五把橹在水里这样强力地划动,船身就飞快地前进了。有时在船头加一把桨,一个人背心向前坐着,把它扳动,那自然又增加了速率。只听得河水活活地向后流去,奏着轻快的调子。船夫一壁划船,一壁随口唱绍兴戏,或者互相说笑,有猥亵的性谈,有绍兴风味的幽默谐语,因此,他们就忘记

英汉对照
English-Chinese
中国文学宝库
Gems of Chinese Literature
现代文学系列
Modern Literature

jokes and humorous Shaoxing banter to take their minds off their exertions, and this also provided an added diversion for the passengers. They liked a race too, and when any boatman ahead of them seemed to be rowing at all hard, one of them would give the order to overtake, and the others would promptly comply with a supreme effort of pushing and heaving, now thrusting forward, now leaning back supine in an apparent fit of madness. When, sure enough, they shortly overtook it, they laughed aloud in celebration of their victory as they fell back into their original pace. The fast rowing attracted the impatient. For instance, the thirty-six li (the "four-nines route") from Suzhou to Luzhi, which took a similarly propelled passenger boat six hours, took a Dangdang boat only four, and even if no pressing business demanded disembarkation two hours earlier, there was after all less physical constriction, and moreover the fare was the same, a hundred and forty cash, or fourteen coppers. (At least, that was the price fifteen years ago; no doubt it has gone up since.)

With a following wind, of course, the Dangdang boats too would hoist sail, a sail compounded of torn clothes, old elegiac couplets, flour sacks and what not with a shape closely approximating to a square, seemingly a little ill-matched in size with the small boat. The mast, erected at the forward cabin door, was a bamboo pole of no great thickness that bent with the strength of the wind, poking the bellying sail out over the side. The natural increase in speed then chopped the water like a motor boat, but invariably worried the more timid, for the roll of the boat brought the lower side almost level with the water and the larger waves splashed spray

了疲劳,而旅客也得到了解闷的好资料。他们又喜欢与旁的船竞赛,看见前面有一条什么船,船家摇船似乎很努力,他们中间一个人发出号令说"追过它",其余几个人立即同意,推呀挽呀分外用力,身子一会儿冲出去,一会儿倒仰过来,好像忽然发了狂。不多时果然把前面的船追过了,他们才哈哈大笑,庆贺自己的胜利,同时回复到原先的速率。由于他们划得快,比较性急的人都欢喜坐他们的船,譬如从苏州到甪直是"四九路"(三十六里),同样地划,航船要六个钟头,"啥啥船"只要四个钟头,早两个钟头上岸,即使不想赶做什么事,身体究竟少受些拘束,何况船价同样是一百四十文,十四个铜板。(这是十五年前的价钱,现在总该增加了。)

风顺,"啥啥船"当然也张风篷。风篷是破衣服、旧挽联、干面袋等等材料拼凑起来的,形式大多近乎正方。因为船身不大,就见得篷幅特别大,有点儿不相称。篷杆竖在船头舱门的地位,是一根并不怎么粗的竹头,风越大,篷杆越弯,把袋满了风的风篷挑出在船的一边。这当儿,船的前进自然更快,听着哗哗的水声,仿佛坐了摩托船。但是胆子小点儿的人就不免惊慌,因为船的两边不平,低的一边几乎齐水面,波浪大,时时有水花从舱篷的缝里泼进来。如

英汉对照
English-Chinese
中国文学宝库
Gems of Chinese Literature
现代文学系列
Modern Literature

through the seams of the awning. Those sitting on the lower side, leaning passively back, were apt to reflect that a capsize would have them in the water first, while those on the upper side would have to exert themselves to stretch out their legs and plant their feet firmly on the deck as the only means of avoiding losing their seats and being toppled on to those opposite. Sometimes, when hoisted in a crosswind, the sail would veer from port to starboard and back, making the boat describe full arcs so that now one side was up, now the other, and causing some of the passengers, seated as if on a kindergarten seesaw, to complain inwardly that "this life is unbearable." But Dangdang boats were not often lost, for the men had drastic measures for dealing with a wind that was really wrong. I was once going to Luzhi in a high wind that filled the sail and almost dipped it in the water, and despite the bad weather the passengers were happy because of the greater speed of the boat, until we entered the Wusong River and held to the windward side of its broad surface, when sudden, wilder gusts of wind swept over us, soaking the sail before lifting it free again, so that the passengers were incapable even of a gasped "oh!", so intent were they on gripping the awning or the wooden seats. There was a splash as three or four of the crew dived in and together dragged down the higher side of the boat while the crew on board lowered the sail, whereupon they clambered dripping on to the stern, took up their oars and rowed for all they were worth without even removing their wet clothes.

On the packet boats one philosophy was shared by rower and passenger alike: you'll-get-thereism. You'll get there anyway, so

果坐在低的一边,身体被动地向后靠着,谁也会想到船一翻自己就最先落水。坐在高的一边更得费力气,要把两条腿伸直,两只脚踩紧在平板上,才不至于脱离坐位,跌扑到对面的人的身上去。有时候风从横里来,他们也张风篷,一会儿篷在左边,一会儿调边,让船在河面上尽画曲线。于是船的两边轮流地一高一低,旅客就好比在那里坐幼稚园里的跷跷板,"这生活可难受",有些人这样暗自叫苦。然而"啥啥船"很少失事,风势真个不对,那些船夫还有硬干的办法。有一回我到角直去,风很大,饱满的风篷几乎蘸着水面,虽然天气不好,因为船行非常快,旅客都觉得高兴,后来进了吴淞江,那里江面很阔,船沿着"上风头"的一边前进。忽然呼呼地吹来更猛烈的几阵风,风篷着了湿重又离开水面。旅客连"哎哟"都喊不出来,只把两只手紧紧地支撑着舱篷或者坐身的木板。扑通,扑通,三四个船夫跳到水里去了。他们一齐扳住船的高起的一边,待留在船上的船夫把风篷落下来,他们才水淋淋地爬上船艄,湿了的衣服也不脱,拿起橹来就拼命地划。

说到航船,凡是摇船的跟坐船的差不多都有一种哲学,就是"反正总是一个到"主义。反

英汉对照
English-Chinese
中国文学宝库
Gems of Chinese Literature
现代文学系列
Modern Literature

what's the hurry? Where's the big deal if you're late, as long as you haven't singed your eyebrows? So the crew clamped foot-long pipes between their teeth, shut their eyes and took the odd drag when they thought so, and when they'd smoked one pipe, they lazily twisted their tobacco, filled up and smoked another. Unlike the Dangdang boat crews, they rarely numbered under forty. After their leisurely smoke, they got up, saw to the rigging and brewed a communal pot of tea. They were far from considering themselves just there to sail the boat. They had to sit and chat too, and hope began only when they arrived back from delivering letters and "pole-loads." Fortunately the passengers were in no hurry either and arrived in ones and twos after ten minutes, or after twenty or thirty minutes had elapsed, got on board, then got off again to buy snacks and have tea, which took a further ten minutes to a quarter of an hour. Some bought spirits, dried beancurd and peanuts to tipple the journey away alone; others bought nothing, their only encumbrance being their own everflowing mouths, jabbering away before they were even settled in the search for a suitable adversary. For them, late arrival — indeed arrival at all — was of no consequence. Those used to steamers and trains had to make an effort to curb their instincts when taking the packet, whose enigmatic progress could otherwise lead at the least to days on end of utter boredom.

The packets, much larger and broader in the beam than the Dangdang boats, had square cabins built of wood rather than the rush matting of the latter. The crew found shelter from sun and rain under the spacious stern awning, while the forward and mid cabins

正总是一个到,要紧做什么?到了也没有烧到眉毛上来的事,慢点儿也呒啥。所以,船夫大多衔着一根一尺多长的烟管,闭上眼睛,偶尔想到才吸一口,一管吸完了,慢吞吞捻了烟丝装上去,再吸第二管。正同"啙啙船"相反,他们中间很少四十以下的人。烟吸畅了,才起来理一理篷索,泡一壶公众的茶。可不要当做就要开船了,他们还得坐下来谈闲天。直到专门给人家送信带东西的"担子"回了船,那才有点儿希望。好在坐船的客人也不要不紧,隔十多分钟二三十分钟来一个两个,下了船重又上岸,买点心哩,吃一开茶哩,又是十分或一刻。有些人买了烧酒豆腐干花生米来,预备一路独酌。有些人并没有买什么,可是带了一张源源不绝的嘴,还没有坐定就乱攀谈,挑选相当的对手。在他们,迟些儿到实在不算一回事,就是不到又何妨。坐惯了轮船火车的人去坐航船,先得做一番养性的功夫,不然,这种阴阳怪气的旅行,至少会有三天的闷闷不乐。

　　航船比"啙啙船"大得多,船身开阔,舱作方形,木制,不像"啙啙船"那样只用芦席。艄篷也宽大,雨落太阳晒,船夫都得到遮掩。头舱中舱

were the domain of the passengers. In the forward cabin one sat cross-legged, but the mid cabin had benches placed across it on which one could sit with one's calves upright unless there was freight stowed under the benches, in which case the passengers just had to sit with their legs up. The only way to open the single-pane windows was to take them out, otherwise they remained closed. Generally one was opened on either side, so that the air inside always smelt rather unpleasant. If the journey became tedious, a glance round at the old oarsmen under the stern awning convinced one that one's own tedium was the real thing. The space between their forward and backward strokes was not large and argued not the slightest exertion, while they gazed blankly at the bank, only the footprints worn in the deck indicating the years they had done so, yet seemed to experience no tedium on this old, daily route whose every stone and blade of grass was familiar to them. Compared with this, what did a slower, duller trip mean to the passengers? For speed you could only hope for a following wind, when the great sail would be hoisted between the forward and mid cabins to the top of its thick, long wooden mast where, supported on a multitude of bamboo struts, it took the wind and advanced in majestic style. The windiest days would waft one from Suzhou to Luzhi in three and a half hours. The passengers, though, were inveterate you'll-get-thereists and harboured, for all their exclamations about a "rare day," what amounted to resentment at the strength of the wind and the speed of the boat, and they all wore expressions of disappointment as they disembarked. Should they encounter a direct head wind, the packets would stop running,

是旅客的区域。头舱要盘膝而坐。中舱横搁着一条条长板,坐在板上,小腿可以垂直。但是中舱有的时候要装货,豆饼菜油之类装满在长板下面,旅客也只得搁起了腿坐了。窗是一块块的板,要开就得卸去,不卸就得关上。通常两旁各开一扇,所以坐在舱里那种气味未免有点儿难受。坐得无聊,如果回转头去看艄篷里那几个老头子摇船,就会觉得自己的无聊才真是无聊。他们的一推一挽距离很小,仿佛全然不用力气,两只眼睛茫然望着岸边,这样地过了不知多少年月,把踏脚的板都出脚印来了,可是他们似乎没有什么无聊,每天还是走那老路,连一棵草一块石头都熟识了的路。两相比较,坐一趟船慢一点儿闷一点儿又算得什么。坐航船要快,只有巴望顺风。篷杆竖在头舱与中舱之间,一根又粗又长的木头。风篷极大,直拉到杆顶,有许多竹头横撑着,吃了风,巍然地推进,很有点儿气派。风最大的日子,苏州到甪直三点半钟就吹到了。但是旅客究竟是"反正总是一个到"主义者,虽然嘴里嚷着"今天难得",另一方面却似乎嫌风太大船太快了,跨上岸去,脸上不免带点儿怅然的神色。遇到顶头逆风航船就停班,不像"啥啥船"那样无论如何总得用人力去

unlike the Dangdang boats, which would brave anything by dint of brawn. Passengers would arrive at the wharf to find a lone boat and not a sign of the men, realize they had stopped running and turn back unperturbed. One day the wind would be bound to drop and the packet would sail. I, with all my letters to send, could not share their calm, and whenever the janitor returned the mail I had dispatched with the news that the packet was not sailing that day, I knew I was in for a whole day of aggravation.

December 20, 1934
Translated by Simon Johnstone

拼。客人走到码头上,看见孤零零的一条船停在那里,半个人影儿也没有,知道是停班,就若无其事地回转身。风总有停的日子,那么航船总有开的日子。忙于寄信的我可不能这样安静,每逢校工把发出的信退回来,说今天航船不开,就得担受整天的不舒服。

Ox

I used to see oxen every day when I lived in the country for a few years. And yet even now what stands out most clearly in my memory are their large eyes. In the winter an ox would be tethered by the gate to catch the sun. It would lie there, incessantly chewing its cud, and its eyes seemed to be even larger than during the busy season. There is a great deal of white in an ox's eye which gives it an awful pallor. When I say "awful pallor," perhaps it is because of the overlying network of bloodshot veins. I believe the only possible comparison for this combination of colours is a scene such as when the silence of a corpse is combined with a mourner's cries. An ox's eyes are too big and they bulge too much, so much so that they frighten me. Whenever I entered the courtyard and passed the ox I was always very heedful of its two large bulging eyes staring at me. The way it stared and stared could not but make me think that it could suddenly get up and charge me. I truly felt there was hate in those eyes. I could understand why it stared at me and always kept my distance as I skirted around it. Now and then I would glance warily at it to see if it would make a move, but I only ever saw it stare dumbly. Yet I still felt as if there were something in those eyes to make people uncomfortable on seeing them.

There were many children in our courtyard — lively, artless and

牛

在乡下住的几年里,天天看见牛。可是直到现在还像显现在眼前的,只有牛的大眼睛。冬天,牛拴在门口晒太阳。它躺着,嘴不停的磋磨,眼睛就似乎比忙的时候睁得更大。牛眼睛好像白的成分多,那是惨白。我说它惨白,也许为了上面网着一条条血丝。我以为这两种颜色配合在一起,只能用死者的寂静配合着吊丧者的哭声那样的情景来摹拟。牛的眼睛太大,又鼓得太高,简直到了使你害怕的程度。我进院子的时候经过牛身旁,总注意到牛鼓着的两只大眼睛在瞪着我。我禁不住想,它这样瞪着,瞪着,会猛的站起身朝我撞过来。我确实感到那眼光里含着恨。我也体会出它为什么这样瞪着我,总距离它远远的绕过去。有时候我留心看它将会有什么举动,可是只见它呆呆地瞪着,我觉得那眼睛里似乎还有别的使人看了不自在的意味。

我们院子里有好些小孩,活泼,天真,当然

英汉对照
English-Chinese
中国文学宝库
Gems of Chinese Literature
现代文学系列
Modern Literature

of course full of mischief. In the spring they caught butterflies. In summer they hooked frogs. When the millet was ripe there were fat grasshoppers everywhere which they would grab and roast on the range to eat. In the winter when there are no small creatures to be found they play with the oxen instead.

I have seen an ox teased into anger by them on many occasions. It will circle the wooden post to which it is tethered, going round and round. With its head lowered, horns at an angle and eyes staring out beneath, it looks ready to turn heaven and earth upside down with its charge.

This is how the children play: they stand at a distance, pick up stones and throw them at the ox. At first the stones are not all that big and when they hit, the ox's hide immediately gives a shiver all over much as when the corners of our mouths tremble. Gradually however the stones get bigger and the ox turns its head to stare at you on being hit. If there is one kid who is particularly brave and smart he will go off to the bamboo grove to fetch a stick. Then, stretching out as far as he can, he will tease the ox's tail and poke at its hindquarters to incite it into a fury. However, I have never seen any of them jab at an ox's head. To my way of thinking, even though they are just kids, they are also made to feel uncomfortable by the look in that big pair of eyes.

The end of the game comes when the ox stands up and the kids let out a shout and scatter in all directions. I have seen scenes like that countless times.

On one occasion a hired-hand came out to work in the courtyard. He was around thirty but still as fond as a kid of playing

也顽皮。春天,他们扑蝴蝶。夏天,他们钓青蛙。谷子成熟的时候到处都有油蚱蜢,他们捉了来,在灶膛里煨了吃。冬天,什么小生物全不见了,他们就玩牛。

有好几回,我见牛让他们惹得发了脾气。它绕着拴住它的木桩子,一圈儿一圈儿的转。低着头,斜起角,眼睛打角底下瞪出来,就好像这一撞要把整个天地翻个身似的。

孩子们是这样玩的,他们一个个远远的站着,捡些石子朝牛扔去。起先,石子不怎么大,扔在牛身上,那一搭皮肤马上轻轻的抖一下,像我们的嘴角动一下似的。渐渐的,捡来的石子大起来了,扔到身上,牛会掉过头来瞪着你。要是有个孩子特别胆大,特别机灵,他会到竹园里找来一根毛竹。伸得远远的去撩牛的尾巴,戳牛的屁股,把牛惹起火来。可是,我从未见过他们撩过牛的头。我想,即使是小孩,也从那双大眼睛看见使人不自在的意味了。

玩到最后,牛站起来了,于是孩子们轰的一声,四处跑散。这种把戏,我看得很熟很熟了。

有一回,正巧一个长工打院子里出来,他三十光景了,还像孩子似的爱闹着玩。他一把捉

英汉对照
English-Chinese
中国文学宝库
Gems of Chinese Literature
现代文学系列
Modern Literature

around. He grabbed one of the children and said, "Don't run away. If you all run away when you see an ox what'll happen when you want to be a farmer one day?" He looked at me and said with a smile, "Really, you don't need to be scared of an ox. See how big he is? But he won't charge you — an ox's eyes are different."

This is what the hired-hand told me: "For instance, we just see this wooden stake, but from an ox's point of view it looks like a pillar holding up heaven. Or take a couple of acres of land, from an ox's point of view they just go on and on. The things an ox sees are all much bigger than they really are, much bigger. As for us, we look as tall and as big as the four Heavenly Guardians to him. He gets scared when he stands in front of us and doesn't dare resist. However you might grab him he still won't resist. He thinks we can kill him with just a flick of our fingers, or just lift our little toe and kick him into the clouds; when we breathe out it's like rain. All he can do is obey our orders for, come rain or shine, whatever the season, we must plough and so he must plough and that's all there is to it. Don't you think it's lucky, sir, that an ox should have eyes like that? Otherwise, he'd never take orders from you. A big one like that with such strength could give you a kick that would hurt for many a day. Five of us couldn't hold out against one ox, that's for sure, but luckily for us, in his eyes only one of us could stand up a dozen of them."

After that, whenever I went in or out of the courtyard I always made a point of looking at the ox's eyes for now I understood what it was that made people uncomfortable. Those muddy yellow pupils and that constant forward-looking gaze both hold a fear which

住个孩子,"莫跑,"他说,"见了牛都要跑,改天还想吃庄稼饭?"他朝我笑笑说,"真的,牛不消怕得。你看它有那么大吗?它不会撞人的。牛的眼睛有点不同。"

以下是长工告诉我的话。

"比方说,我们看见这根木头桩子,牛眼睛看来就像一根撑天柱。比方说,一块田十多亩,牛眼睛看来就没有边,没有沿。牛眼睛看出来的东西,都比原来大,大许多许多。看我们人,就有四金刚那么高,那么大。站到我们跟前它就害怕了,它不敢倔强,随便拿它怎么样都不敢倔强。它当我们只要两个指头就能捻死它,抬一抬脚拇趾就能踢它到半天云里,我们哈气就像下雨一样。那它就只有听我们使唤,天好,落雨,生田,熟田,我们要耕,它就只有耕,没得话说的。你先生说对不对,幸好牛有那么一双眼睛。不然的话,还让你使唤啊,那么大的一个,力气又蛮,踩到一脚就要痛上好几天。对了,我们跟牛,五个抵一个都抵不住。好在牛眼睛看出来,我们一个抵它十几个。"

以后,我进出院子的时候,总特意留心看牛的眼睛,我明白了另一种使人看着不自在的意味。那黄色的浑浊的瞳仁,那老是直视前方的

英汉对照
English-Chinese
中国文学宝库
Gems of Chinese Literature
现代文学系列
Modern Literature

transforms the hate in their eyes to pathos. From an ox's point of view it would be worthwhile losing those eyes and going blind, for then it would be free.

December 21, 1946
Translated by Alison Bailey

眼光,都带着恐惧的神情,这使眼睛里的恨转成了哀怨。站在牛的立场上说,如果能去掉这双眼睛,成了瞎子也值得,因为得到自由了。